D0461194

# JINXED

⟨ AMY McCULLOCH ⟩

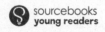

sourcebooks
young readers

First published in the United States in 2020 by Sourcebooks
Copyright © 2018, 2020 by Amy Alward Limited
Cover and internal design © 2020 by Sourcebooks
Cover art © Vivienne To
Cover and internal images © KOHb/Getty Images

Published by Sourcebooks Young Readers, an imprint of Sourcebooks Kids
P.O. Box 4410, Naperville, Illinois 60567-4410
(630) 961-3900
sourcebookskids.com

Originally published as *Jinxed* in 2018 in the United Kingdom by Simon &
Schuster UK.

Library of Congress Cataloging-in-Publication data is on file with the publisher.

Source of Production: Maple Press, York, Pennsylvania, United States
Date of Production: November 2019
Run Number: 5016685

Printed and bound in the United States of America.
MA 10 9 8 7 6 5 4 3 2 1

*To Sarah, Wonder Woman*

# PROLOGUE

SHE BURST THROUGH THE TREES, CRADLING THE creature in her arms.

The whine of a pulse gun sounded in the wood; she ducked and the shot flew over her head, obliterating the trunk of a beech tree in front of her. Panic rose in her throat. They weren't just out to destroy the creature.

They were going to kill her too.

She kept running, her feet slipping inside the blue, plastic overshoes she hadn't had time to remove before bolting from the lab. She'd known this day would come—she'd crossed the line so far, it was no longer even a mark on the horizon. But she still hadn't been ready.

How could she ever be ready to lose what she'd been working on her entire life?

The creature vibrated against her chest, a red light pulsing against its hot, metal skin like a heartbeat. It wriggled in her arms, trying to escape—as if it too knew what was coming—but she tightened her grip. She just had to make it to the other side of the ravine to the emergency car that would take them to safety.

The next shot hit her shoulder, and she wasn't sure who

screamed louder: her or the creature. She stumbled, one leg collapsing underneath her as her foot sank into a crevice hidden by a carpet of fallen leaves. She dared to glimpse down, and her heart almost stopped—the creature's metal body was smoking, the acrid stench of burned electronics filling her nostrils. The pulse guns were doing their job: destroying it from the inside out.

She pulled her foot free and pressed on. The bridge was so close, she could feel the rumble of trains as they passed underneath. Yet the heavy boot steps of the men behind her were louder still.

"Come on, come on," said the voice crackling in her ear.

She must have come into range of her partner's communication device. She forced her legs to pump harder, ignoring the sticky, wet stab of pain in her side…

Barely had her toe crossed the threshold onto the bridge when alarms wailed, hidden IP protection sensors blaring from the tree line. Traps sprung from the ground—nets that coiled around her legs, tripping her up. "I'm down," she screamed into her earpiece. "Help me!"

"Cutting comms, link destruction in process." Almost as an afterthought, he added, "Sorry." And then the line went dead.

Another pulse thumped her in the back, launching her forward and sending the creature flying from her arms. She had no choice but to watch as the smoking hunk of metal disappeared off the side of the bridge. Her assailants ran past her now, flinging themselves at the railing, leaning out over the edge and watching the blaze of sparks sent up as the metal monster hit electrified track.

It was gone. Her life's work—destroyed.

The men turned back to her, gun barrels leveling at her head. She closed her eyes and accepted the inevitable.

Down on the tracks below, the creature shuddered with one final pulse of life. As a train thundered down the tracks toward it, it only had the energy for the faintest sound.

It purred.

# PART ONE

# JINX

1

SMOKE RISES FROM THE TIP OF THE SOLDERING iron, my eyes watering as I stare at the motherboard through the microscope. I don't dare blink, not until I finish melting the silver solder with its rosin core flux into miniature peaks, connecting the loose components together.

I count the seconds in my head as the solder dries. *One, two...*

The butterfly lifts its delicate mechanical wings, opening and closing the intricately detailed triangles of metal as it runs through system checks. *Whirr. Click.* A small vibration signals the okay.

"Yes!" I jump to my feet and dance, rocking my hips in time to the victory music in my head.

Mom rushes in from the kitchen. "You did it?"

"Why don't you check?"

She nods and says, "To me, Petal." It takes a second for the command to register, but the butterfly flaps its wings, lifting up to land on her hand. Mom's face glows, reflecting back the stream of texts and emails that Petal projects onto the flat of her palm. "Looks like she works to me!"

I grin. "Okay, one final thing." I take Petal from Mom, gently placing her back under my microscope as I sit back in my chair. My work is flawless—so neat the repairs are barely visible. Taking it to the Moncha vet would have taken hours (and cost a fortune), but I've finished in less than an hour.

Satisfied, I snap the casing back over the exposed electronics. "There. Good as new."

"Thank you, honey!" Mom wraps her arms around me, planting multiple kisses on my forehead. I groan in mock mortification, but my face heats up with the warmth of her praise.

It's not *that* big a deal. I've had a lot of practice with Petal. The butterfly baku is one of the bestsellers for Mom's demographic, and insects in general are the least complex models on the market, offering the bare minimum of functions like text and talk, a browser, and GPS. The butterfly is extra popular because of the ability to customize its wings. On the flip side, the wings are flimsy, prone to snapping with the tiniest snag, which in turn damages the internal electronics. Petal is a perfect example. She got caught when Mom unwound her scarf and her projector malfunctioned.

"You're welcome. Remember to unleash her as soon as you get inside next time."

"I don't know what I'd do without you, Lacey. Your repair is better than any of the vets could do." Mom smiles as Petal flies back up to settle on her shoulder, her hand still lingering on my back. "You find out today, don't you?"

I cringe. I thought she had forgotten. To my surprise, even *I'd* managed to forget about it for an hour. Fixing things does that for me. My mind focuses in on the problem—in this case, a loose wire and a wonky PCB connection—and the rest of the world falls away.

Even the fact that any minute now, I'm going to receive the biggest news of my twelve-year-old life.

"Yup." All moisture evaporates from inside my mouth, and I try in vain to return the smile. I sense hesitation from Mom, her fingers drumming a pattern up and down my spine, so I stand abruptly from my chair. "Better put this stuff away," I say, gesturing to the tangle of silver wire and machinery.

Mom gives me one final kiss on the top of my head. "Whatever happens, you're still the best companioneer in *this* household." She heads over to the sink, Petal fluttering up to the leash behind her ear, where she plugs in to charge. Mom bobs her head in time to some invisible music, and I assume Petal has started streaming her favorite playlist.

I wipe the end of the soldering iron with a sponge and pack it away, closing the case with a decisive click. Some people ask for bikes or gift cards or books for their birthday. I asked for a soldering iron. I had researched a store on the outskirts of town that sold refurbished electrical tools and casually added it to Petal's GPS database—and Mom had taken me there on my eleventh birthday.

Monica Chan—who invented the bakus and lent her name to Moncha Corp, now the largest tech firm in North America—had one when she was a kid. I'd read that somewhere. If it's good enough for her, it is for me too.

As Zora, my BFF, would say, *That doesn't make you special—it makes you weird.*

She's right.

I carry my kit and microscope back to my room. Mom normally hates it when I solder in the condo—the metallic smell seems to sink into everything from the pillows on the sofa to the rice in the cooker—but when it's her own baku that needs repairing, she makes an exception.

That's too often for my liking. The level one insect bakus are renowned for being a bit…*buggy*. If I had my choice, I know exactly what baku I would get. I'd go straight for one of the originals. One of the level three spaniel models, with cute floppy ears and a tail that works as a selfie stick. If I close my eyes, I can picture hanging out with my baku in my room, teaching it to play games, helping me with my homework, and cuddling up with it at night. *But you only get a spaniel baku if you get into Profectus*, my brain reminds me.

My dream school—Profectus Academy of Science and Technology—was founded by Monica herself, and operates as a division of Moncha Corp. Profectus students are fast-tracked through all the education they need so they don't have to go to university—after they've graduated, they can be hired straight away by Moncha Corp. The Academy offer grants to incoming students who can't afford the minimum level three baku, and I need one. Otherwise, the only baku I can afford is a puny level one.

I take a deep breath.

I've done everything I can to make it happen. I have near-perfect grades, checked off all the extracurriculars, participated in science fairs and early-bird band, and volunteered for an environmental charity to pad my admission application.

Zora once told me I was locked in for a place because no one worked as hard for it as I did. If only it were that easy. It's not like I'm Carter Smith, the son of Eric Smith—Monica's business partner and co-founder of Moncha. Carter is also in our grade at St. Agnes, and even though I beat him in all our classes, and in two science fairs, I know he'll get in without a fight.

*Whereas* my *dad…*

I twist the ring on my finger, the only object I have left of him.

*…is just a liability.* I don't let myself think about it anymore. Besides, Mom and I, we owe Moncha *everything*. They gave us a place to live when Dad disappeared, gave Mom a job, and provided childcare for me while she worked. Without Moncha, I wouldn't have met Zora.

No matter what, I want to work for the company—I'll sweep Moncha floors if I have to, a practical dung beetle baku at my side. But if I truly let myself dream, I know what I want to do with the rest of my life. It's not only about working for Moncha. I want to be Monica Chan. I want to be a companioneer, one of the people working on the bakus. I want to design new animals, innovate for existing ones, and implement even more amazing features. Every day would be a challenge.

But the first step to get there is acceptance into Profectus. Although in theory, Moncha could hire companioneers from anywhere, for the past decade (since Profectus has been open), every companioneer hire has been a graduate of the academy. The middle school feeds into the high school, and all students are rising stars in science and technology fields.

*You'll know soon enough,* I remind myself. I gently place everything on my desk. *But maybe I should check...*

I bounce onto the bed and tap my phone screen to wake it up. No email from Profectus. But I have missed a Flash from Zora. *"BYE BYE!!!"* is scrawled in her fingertip-writing as a boomerang clip plays on a loop of her throwing her phone from the edge of a boardwalk.

I swipe the screen so I can see the next Flash—a still of the splash her phone makes in the lake, with the caption *#PhoneMurder*.

I snort a laugh and collapse back onto the nest of pillows. #PhoneMurder is the latest craze—the wanton, totally unnecessary (but often hilarious and creative) destruction of your old, government-granted smartphone, filmed by a newly acquired baku, and shared online. Things got out of hand when a Flashite committed #PhoneMurder by dropping his device from the top of the tallest building in the city and almost caused *actual* murder by phone. Still, the video got over ten million hits, so he'd probably consider it a win. Thanks to his status as an incoming Profectus student, he was released from police custody with only a warning.

Within the space of a few seconds, I film a video of myself drawing a fake tear dripping down my cheek, select the puppy-ear filter, type *"RIP ZORA'S PHONE"* as a caption, and send my reply. This is the distraction I need.

If Zora is destroying her phone that means she must have chosen her baku already. My next message to her is a giant question mark. Okay, I send her about fifteen of them.

*"I chose...a dormouse!"* Zora's next selfie shows her hugging the cutest baku I've ever seen, a tiny ball of soft, matte-gray metal fur, pointed nose, and oversize eyes. It's curled up in a ball next to her cheek, its long tail extended to take the picture, her dark brown skin glowing gold from the sunlight reflected off the lake. She looks so happy; I can't help but smile with her. A dormouse is a level two baku—better than I can afford, but not good enough for a place at Profectus—but going there was never one of Zora's goals. She's continuing on at St. Agnes and experimenting with programming on the side.

*"His name is Linus, and I can already tell we're going to be best friends for life. Well, not better friends than you and me, but you'll know what I mean as soon as you get your own. Tell me as soon as you hear anything!!!"* reads her next message.

*"Of course,"* I shoot back. I stare at the photo of her and Linus together a little longer, my throat feeling tight.

Then it comes in. The alert. I can only read a tiny portion

of the subject line, and it gives nothing away. **LACEY CHU: PROFECTUS APPLICATION STATUS**

My heart hammers inside my chest. The slim, rectangular device feels so old-school in my suddenly clammy palm, but then... This is it. The very last time I will use it. Before I choose a baku of my very own. Level one or level three.

A single tap opens my email app where, in bold letters, is the message I'd been waiting for.

I click open.

*Dear Miss Chu,*

*We regret to inform you that...*

The phone flies out of my hand like it's heated to a thousand degrees. It bounces off the corner of my bed frame and onto the floor, where—just like that—the screen shatters into a million tiny pieces.

Exactly like my dreams.

2

"I'M SORRY, WE'RE SOLD OUT OF THE PRAYING mantis." The vet doesn't even look up at me as he stares at the information provided by his Labrador baku. They're standard-issue for employees of the Moncha store (and most service industry professionals), always helpful, with smooth, black, digital fur that makes reading information off their backs easy.

I feel a twinge of jealousy at the sight, and then a wave of embarrassment for envying a Moncha store employee. They call themselves *vets* because they think it's hilarious, as if they have real medical degrees or something, but the actual geniuses behind the bakus are the companioneers, not the faux-hip guys in white lab coats and lens-free, plastic-rimmed glasses with no real understanding of what makes their bakus tick.

But the truth is, this vet is still going to have a better baku than I will.

"This is a waste of time," I say to Zora, turning away, but she grabs my arm and drags me back around to stare at the screen on the glaring white counter.

"No way am I standing in line again," she hisses. Then she turns her sweetest smile on to the vet. On the counter, one of Moncha's slogans glows to life: *Moncha: We always have your bak(u).*

Well, it doesn't have *my* particular baku, but that's apparently beside the point.

"So…no praying mantis and no dragonflies. What *do* you have in stock?" Zora asks. Linus sticks his head out from underneath her collar and twitches his nose at me. I wrinkle mine in response and poke my tongue out. Linus ducks back under the fabric, and Zora shoots me a look over her shoulder. I roll my eyes but pay attention to the vet once again.

"We have butterflies and scarabs in the insect department," he says, bringing up my options on the screen. "If you want to move up to level two, small mammals, the selection is a lot bigger…"

I grimace. Without the Profectus grant, all I can afford with my savings is a level one insect. "I'll pick something another time," I say through gritted teeth, not feeling inspired by any of the options.

"You can't, because you smashed your phone, remember? You need something *now*." Zora grabs my arm again to stop me moving.

I sigh. I know she's right, but my mind is still refusing to accept reality. I rub the sore spot behind my ear where the leash has been installed. I'm committed now, and I have to choose something. *I can always upgrade in a few years, when I've saved up a bit more money…*

The vet stares pointedly over my shoulder at the long line snaking its way out the door behind me. I take a deep breath and force myself to focus. "Okay, I'll take a scarab," I say, pointing at one on the counter's screen. Its carapace is greenish-purple, iridescent like an oil slick. It's kind of pretty. Scarabs are known for having flight issues (something about the way the wings fold up) but I don't want the same baku as my mom. That would be too sad.

"Coming right up. Rolo and I will go get one for you." He snaps his fingers, and his retriever baku follows him obediently to the stockroom.

Once the vet and his baku are gone, I turn my back on the counter and cross my arms. "Well, this sucks."

Zora nudges my shoulder. "Can I give you a hug?"

She knows I'm not normally the touchy-feely type, but I nod—every hug is worth its weight in gold right about now. The sting of the Profectus rejection is a raw hurt, an open wound that refuses to heal over. I keep going over it in my head.

*Did I fail a portion of the test?*

*Which part?*

*If I'd studied harder…*

*Or maybe the competition this year was too much…*

Yet as much as I want to pretend it was a mistake, or forget the email ever came in, Zora's right: I barely lasted the morning without the internet (is internet withdrawal a thing? Because I was all shaky and sweaty without being able to check my Flashes) and I can't show up to school with a broken phone. I need a baku. It's not even a social standing thing anymore. At St. Agnes (where I'll be forced to stay now that I wasn't accepted into Profectus), once we enter seventh grade, all our textbooks are stored in baku-encrypted software, and homework assignments are sent to our bakus directly. It's the trade-off of living in Monchaville. It's not really called that, but it might as well be. Moncha provides our housing, health care, and education—it's a corporate mini-city within Toronto, occupying almost the entire eastern half of the city. And a requirement of living in Monchaville is that you have your own baku. Not that that's a big deal anymore. Almost everyone in the country has one.

Another slogan appears where my elbows are touching the countertop. *Bak-up your life... Moncha's newest cloud software included with every new baku.* This time, a picture of Monica flashes up, with her signature asymmetrical bangs cut into a diamond pattern, almost like a reverse crown. Mom has a story of when I tried to cut my hair into the same style...and that's why I had a pixie cut for half of second grade.

Seeing Monica's face makes me smile. The story behind bakus is ingrained in our cultural history, and Monica Chan is its main protagonist. There's even a Hollywood-produced miniseries about her journey, called *(Wo)man's Best Friend.* I stream it whenever I'm feeling low or uninspired—and I dread to think how many times it's been logged that I watch it.

The story goes that Monica grew up glued to her smart-phone—so much so that it began to be detrimental to both her mental and physical health. During her doctor-mandated phone break, she wandered the streets and found herself watching people walking their dogs in High Park. She realized what she'd been missing all along: a companion. If her smartphone was going to be by her side all the time, why not have it be cute and interactive? Something she could love and feel comforted by? But that could also be useful— helping her keep track of her life and her calendar, stay in touch with her friends and family, and access her social media and the internet and everything else she needed.

She got to work in the storage locker of her apartment building because her parents didn't have a house with a garage (I bet her mom couldn't stand the smell of solder either). They squeezed their entire family into a two-bedroom condo, just like my family's. She designed a robotic pet with all the features of a smartphone and called it a "baku" because of a story she'd heard from her Chinese grandmother about creatures made up of the leftover parts of other animals. Her first model, affectionately known as Yi (the Chinese word for *one*), was built out of the screen from her portable gaming device, her old smartphone's motherboard, and metal parts she could scrape together from old toys and electronics. She went door-to-door in her apartment building, asking her neighbors to give her any old bits of tech destined for the scrapyard.

She took her design to a board of reality television investors, who threw money at her and turned her—and her baku—into a viral sensation overnight. Before long, Moncha was up and running in a small co-working space in Toronto's Discovery District, alongside crowdsourced taxi services and the latest health-tracking software. It opened its first factory east of the city and kept expanding, taking over buildings and multiplying like mold in a petri dish as bakus became *the* must-have device around the world. Monica bought her old condominium building to help provide housing for her employees, then started her own school for her employees' kids, acquired a local hospital to provide health care, and quickly, Monchaville was born.

A loud crash from beside me snaps me from my thoughts. Zora gasps, and when I look up, my jaw drops too. On the counter two down from ours is a stunning high-level baku—an eagle—its wings spread so wide, they've knocked over a display case of customizable butterfly wings. The companioneering work on display is on a level beyond anything I've seen. The feathers are made up of individual filaments of steel sprayed gold, giving it a rich, sparkling texture. It tosses its head—so lifelike—and lets out a screech that almost pierces my eardrums. It's magnificent. It's absolutely top-of-the-line. Must be at least level four, if not level five.

Who could *afford* something like that?

I get my answer. The eagle folds its wings and, staring wide-eyed at his new baku, is a guy in a Profectus-branded jersey.

"Lace?" Zora whispers in my ear. "I think you're drooling."

"What?" I drop my head and wipe my mouth, in case she wasn't joking. "That baku is amazing."

"That's not the only thing that's amazing. He is cute," Zora says in a low voice, wiggling her eyebrows at the guy, making me snort.

She's not wrong. I dare one more glance. The guy is older than us and tall—with close-shaved black hair that's just starting to lift into small curls. His teeth are bright white against his dark skin as his lips split into a giant grin.

I'd be grinning like that too if that beautiful bird was destined to be my baku.

"Tobias, my man!" comes a shout from behind me. Another guy—also in a Profectus jersey, but this one so new I see the price tag sticking out the back—barges past me, knocking me into Zora, and then both of us into the counter.

"Watch it!" I snap. "There's a line, you know."

The guy doesn't turn around, but his baku does. An ugly pig snuffles at our feet, pawing at the ground. It has two huge tusks, and it sways its head menacingly—not a pig, then, but a boar. I leap back, letting out an involuntary yelp.

"Rein it in, Carter," says Zora, who recovers faster than me.

My neck snaps around so fast, I almost get whiplash. *Carter?*

I don't know why I'm so surprised. Despite the fact that I beat him in almost every class—much to his annoyance—his acceptance into Profectus was a signed, sealed, and delivered thing.

He saunters over, smirking at me.

"Zora? Is that you—and Lacey?"

I cringe as he says my name. I wish with all my heart now that I had taken the subway out to some distant Moncha store where I wouldn't run into people I know. Especially not this particular person.

"Admiring my new baku, are you? When I got my Profectus acceptance last night, I got him *right* away. Meet Hunter—he's a level four, in case you didn't know."

I grimace, despite myself. Trust him to get a level four baku without having to earn it. I wonder if he even knows how to operate it properly. And his dad probably got one of the companioneers at Moncha to customize it for him. My body aches with jealousy. "Choosing your baku, are you?" He leans his elbow on the counter, tilting his head to one side. "What are you going for?"

"Oh, uh…" I try to calculate the time it would take for me to bolt to the door. Internet or no internet, anything is better than the humiliation I'm about to face if…

"Here's your beetle, miss."

The vet's timing couldn't be worse. He sets the tiny box down on the counter, the beetle baku trapped in a white plastic mold, clearly visible through the transparent opening in the front. Carter's eyes bulge out of his head. I don't know whether he's going to explode from confusion or glee—or both, as the realization dawns. Then, he begins to laugh. He laughs and laughs, as my face burns with embarrassment.

I turn away from Carter, but not before I notice that everyone in the store is looking at me, including the cute guy Tobias with the eagle baku.

"You didn't get in, did you? Oh, Lacey—all those years of being a total nerd, wasted!" Carter says, before laughing even more.

"Come on, Zora," I mumble, snatching the beetle off the counter, and this time, she doesn't try to stop me.

"Hey, don't you want me to show you how to leash it?" the vet calls after us.

But Zora and I are already out the door.

3

"HE'S A JERK. FORGET ABOUT HIM," SAYS ZORA,
once she catches up to me. She slips her arm around mine, forcing
me back to a more normal pace. But I don't want to slow down.
Everywhere I look in the mall, I see people with their higher-level
bakus—mechanical dogs and cats either trotting at their heels or
leashed up on their shoulders—and it's a constant reminder of what I
can't have. I make a beeline for the exit, craving sunlight and fresh air.

I'm still shaking, Carter's laugh a soundtrack to my steps that
I can't turn off. I'm simultaneously humiliated and annoyed that
I've let him get to me. My new beetle baku is still trapped in the
box in my hand; I can't bear to look at it yet. "Let's go somewhere,"
I say to Zora once we're through the revolving doors and outside.
"Somewhere…to escape from here."

"I know a place. I'll get directions." She holds her palm out as her
dormouse sneaks down her arm, projecting directions on her fingers.

I shove the beetle into my backpack. Zora shoots me a look, but doesn't say anything. I avert my eyes, focusing on the zipper of my bag. I can tell by the gentle rattle of the beads at the bottom of her braids that she's shaking her head at me.

By the time I stand again, though, she's over it. That's what I love best about Zora. She's the least emotional person I know. It's one of the things that makes her such a great coder. She sees everything as if it's an algorithm, including our emotions.

"This is your body's built-in response to stressful stimuli," she'd told me when we first met, while I was crying in the elevator after getting a B on a test in third grade, and I blinked at her as if I couldn't believe I'd found another eight-year-old as nerdy as I was. She'd just moved into the same condo building with her parents and three high-maintenance sisters. I'd always been the loner kid in class—the one who took everything (especially my grades) a bit too seriously, who was always hungry to learn more about engineering, to be the one the teacher always knew to call on. Zora was the first person who was as passionate about something as I was.

No other person has ever understood me like she does. We lock together like pieces of a very specific jigsaw puzzle. She pushes; I pull. She codes; I build. My creations would be lifeless without her code and her code formless without my builds. And because we live in the same building, she's always hanging out in my unit—helping me not get too lonely when Mom is at work, and even hanging out with Mom when I'm tinkering in the basement. She's more like a sister than a friend—she calls me a sister that she *chose* rather than was born with—and I don't know what I'd do without her.

There is no specific border for when we leave Monchaville, no massive gate or wall, but there's a definite *feeling*. A gentle shift in energy from one side of the road to the other. I think it's because of how clean everything is in the part of town that is run by the company. They took over responsibility from the city for all the maintenance of the ten-block (and expanding) rectangle in exchange for preferential planning permissions and the right to override specific bylaws. I saw an article in a regular city paper once that said the sidewalks and pathways around Moncha are embedded with anti-trademark-infringement alarms that trigger if someone attempts to steal anything, and that there are security bird bakus flying over every square inch. I don't know if any of the rumors are true—I've never seen any unusual-looking birds or heard an alarm, but the Moncha guard—the security team—are ever-present, keeping the streets of Monchaville safe.

Tales of surveillance bakus and alarms go against everything I've read about Monica Chan—she doesn't seem paranoid about copyright infringement. We've had loads of talks in school about how important it is for us to experiment and play—that's how technology makes its great leaps forward. And no company in the world has yet been able to replicate the bakus to any reasonable standard. There was a disastrous version that came out in Germany—the animals were all based on mythological creatures (that part was totally cool)—but they bugged out and started twitching, scrambling text messages and rerouting all websites to illegal darknet stuff. One even attacked its owner. They had to shut down production within a week. Once again, there were rumors that it could have easily been Moncha's ace code creators that infected the German hosts, but viral code wouldn't explain the weird mechanical tics.

In the decade that bakus have been around, there haven't been any major glitches. The neuroleash technology is no more invasive than an ear piercing. The best part is that even older bakus can be upgraded, incorporating any developments in the technology, under lifetime Moncha warrantee. Their spread around the world has been so rapid and prolific, there isn't any need for competition. And if you want to work for a cutting-edge technology company, there is only one choice: Moncha.

There has only ever been one choice for me, that's for sure. Except now, the spark of hope is accompanied by a wave of crashing disappointment. I wonder if that feeling will ever go away, or if I'll be left with this regret for the rest of my life.

When Linus indicates we should turn left, I realize where Zora is taking us. I grin with delight. The river valley trails. The river valley slices through the city center like a river of green, an oasis of calm in the busy metropolis. It's one of my favorite parts of the city. You can look down into it and pretend you're in the middle of the wilderness. I have a blurred memory of being on my dad's shoulders as we hiked down toward the tracks and—

I immediately curse my brain and scrub it of all mention of my dad. I do not need to go there. Not today. Today has been filled with enough disappointment.

"Everything all right?" Zora asks, and Linus tilts his head in strange synchronicity. He's only been hers for a day, and yet already he's adopting her mannerisms and becoming as much a part of her as the line of earrings dotted up her earlobe.

"What do you mean?"

She tilts her head and stares at my hand. "You're rubbing your ring."

Heat rises in my cheeks, and I snap my hands apart. She's right. Whenever I touch my dad's old engineering ring—the last piece of him I have left—something is up.

The iron rings are a Canadian engineering tradition. Supposedly forged from the iron of a collapsed bridge, it's a reminder of the immense responsibility borne by engineers to keep the safety of their work in mind. It's supposed to be worn on the left pinky, but my hands are much smaller than my dad's. I wear mine on my thumb. Besides, I'm not an engineer yet.

*And maybe now, you never will be—not for Moncha Corp, anyway*, says a small voice in my head.

I push the thought away.

"Oh, I'm fine," I say. "This was the perfect place to come. I love it here." I throw my arms wide and twirl around under the canopy of leaves, hoping to distract her.

It works. She closes her eyes and takes a deep breath. "It's pretty great. And if we head across the bridge, it's a shortcut downtown, so we can get some bubble tea."

There's a suspension bridge in the middle of the park that crosses over the high-speed rail tracks. "Excellent plan," I say. I stare at the pattern of shadows created by the leaves on her face and arms, her skin shining burnished copper where the sun hits it. I feel a twinge of sadness that she's off to an advanced coding course this summer. It's an amazing opportunity for her.

"When does your program start?" I ask, wanting to know exactly how many days I have to hang with Zora before she leaves me for two whole months.

"Hmm?" She opens her deep brown eyes and levels her gaze at me. "Oh…beginning of next week. Are you going to miss me?"

"Are you kidding?" I stop in my tracks. "What am I going to do with my summer without you?"

She pokes me in the ribs. "Maybe you'll *enjoy* yourself. It's the summer. You've worked hard all friggin' year. You're allowed to take a break and relax."

"Right…" *Easy for you to say, but you get to do the thing you've been wanting to do your whole life. Whereas for me…* The words balance on the tip of my tongue, but I don't let them spill off the edge.

Laughter reaches us from behind, the low chuckle of inside jokes and bad puns. Zora looks over her shoulder. "Oh no," she says, her shoulders tensing.

"What is it?" I turn around too and immediately see the source of tension: the twitch of a robotic boar nose coming up behind us. Their bakus must have directed them down the same shortcut into downtown.

"Oh look, it's beetle brain and her rodent friend," says Carter, his voice laced with smugness as he approaches. He's accompanied by a few guys I don't recognize, all with level three bakus and also in Profectus shirts, and Tobias. At least *he* has the decency to look ashamed at his friend's blatant taunting, staring off into the trees and refusing to make eye contact. As if I'm looking at him anyway. My eyes drift over to the sight of his beautiful eagle baku, my stomach clenching with jealousy.

"Ignore Carter," whispers Zora, holding her chin up high. Linus quivers inside the hood of her jacket. We slow our pace, hoping they'll pass us by.

"Now, seriously though," says Carter, holding his hands up in front of him as he steps in front of us, forcing us to stop. Reluctantly, I hold his gaze. "I'm kinda disappointed that you're not going to be at Profectus next year. You were by far my closest competition in our class. I guess now I get to see what the *actual* smart kids are like. So did you flunk the exam?"

Beside me, Zora bristles, all four-and-a-half feet of her stocky frame, and she glares at me expectantly, her expression in her deep-brown eyes screaming: *You can't let him get away with saying that!*

But my treacherous brain draws a blank at anything witty or creative. Instead, I mumble nonwords, drop my chin and my eyes, and keep on walking, speeding up this time. My cheeks burn with shame.

Zora doesn't immediately follow, and I whisper a silent prayer for her to *drop it*, and a few seconds later, she's hurrying to catch

up with me. "I preferred him without that baku," Zora hisses in my ear, and—as if he's heard us—we hear a huff and snort from the boar behind.

"He'll probably upgrade him in no time." Despite myself, I sneak a glance over my shoulder. It's true: Carter is like a different person with that boar by his side. He's standing taller, his stance wider, and his blond hair less lank and greasy on top of his head. The Profectus makeover. It's a thing.

"Come on, guys," he shouts after us. "This might be the last time we see you—soon we won't exactly be traveling in the same circles." He's tossing a ball up and down in his hand—I recognize it as a baku training tool, so owners can play "fetch" with their bakus like with a real pet. "Unless I need someone to come and clean my house. Isn't that what beetles do? The grunt work of the animal world?"

"What does that make you, a garbage disposal like your pig?" The words fly out of my mouth before I can stop them. I might hate my little beetle, but that doesn't mean I'm going to give Carter permission to dis him.

A flare of red creeps over Carter's pasty skin, rising up from his collar to his cheek like an angry tide, and his fist closes over the baku ball. We don't want to see his reaction rise any further (satisfying though it is). I know full well I might have just poked an angry bear...or boar. I pull Zora forward.

"I'll have you know pigs are highly intelligent and resourceful creatures!" Carter's screechy voice follows us down the trail. "Come back! Don't you want to see what a level four baku can do?"

We ignore him, half running, half walking until we are out of sight and earshot before we relax.

Once upon a time, I would have loved to see a level four baku at work—especially something as complex as a boar model—but now, I only want to get away. I hate how small Carter can make me feel. Less than twenty-four hours since I got the rejection from Profectus, and already it's like my dreams have shrunk down from sky-high to subterranean.

There's a snapping of twigs and leaves behind us, a sinister snarl.

The boar is back. I reach out and grab Zora's hand—the boar baku might be intimidating, but he can't hurt us or Linus—he's not programmed that way. If we can get across the bridge and into the city, we can lose them for good. I start to run.

At first, Zora surges forward with me, but then her palm slips from mine. There are angry shouts from behind us and then a piercing screech from the eagle. I stop and spin around, already halfway across the bridge.

Tobias's eagle soars over the top of Zora's head, so close his wings brush her hairline, and he snatches something too small for me to see out of the air in his talons. She screams with fear, but she's running so fast, she stumbles over her flip-flops, skidding out of control, and she lands with a thump on the metal surface of the bridge. Something escapes her collar then bounces once, twice, and over the edge and down into the valley.

Out of instinct, I grab the closest thing I can find—a pine

cone—and whip it at the eagle to get it away from Zora. My aim, surprisingly, is good. The pine cone rattles against the eagle's golden wings, sending it off-balance.

Then I hear Zora's panicked scream: "Linus!"

*Oh no.* My throat drops into my stomach and I race to Zora's side, leaning out over the railing as Carter, Tobias, and the rest of his friends run past us on the bridge, disappearing into the forest the other side. Cowards.

But her brand-new baku is absolutely nowhere to be seen.

4

"NO!" CRIES ZORA. SHE'S SHAKING, HER HANDS clawing at her collar and at the leash around her ear, as if praying to find Linus tucked away in a fold somewhere. "Linus? Linus, are you there?"

But if he were there, he would have answered. Instead, there's a deafening silence.

She grabs my hands, pulling herself to her feet. "Lace, I can't lose him! I just got him. All my savings…"

"I know." I take a deep breath. I know *exactly* how hard Zora has worked to save up for her baku, and I'm not going to let Carter and his friends take that away from her. I look down toward the valley floor and the railway tracks—then at my feet encased in their sturdy boots and Zora's feet in flip-flops. I know what I have to do. I turn back to Zora, pressing my phone into her palm. Even though the screen is broken, it still works. "Call Moncha guard. Tell them what happened."

She stares at the phone through tear-filled eyes, her forehead wrinkling in confusion. It looks laughably old-fashioned in her hand already. But then she sniffs and closes her fingers tight around the handset. "Okay."

"Good," I say, before pulling my sleeves down so they cover my lower arms and tightening up the straps on my backpack.

"Wait, where are you going?" she asks.

I climb up onto the metal railing. "I'm going to find Linus." Without waiting for her response, I swing my leg over and hop down onto the overgrown slope on the other side. Zora hesitates—I can tell she wants to follow—but she does the mental calculations in her head. She can't clamber down into the ravine in her footwear. "I'll be fine," I tell her, and after another second she agrees.

"Thank you!" she shouts after me.

I start my hike, pushing aside the shrub, trying not to think about the ticks and bugs that lurk in the long grass. I hear the start of Zora's conversation with Moncha guard. "Hello? Yes, I'd like to report a lost baku ..."

The deeper I get into the ravine, the steeper it becomes, and Zora's voice fades away as I concentrate on my footing. Stupid rational thoughts crowd my brain, like: *How am I going to get back up out of here?* and *Why did I leave my phone behind?* I push them away again. When I look back up at the bridge to try and make sure I am following Linus's most likely flight path, I can barely make out the metal railings. From here, it looks as if I am in a forest—all I can see are the tops of the trees and the shrubs and the blue sky. It could be peaceful.

Then, I'm almost forced to my knees. There's a loud screech of iron against iron and a strong gust of wind as a train hurtles by on the tracks below. I hope the baku wasn't thrown as far as the tracks. He would be squashed dormouse parts if that were the case, and impossible to fix.

It's amazing how quickly Zora has bonded with Linus—it's one of the magic side effects of the bakus that Monica Chan said she never could have predicted. Of course, she had known that having a companion would be part of the robot's appeal—but what started out as a tool to help her overcome her smartphone addiction exploded once it hit the mass market. People really came to *love* their bakus. And Monica was keen that she built each machine to last, with upgrades fully backward compatible. She herself still had her first-gen model—a slinky cat by the name of Yi—and the Moncha marketing machine played on that for their slogans. *A baku is for life—so get one for Christmas.*

My own grandma would tell me stories of how people used to be addicted to their phones, sitting at the dinner table scrolling on tiny screens rather than talking to each other. And they had to be charged every single day, tying you to the wall. Sometimes, if you used them too much, they even lost charge in the middle of the day and you were stuck, phoneless, until you could find an outlet.

That was the Moncha breakthrough *part two.* She always

credited her business partner, Eric Smith, for the discovery, even though I'm positive she had more to do with it than him. Still, *together* they discovered a way to convert the natural kinetic energy of human movement into battery power for the bakus. Combined with solar backups, as long as a baku spent some time being "leashed" to their owner, they kept their charge. The leash was a strange concept to get used to at first, but the procedure to install it was no more invasive than an earring. One gun and done. I'd had my leash put in that morning—I just hadn't connected the beetle to it yet. But once I did, maybe I would bond with it.

*Beetles are the best bakus. They take up hardly any energy; they don't even need to be leashed every night. They're virtually indestructible. They're super customizable. Beetles are the perfect companions.*

Yeah. Says everyone who can't afford anything different.

I think about Companioneers Crescent, the road we would have moved into had my dad not…disappeared.

If I'd gotten into Profectus, I could have given Mom and I another shot at a great life. A big house. A job for as long as I want. Lifelong benefits. But once I graduate from St. Agnes, I'll have to leave Monchaville, or else get a Moncha job suitable for a beetle baku owner.

My beetle. I need to think of a name for him. Anything except Beetlejuice or Crawly. People are so unimaginative. Maybe I'll call him Speck. Because compared to other bakus, he's a tiny bit of machinery.

My foot slips on the muddy ground, and I steady myself by

grabbing a branch. If my calculations are right, Linus should have landed nearby—but who knows how far he might have continued to roll down the hill.

Bakus have built-in distress signals for if they're away from their owner's side or if they're broken. My ears prick as I hear a telltale beep—not as strong as a normal signal, but maybe the fall damaged that too.

"Linus?" I call out. The bakus are programmed to respond to their names. Sometimes it doesn't work so well with someone other than the owner's voice, but the beeping speeds up like a chew toy on steroids—I'm sure it must be him. I crash through the overgrown foliage, trying to locate the source.

Then I see him, so small he's caught in the center of a huge leaf, right where the foliage meets the stem. I push the leaf down and scoop the little mouse up in my palm. He doesn't look in too bad shape—his tail is a bit bent, and I'll have to take some test pictures to see if the camera still works, but I'm confident I can fix him.

"There, there, Linus," I say, even though it feels a little absurd to be comforting a robot. He seems to appreciate it though, twitching his nose before he gives a final wheeze and all electronic life leaves his eyes. He needs to be leashed before I can assess him anymore. Now to find a way out of here.

I place Linus in my jacket pocket and search for a path back up the hill.

The leaf I'd been leaning on snaps as I shift my weight. Before

I can grab anything else, I tumble, my shoulder colliding with the ground as I catapult forward and slide deeper down into the ravine.

I dig in with my feet, trying to stop my fall toward the railway tracks and super-high-speed trains at the very bottom of the valley. I grab at every passing branch and plant, slicing my palm in the process, but I can't think about it before I launch off a small concrete wall and land on the stony ground below. Something crashes down beside me.

I wait a beat, then another, my breath coming in hard, fast gasps as I brace myself for pain. Yet I can't stop for too long. I hear the whine of an approaching train, and my feet are way too close to the tracks. I yank them in, curling my arms around my knees, my back up against the wall. I close my eyes, and the train whooshes by me.

5

IT SEEMS TO LAST FOREVER, THE SCREAM OF THE wind and the debris hitting my face, but eventually, it passes. I take a deep breath that fills my lungs. I'm not hurt—or at least, nothing is broken—but I'm going to ache in the morning.

My hand snaps to my pocket. I almost don't want to look inside but I do, and breathe a sigh of relief—Linus doesn't look much worse for wear after my fall. He's survived one big drop already—I guess another didn't do him any more harm.

My heart jumps as I see a smear of red on my jeans, my jacket… everywhere. Blood. It's coming from my palm where I sliced it on the way down. The wound is sharp and clean and gapes like a mouth—my stomach turns looking at it. I pull out an old gym T-shirt from my backpack, which I awkwardly wrap around my hand to staunch the blood. I need to get home. Now.

The benefit of being by the railway tracks is that I know there must be steps for workmen down into the valley. I can follow them back up to the main road.

As I swing my bag over my shoulder, I hear a trill of electronic beeping. My instinct makes me think of Linus, but it can't be him—he's powered down.

Then I see it. At my feet is a crumpled pile of black metal—the thing that fell down next to me. One side is slick with bright red blood—mine, I realize. This is what I must have sliced myself on.

"Stupid piece of junk," I say, kicking it with my boot. It seems to make a tiny mewl of pain—but I must have imagined it. It rolls over against the concrete, revealing a gaping hole, gray and charred around the edges. It looks like it's been through the mill.

Something catches my eye, and I kneel to look closer. I blink rapidly, my brain hardly processing what my eyes are seeing. It's the Moncha logo. At least, I think it is—it's distorted and half-hidden by what look like scorch marks. But Moncha-made metal can be useful— especially when it comes to doing unauthorized repairs on bakus.

The railway lines hum again, and I don't give myself any more time to think. I scoop the metal contraption into my bag, shoving it to the bottom beneath my smelly gym uniform and the new beetle baku I've just bought. There might be parts to sell or salvage, if nothing else.

Then, without wasting any more time, I climb the steps back up out of the valley.

The top is blocked by a gate, but I clamber over it without too much trouble, relieved to be out of the woods. It takes a while to orient myself—without a phone or an active baku, I feel cut off, as if I'm missing a limb. I've come out on a quiet residential road, towering apartment blocks all around, but the signs mean little to me. I don't normally travel anywhere without GPS.

How did people handle it before? With physical telephone boxes on the side of the road that needed change to make a call or actual maps that didn't provide automatic directions…

My hand throbs where I've sliced it. I swallow and spin around 360 degrees. This can't be too difficult. The city is built on a grid. I'm not in Monchaville, so that means the ravine is east. If I walk away from it—west—I'll find a main road and from there, a subway station.

I adjust the straps on my bag, face what I *hope* is west, and start walking.

"Hey, you there!" a gruff voice calls from behind me.

I spin on my heels, and my heart lurches. Three men are jogging up to me in perfect synchronization, coming from the same set of stairs I used to climb out of the ravine. Three vicious-looking panther bakus are at their heels, sleek and efficient. No attempt has been made to make them look remotely like real animals. They're all sleek, metal plates, exposed pistons and wires, flashing yellow eyes and razor-sharp claws. The men wear full face masks and black uniforms, but I don't see the distinctive Moncha logo or a police badge on their shoulders. One of them lowers his visor enough to reveal dark brown eyes under his bushy black brows.

"Don't move. Moncha guard." He flashes his badge at me so quick, I barely register it. It did look vaguely like the logo, so I stay put. My feet are rooted to the floor anyway. I've never once been in trouble with the police or the Moncha guard.

The man flicks his eyes up and down, taking in the state of me. I can't imagine what he must be thinking. The T-shirt wrapped around my hand is bloodstained, I've got bits of tree and dirt stuck in my hair, and my jeans are all torn up—not in an artful way.

In an *I've-just-tumbled-down-a-ravine-trespassing-on-train-tracks* kind of way.

"We need to see your baku."

"I'm sorry," I stutter out. "I didn't mean to trespass. My best friend's baku fell down into the valley, and I went to find it…"

"Your baku, please."

"I…I don't have one yet—"

"Active baku indicated in—" The man talks over me, and the panther baku steps forward.

Then I remember. Linus. I quickly grab him from my pocket. "This is the baku I have on me! He belongs to my friend, Zora Layeni."

The panther stalks forward and sniffs at Linus. A stream of information appears on his back, which the dark-eyed man leans over to read.

"Property of Zora Layeni. Reported missing forty-five minutes ago. What's your name?"

"Lacey. Lacey Chu."

"You're on the approved list." He steps back and stares at me. "Did you see anyone else while you were down there? Or see any other bakus?"

I shake my head, my legs trembling. "No…no one! I just grabbed Linus and came straight out again."

The panther circles me, and the man waits for several of my loud heartbeats before waving his hand. "You're free to go," he says.

"Thank you, sir." I nod, then turn and start walking in what I hope is a normal manner. They don't seem to care that I was down in the ravine at all.

I've barely taken ten steps when I hear a snarl behind me.

"Wait, Rex IXX has detected another baku in the backpack." The unmasked man strides forward, grabbing my bag and forcing me to stop. Before I have any chance to protest, he rips it down off my shoulders. He opens the zipper, and my beetle baku, still in his packaging, tumbles to the floor.

My mouth goes dry. I'd forgotten about the beetle. And even though I don't think I've committed any crime, my heart pounds with fear. These guards look deadly serious, and I don't want to look like I've deliberately deceived them. "Please—I forgot because I haven't had the chance to register the beetle yet—I only got him this morning…"

"Her story check out, Jones," says one of the other guards, and my shoulders slump with relief. "Receipt from the Moncha store is stored on the cloud registered to a Lacey Chu. Let's go. Boss has sent us through another lead."

He grunts, tossing the backpack at my feet, and I drop to my knees to scoop the beetle baku back into the bag. The men take off in the opposite direction, running in sync.

When I touch my face, it's damp with tears. It doesn't seem like this day could get any worse.

6

"LACEY, WHAT TOOK YOU SO LONG? I WAS WORRIED..."
Mom's words die in her mouth as she rounds the corner and takes
in my ratty appearance. "What happened to you?"

I drop the backpack with a thud on the floor and don't reply—
just groan.

"Let me look at that hand." Mom leads me through into the
kitchen and sits me down firmly by the shoulders. She unwinds the
makeshift T-shirt bandage from my wound and hisses a breath at
the sight of it, then clucks her tongue against the roof of her mouth.
"Don't move," she says, as she disappears into our bathroom and
then returns with antiseptic solution.

"Ow!" I cry out as Mom cleans the wound.

She turns my palm this way and that. "You'll live," she says
with a sigh. "Any deeper and you might've needed stitches. That
would have put an end to your intricate soldering days for the

summer. What were you thinking?" She leans forward and pushes my hair off my face, scanning my head for other scrapes or cuts. "Are you hurt anywhere else?"

"No, I'm fine." I lean back to push her away, my hand throbbing.

She folds her arms. "Well, good. That means you can explain to me how this happened."

I wince. "Zora and I ran into Carter."

"Lacey!" Mom's tone is sharp. While she knows a bit about our rivalry, she's more concerned that I don't tick off the son of the second-most-powerful person in Moncha Corp.

"What? He and his friends were being jerks. Zora got spooked by one of their bakus and accidentally dropped Linus down into the ravine. So I went to get him."

"Oh, honey," says Mom, disapproval warring with admiration on her face. "And Linus is all right?"

I pull him out of my pocket to show her. "He's a little banged up. I'll go downstairs and take a look at him, but he should be fine. I'm just so mad at those guys. And the fact that Carter got into Profectus and not me. Where's the justice in that? I'm twice the engineer he is, and my grades are always better…"

Mom's mouth draws into a thin line, any residual admiration disappearing. It's disapproval all the way now. I'm sure the V-shaped frown marks at the top of her nose have been caused solely by my obsession with getting into Profectus. She knows my motives are good, but I think the obsession reminds her of my dad…and that didn't end well. All I know is that when I was around five years old, he had some kind of nervous breakdown, leaving Mom and I, never to be heard from again. I don't know the whole story because I've never pressed, but my intense drive can be triggering for Mom.

"St. Agnes isn't the end of the world, and you'll have Zora with you. You can still be an engineer."

"Just not for Moncha," I mutter.

Her expression softens, and she reaches out to stroke my hair. "No, not for Moncha. And if we have to move, we'll move. Sometimes you have to change your dreams, Lacey. No matter how hard you work, sometimes things won't go your way."

I want to protest, but I also know better. "I'm going to shower and then go to my cave, okay?"

"Okay, honey. But take a plate of food with you. You've had a shock today, and you need your brain fuel."

"Not for St. Agnes, I won't," I mumble, dashing away to the bathroom so Mom can't groan at me.

The heat of the shower scrubs the dirt and leaves from my hair and skin, but leaves me feeling raw. The fact that the choice has been taken out of my hands is what makes it even worse. I sigh. I just have to find a new dream. And if I can't be an companioneer for Moncha, then I'll be a...

My mind fails to come up with even a halfway decent alternative.

At least I'll be with Zora, I remind myself, as the water around my feet finally runs clear.

Out of the shower, I throw on an old plaid shirt and some black leggings, winding my dark hair into a bun to dry naturally. I don't have a phone to text Zora on, so I shoot her an old-school email on my ancient laptop, telling her I've found Linus and I'll bring him around to her unit tomorrow after I've fixed him up.

She responds almost right away with a series of "Praise the Lord" emojis. She has a real nostalgia moment whenever we email and fills the screen with as many emojis as she can.

I head into the kitchen and pick up a pot of ramen noodles. I nuke them in the microwave and pour the slimy concoction into a thermos, then pick up my backpack while yelling goodbye to Mom. The television blasts the theme song to her favorite show as I shut the door and head to the elevator. I press the button for the basement level.

It's time to work.

The elevator doors open into the underground parking lot, but I'm not there for the cars. Every apartment in the building is allocated its own small, rectangular storage locker. Most people keep bikes, tents, or ski equipment down here, but I convinced Mom to let me turn our locker into my own personal workshop. At first, she wasn't happy with me being down here by myself, but the space can only be accessed by residents or approved guests— and I've installed a direct phone line back to the apartment so Mom can contact me at any time. When she saw how happy I was, she let me stay. It's a bit like being in a big cage, but I've hung so much stuff off the wire mesh fencing that I've created a cozy, warm space. And I almost never see anyone down here. It's just me and the unwanted clutter. Exactly how I like it. My cave.

Bill Gates, Bill Hewlett, and Steve Jobs may have had their parents' garages, but Monica Chan and I have our condo lockers.

"When you have the drive to invent, you find the space to make it happen"—one of my favorite Monica quotes.

I installed a thumbprint scanner in addition to the normal padlock for extra security. Occasionally it's buggy and I have to force my way in, but this time I press the pad of my finger against it and it opens easily.

Home sweet home.

The place is an Ariel's grotto of electronic equipment and tools, including my precious soldering iron I'd used to fix Petal upstairs. I have drawers filled with silver wire and screws of all different sizes, PCBs stolen from broken equipment or rummaged from yard sales (we still call them that, even though none of us have yards—it's mostly people selling unwanted junk on the advertising boards of our building). I have large sheets of thin metal for when I make repairs, rolls of different filaments for my 3-D printer, an old TV so I can watch my favorite K-dramas as I work, some computer monitors for Zora to look at code on, and a bookshelf filled with old manuals and scavenged textbooks.

In the far corner is a camp bed. Mom doesn't like it when I sleep down here, but sometimes I work until my eyes droop, and there's no way I can make it to the elevator without nodding off. As long as I'm prepared to grovel in the morning, I can get away with it.

Above the bed is the cheesy vision board Zora made me put up. It was a school assignment that we took to another level—we'd been tasked with creating a collage of images to define our specific goals for the future. We kept our school ones quite generic and boring, but made special versions for ourselves that were much more precise.

Mine has pictures of Hong Kong, Tokyo, and Seoul—the dream trip I want to take after graduating from high school. I've researched train routes, accommodations, everything.

It has a photo of a spaniel baku, my dream companion.

It has pictures of Profectus Academy, of students walking through the huge two-story-tall doors, into the hallowed hallways, and then graduating as new Moncha employees.

It has a screen grab of the research and innovation lab at Moncha, where I dreamed of working as a companioneer.

And it has a portrait of Monica Chan herself, standing, arms folded and looking powerful, signature bangs on point, in front of the next generation of bakus.

I kneel forward on the squeaky camp bed to take the pictures down—even the ones of the trip. I'll never be able to afford to go now. I blink back tears. It's hard to look at the gaping hole left on the corkboard.

Taking a deep breath to pull myself together, I dump the clippings in the garbage can and get settled at my scratched-up glass-top desk. I place Linus down on my workstation and pull up the typical schematics for a dormouse baku on the nearest screen.

You can find anything on the Moncha cloud, but most people don't mess with their bakus, as Moncha-approved vets will only work on bakus that haven't had any unauthorized repairs. Zora, however, trusts me.

The work takes my mind off Profectus, and it takes me a good hour to get Linus's tail straightened out, manipulating the metal back into shape with the help of a heated clamp and the soldering iron. He looks almost as good as new. I can't check the movement or camera until he's charged, so I leash him to the electrical outlet using an old cable of Petal's. It's not nearly as fast as leashing it to his owner, but it will work.

I rub my eyes, the impact of the roller-coaster day finally hitting me. I can't believe I started the day in the Moncha store, getting my leash and picking my beetle baku. Feels like a lifetime ago.

I suppose I should leash my scarab beetle and give him a name so he can start learning my behaviors and downloading my feed from the Moncha cloud.

Ringo? Too retro.

Herbie? Too eccentric.

Dune? Too geeky.

I'm stalling, and I know it. I lift the backpack up, groaning at how heavy it is. When it lands on the desk with a resounding thud, I remember the hunk of twisted metal I carried home with me. That's what's weighing the pack down. With a lot more excitement than before, I tear into the backpack, tossing the beetle up onto a shelf, still in his box. I'll leash and name him later.

I tip out the crumpled metal, pulling away bits of dirt and leaves that cling to the surface. It has no distinguishable form, but my instinct was good—there is something really valuable here. The metal that isn't covered in either my blood or scorched by some sort of burn mark is dark as onyx, a deep, rich black that I can almost see my reflection in. I stare at it without touching it, trying to figure out where to begin.

The hole gapes like a mouth. I can't figure out what would have caused a "wound" like that. Certainly not being run over by a train or a falling from a height.

Finally, I realize the metal is curled in on itself around the hole—I'm going to have to unravel it to see if there are any parts to salvage. Unfortunately the burn means the beautiful black metal itself is pretty useless and will just end up in the garbage.

Junk. I wasted all that time and energy carrying home junk.

No point being delicate with it now. I take the metal in my hands and wrench it apart. It refuses to budge at first, and I think about getting a hammer from the toolbox, but then finally it gives.

I gasp.

There, tucked into the burned space, is a face.

7

NO QUESTION ABOUT IT: IT'S DEFINITELY A FACE.
The eyes are open, one lid dented, the nose is smooshed and pointing off to one side, but its little triangular ears are in almost perfect
condition.

It's the ears that get me. The rest I might have written off. But
those ears are perfect. They're a level up in design I haven't seen before,
with tiny filaments spun out into simulation fur, soft but strong, and
most likely vital sense receptors like they are in real cats.

That's what this hunk of metal is. A cat baku.

A very expensive cat baku, if the quality of the materials is any
indication.

I run my fingertips over the ears, half expecting them to twitch
in response. But they're lifeless.

Now that I know what I'm looking at, the crumpled heap makes
much more sense. My blood is on the tail—that's what sliced my

palm when I was down in the ravine. The gaping, scorched hole is on the right side, where the ribcage would be—and where a lot of key tech would be stored. Maybe in real animals, it makes sense to have the majority of the thinking tech in the head, but that's not how it works with bakus—the motherboard is in the main body, not the head. It's a shame, as that probably means the poor thing is unfixable.

My eyes widen as my fingers run over the cat's broken body, gentle now as if I were diagnosing a real animal. The tech on display in front of me is unbelievable. I can barely stop turning it over and over in my hands, finding something new to marvel at each time. The metallic strands that cover its body are so thin, they have the smooth texture of real fur. As I attempt to follow the connections down through the body, I can see that each one of them would be charged with gathering different types of data—maybe weather conditions, or solar energy power, or measuring information from its owner, like resting heart rate or core internal temperature. A lot of bakus have these sorts of capabilities, but I've never seen them encased in such an elegant shell.

I swallow and take my hands off it, placing my palms on the glass. Someone must be really missing this baku. I can't help but wonder how it ended up down near the train tracks…or how it got such a huge hole in its side.

I bite my lower lip. I should really return it to a Moncha store to see if they can run any tests to see who the owner is. I could go in the morning.

*Or*, a naughtier voice in my head says, *you could wait to see if anyone comes looking for it.* If there's still a functioning tracking beacon within the baku's shell, then someone will arrive to claim it. If not…then who would know? It's as good as mine, just the same as any of the other tech I've scavenged.

My guilt temporarily set to one side, I get to work.

For the next couple of hours, I clean the baku up, scouring off the scorch marks with a wire sponge and wiping off dirt and dust that has collected around the metallic strands of "fur." Every now and then, I gasp. I keep uncovering tiny, beautiful details in the machine's bodywork, elements with an impeccably smooth finish I know couldn't have been accomplished by a machine. No, someone handmade this. Crafted it. Soldered and manipulated the metal and electronics with the skill of a sculptor. I feel like an apprentice studying the long lost work of a master.

"Got something good in there, kiddo?"

I almost leap out of my chair at the sound of the deep, male voice. But I instantly breathe a sigh of relief. It's only Paul. He looks the part of a scary intruder—he's got a scraggly gray beard and a ruddy, often grease-stained face, with piercing bright blue eyes that gleam out from beneath the bushiest eyebrows I've ever seen. But he's harmless. He's my fellow basement tinkerer, hobbyist DIY-er, and cave dweller, always puttering around and fixing things other people throw away. Old technology that they have no use for. He's got the best collection of telephones I've ever seen. He even has an old fax machine. Positively ancient.

Sure, he scared me half to death the first time we met, sticking his chubby fingers, blackened by dirt and calloused from hard work, through the holes in my wire mesh cage and giving it a shake.

He says he did it to get my attention, since calling my name didn't seem to work. I get it. I dive deep into the zone when I'm working, and it's almost impossible to drag me back to the land of the living. With my safety goggles and headphones on, the rest of the world disappears. It was that laser-like focused intensity that was supposed to get me into Profectus. *Oh well.*

Paul and I are comrades in engineering. Still, I find myself turning my back on him as he peers in, blocking his full view of the broken cat baku. I've overlooked some of his…less than legal DIY jobs, the things I've seen gathered in his locker that I know don't belong to him, so I'm sure he wouldn't breathe a word. But my body is tense and defensive of my find.

I feel protective of it.

"Oh, just a bit of junk I found on the street, you know how it is."

"Sure do." His lemur baku climbs up the wire fencing and peers in. George is a pretty advanced baku for a guy like Paul to own—level four, at least—but he won't tell me what his job was at Moncha before his accident. Paul only has one arm. I assume that George was his upgrade baku once he got on disability. "That's why I need a baku with opposable thumbs!" is his long-running joke.

"Well, I'm turnin' in for the night. You need anything?" We

often remind each other to do normal things—like eat and drink. Tinkerers understand.

I gesture to the thermos, then lift a pair of chopsticks to fill my mouth with cold, slimy noodles for good measure. "All good," I say, the words muffled by ramen.

He chuckles. "Well, all right then. Don't stay up too late now."

"Night."

"Night."

George lets out a series of beeps.

"Wait, did you get your baku today?" He pronounces it the old way, "back-you" rather than the more modern "back-oo."

My heart skips a beat. I don't remember telling him anything about a baku. Maybe George was able to see the cat on the table and showed a picture to Paul and…then I remember. The beetle. "Oh yeah. I'll show you tomorrow since I haven't leashed it yet."

Paul frowns. "But George tells me there's a live baku in there."

I pause. "Oh! That must be Linus. That's Zora's new baku. I fixed him up for her and just leashed him to charge."

"Huh. Always thought you'd be the type to leash yours right away. Leash it, name it, then take it apart. You're going to run circles around anyone at that school."

"I…" I don't have the heart to tell him I didn't make it into Profectus. It feels like disappointing too many people in one day. "I'll show you tomorrow," I repeat.

He pauses for a beat, apprising me beneath those bushy brows, but to my relief, he nods and walks away, George leaping onto his shoulder.

"Good night, little tinker!" he calls out as he walks.

When I no longer hear his footsteps, I hunch over my desk. I work on the broken baku for another couple of hours, until I straighten out as much of the creature's body without resorting to electronic tools. Now I can do a proper damage assessment.

One of the key finds is that the leash connection is intact. Excitement tingles in my fingers. If this works—if the baku is able to carry a charge, despite the gaping hole in its belly—then that means I might be able to bring it back to life. Holding my breath, I take the leash and plug it into the electrical outlet.

I wait for any sign of life. A light. Movement. A hum. But there's nothing. Frustrated, I pull open the drawer closest to me and dig around for my multimeter. I attach the probes to various parts of the baku, but despite it being plugged in, I can see no sign of any response. My shoulders slump with disappointment. It's such a shame. To have something so beautiful go to waste. I pull the leash from the outlet and sigh.

Then an idea strikes me. It's a bit of a wild one—there's no reason why it should work. But bakus are not designed to be charged from a power outlet. They're designed to work with humans. I have a brand-new leash hooked around my ear, ready and waiting. Maybe...

I lift the end of the cat's leash and hook it up to mine.

As it syncs, my nose begins to tingle, and I sneeze.

At almost the exact same time, the baku's whiskers judder, the first sign of potential electronic life.

"Jinx!" I say to it, laughing. I think all the work is turning me slightly loopy.

When nothing else happens for a good few minutes, I wonder if I imagined the juddering whiskers. I poke and prod at it, staring at it, willing it to make another move. But nothing happens.

Eventually, my eyes feel as if they are going to drop out of my head. I slump over my desk, the events of the day hitting me like a punching bag. Slam, rejection. Pow, forced to buy the beetle. Sucker punch, humiliated by Carter. Knock-out blow, stopped by those terrifying Moncha guards.

Then the final kick while I'm down, seeing Tobias's eagle baku in action and knowing I'll *never* own a baku that cool.

Knowing they'll be at Profectus but not me.

That *they'll* be living my dream.

I know I have to let it go. But not before I let one single final thought dominate my brain, my throat, my stomach.

*It's not fair.*

I don't even make it to the camp bed before I'm fast asleep.

## 8

A FAINT BEEPING ROUSES ME. IT TAKES A FEW
seconds to orient myself, and my neck cricks in protest at being
moved. I paw for my phone on the desk to check the time, but it's
not there.

I blink several times, my body awakening to the world. No
phone. No phone because I smashed the screen. No replacement
phone because I bought myself a baku. But I haven't leashed it yet,
so it can't function as my clock.

The beeping grows louder, echoing around the basement,
and—when it's accompanied by loud, metallic bangs—I recognize
it. The garbage trucks have arrived. And that means I've slept the
whole night in the locker.

Mom is not going to be happy. I quickly pack up my things,
unleashing the broken baku and shoving it into a box before throwing it under the desk. Linus is fully charged, and a quick selfie proves

that his camera and display projector screen are fully functioning. Perfect. His clock readout shows me it's 7:37 a.m. Oops.

I grab my dirty cutlery (I don't want to encourage pests into my locker—especially not if I'm falling asleep down there) and lock up, balancing armloads of stuff with the skill of a juggler. Then I race to the elevator.

When I get upstairs to our unit, my heart is pounding in my chest. "Mom, I'm so sorry—I lost track of time," I shout from the front door.

But when I enter the kitchen, it's not Mom I see first, but Zora. She's perched on a stool at our breakfast bar, while Mom is at the stove. "Oh, hey! I was just about to come down and get you," Zora says, slurping down a bowl of cereal. "How's Linus?"

"He's all good! Back to normal, I think."

"Yay!" she squeals. "I came by last night, but your mom said you were working, so I didn't want to disturb you."

I place Linus down on the counter, and he scurries over to Zora. She lays down her palm and he leaps onto it, rushing up her arm to the leash on her ear, making delighted squeaking sounds. "I missed you too!" says Zora.

I bite down on my bottom lip. It's strange to see Zora so… giddy and emotional. The connection she's developed with Linus seems so deep already. I always knew that people developed attachments to their bakus, but I didn't think it would happen that quick. I feel guilty for leaving mine packaged up in his box.

"Oh, here's your phone back," says Zora.

"Thanks!" I say. I relax when my phone hits my palm, tension I was holding in my shoulders releasing. It's wild to have such a visceral reaction to a phone, but there you go. Maybe it's not such a surprise after all that people bond with their bakus.

"What's your beetle's serial number, and I'll store it with Linus in my favorite contacts," says Zora.

"Oh, I haven't leashed him yet," I say. My fingers fly across the cracked screen of my phone, checking updates from social media across different platforms.

"You still haven't leashed your baku? La*cey*…" I know that tone of voice from Mom. She's exasperated. Sometimes she acts as if I'm an alien creature who's landed in her living room, as opposed to her own flesh and blood.

She just doesn't get what that baku represents to me—failure.

I keep on scrolling.

My breath catches in my throat.

There's an email from the Board of Education. It has the same heading as the one a couple of days before. **LACEY CHU: PROFECTUS APPLICATION STATUS**. There's probably a bug in their system, emailing me for a double hit of rejection. Great. Like I need that.

Even though it makes my nose twitch to see the unread notification, I don't open the email. Instead, I scroll through the Flashes from the people I follow. Pretty much all my St. Agnes classmates are getting their new bakus in time for the new school year, and even people with the boring level one insects seem excited.

Suddenly, it's like my phone is an old, dead object in my palm. Looking up at Zora, who is stroking Linus's nose as he projects updates onto her palm, or Mom creating a new recipe with Petal describing every step, I realize how silly I'm being. My phone is just a lump of metal, broken glass, and plastic.

I need a baku.

"I left my beetle downstairs. I better go and grab it," I say.

"Okay, but you come straight back up here, promise me? You've already spent too much time down there. You need more sunshine," says Mom.

"You got it," I reply.

"I'll come with," says Zora, shoveling the last spoonful into her mouth. "If you let me borrow your new baku for a bit, I can upgrade some of your apps as a thank-you for saving Linus."

I shoot her a grateful smile. I want to fill her in on what happened last night—and get her take on the Moncha guard encounter. I can always count on her logical brain to tell me whether I should be more worried about something than not.

Then there's the mysterious cat baku, but I don't know whether I'm ready to tell Zora about that discovery yet.

We walk over to the elevator as I tell her about my adventures in the ravine.

Her jaw drops. "I'd heard they'd stepped up security in Monchaville, but I didn't realize it was *that* bad. And I still can't believe you found him! The probability of that happening was very low," Zora says. "When I work on your beetle, I'll load him up

with some custom apps. I've got a few that I've coded. You'll love it, I promise. Have you decided on a name yet?"

I shake my head. "Not yet, but…" My phone buzzes in my hand and I glance down at the splintered screen.

**MESSAGE FOR LACEY CHU FROM BOARD OF EDUCATION**

I roll my eyes.

"What is it?" asks Zora.

I turn the screen to show her. She kisses her teeth. "What do they want?"

"Probably some kind of error message. I guess I'd better find out."

My finger hovers over the email app on screen. Zora reaches out and squeezes my shoulder.

**LACEY CHU: PROFECTUS APPLICATION STATUS**

*Dear Lacey,*

*We are delighted to offer you a place at Profectus Academy next year. We have registered your level three baku in our system.*

*Congratulations, and we look forward to seeing you in September.*

*Dr. Grant*

*Principal of Profectus Academy*

"WHAT?" I actually scream out loud after I've read the email. I close it, then scroll back to find the original—but it's gone.

Deleted. It's not in my trash folder either. It's as if I never received it. I open the new email again and stare, wondering if the letters are going to rearrange in front of my eyes. But they don't. I'm in, for real.

"What is it? What's happened?" Zora asks.

I try to speak but can't. Zora grabs the phone from my hand.

"Holy baku," she says as she reads the email, her hand flying to her mouth. "But I thought—"

"Two days ago—"

We both start at the same time.

The rejection must have been a mistake all along. I can hardly believe it.

For a moment, there are no words I can find to describe how I'm feeling. Then...

"I'm in, Z. I'm in." Tears shine in my eyes.

She steps forward and gives me a hug.

But then her logical brain takes over and she steps back, holding me by the shoulders. "Wait. I thought you hadn't leashed your baku yet? And it says here they have you registered with a level three?"

My heart sinks. She knows as well as I do that I bought a level one beetle. Nothing like a level three. And she's right, I haven't leashed it yet. Zora scrunches up her nose as if she's trying to hold up the weight of her glasses while she stares down at my phone. She's realizing what I am—that *this* email is actually the mistake. A practical joke. It's just the kind of thing Carter would do—probably in retaliation for yesterday.

Then, her eyes open wide. "Oh my gosh—they're probably sending you a level three baku because you need financial aid! It's a good thing you didn't leash that beetle after all!"

Now she hugs me properly.

I squeeze her back, but my stomach churns with confusion. I *know* that's not how it works at Profectus. They would never just send over a random baku. They would have given me grant money to go out and buy my own.

"Look, there's an attachment," she says. Before I can stop her, she opens it up.

**APPLICANT NAME: LACEY JANE CHU**

**APPLICANT NUMBER: 651**

**BAKU: Level three cat baku "Jinx" (serial number J1NX89)**

**STATUS: INCOMING PROFECTUS STUDENT 2067**

Everything about the form looks perfectly legitimate—and hard to fake. The applicant number in particular—I remember it from when I sent in my application. There is no way that Carter would have been able to guess the correct one.

The level three cat baku statement is what has me chewing my lower lip, however. So many questions buzz into my brain at once, I feel like I'm being attacked by hornets. Yet one thought dominates over all the rest: Could it be referring to the broken baku I found yesterday?

It seems impossible, and yet…if it's true…I can't let anyone know the baku isn't really mine.

Not my Mom. Not the Profectus Board. And not Zora.

"You're in." A grin blossoms on Zora's face. "You're in, Lacey! I knew the rejection was a mistake!" She grabs my arm, and we spin around, bouncing up and down like maniacs.

For a moment I let the truth fade. I'm going to Profectus. *I'm actually going!*

Finally I collapse against the wall, my cheeks stinging from how wide my grin is.

"I can't wait to see your new baku, by the way. I love the name—Jinx. I really want to meet him! Come on, let's go back in and tell your mom." She extends her hand. And reality begins to sink in.

Including one very big question.

*Who on earth is Jinx?*

9

NEWS SPREAD FAST IN OUR BUILDING.

Mom had heard our happy screams and rushed out of the condo to find out what happened. She danced with joy alongside us, but then her face fell.

"Oh, honey, I had everything prepared for a big celebration, but then when your rejection came through I canceled the order because I didn't want to make you feel even worse..." Mom had said after processing the news.

"Oh... I don't need any celebrations!" I'd replied, shifting on my feet. My stomach was still swirling with confusion, and I needed to get down to the basement to make sure my suspicion about the broken baku was true.

"Don't be silly; you've wanted this your whole life. I'm so happy for you."

"Even with...what happened to Dad?" I'd cringed, then. I

rarely brought it up. But if there was any moment it felt needed, it was right after getting my acceptance to Profectus. It's one step away from working at Moncha HQ, just like he did.

Mom shushed me, but she also turned her face away so I couldn't see her get emotional. "It doesn't matter what I think, and it definitely doesn't matter what your father would have thought. Your life is your own, and so are your dreams. I will always support you, no matter what." She'd then kissed me on the forehead and ordered me to change out of the clothes I had slept in. Mom leapt into super hostess mode, Petal darting back and forth between the cupboards, projecting a recipe for a quick celebration cake she could whip up.

Less than an hour later, our unit is filled with Zora's family, neighbors from our floor, even Darwin—the building's manager—all celebrating my achievement. I receive more hugs and kisses than I can process. Even Paul shows up, and he gives me a gruff hug. "Knew you could do it! That probably means I won't be seeing you in the basement much."

"I don't know about that. There might be one last big project over this summer."

He raises an eyebrow. "Anything you need, you know who to ask."

"Thanks, Paul."

"I'm proud of you, little tinker."

My cheeks burn with a mixture of pride and embarrassment at the same time.

After way too much cake, I slip out of the front door and edge along the hallway to the stairwell. If I take the elevator, I'm bound to bump into someone I know. Even though everyone is there for me, the noise and the people and the attention is all a bit too much.

Especially as I'm desperate to get down to my cave and figure out if that broken hunk of metal could possibly be turned into a fully functioning level three baku—or else my career at Profectus might be short-lived after all.

Zora spots me escaping. "Want me to run interference?" she asks, and I'm grateful she doesn't push to come with me.

I smile at her. "That would be great."

"Hey—when do think they'll send the new baku—Jinx, isn't it?"

I play Zora off, even though I hate lying to her. "Oh, they just emailed to say they'd send me the baku right before the start of term—something about not wanting me to get too attached."

She frowns. "That's odd." Then, she shrugs. "I guess you know more about Profectus than I do! But does that mean you won't have a baku all summer long? How am I going to get in touch with you?"

"I'll still have my old phone," I say with a grin. "We'll just have to text each other old-school style while you're away."

"I suppose so," she says. Linus wrinkles his nose in a gesture of solidarity with Zora's skepticism. "I'd better get back to the party and make sure no one asks too many questions about where the guest of honor has gone," she says with a wink.

"Thanks, Zora. I owe you one."

When I get down to the locker, it's quiet. Eerily so. I fumble with the lock—it takes me two or three attempts to open—and once I'm inside, I take several deep breaths to calm myself down. When I feel more settled, I slide the box out from underneath the desk, and there is the baku—still just as broken and messed up as I left it.

*You can't just name a baku by saying a word aloud,* I remind myself. *That isn't how baku registering works. You have to go through the leashing process and input the name, check that it hasn't been registered to a similar baku within a certain radius...all things I was going to do with my beetle.*

Another, louder voice says: *But this has to be Jinx.*

I'd lied to Zora earlier. There's no way that Profectus would send me a level three baku. Which means they think I have one already. So if I don't manage to get one before the start of term, I won't be starting school in September, acceptance letter or not.

I have no money to buy one (a level three is way out of my price range). You can't buy secondhand bakus. So my only option is to fix the one that has somehow fallen into my hands.

I stare at the cat baku, which looks nothing like a cat baku— yet—with those lifeless eyes and gaping hole in its side, the tangle of wires and the broken paws.

The longer I stare, the more certain I am that this is an impossible plan. I'm overwhelmed by how much work needs to be done. Finally, I blink, slumping against the back of my chair.

The baku's one, unbroken eye lazily blinks back.

It's enough to jolt me out of my seat. But I'm *sure* I didn't imagine it this time.

If there's a spark of life, there's a spark of hope. It's all I need. That, and every second of summer vacation I can spare.

Three months to turn this scrap metal into a fully functional baku.

If I can pull this off, it will be a miracle.

10

IT TAKES THE ENTIRE SUMMER, DOWN TO THE FINAL hours. For the first time, I'm grateful Zora has gone off to coding camp and Mom works full-time—it means I got away with working almost nonstop without facing too many awkward questions.

The month of June I'd spent tackling the basics. That one blinking eye kept me motivated, even though it took me another week of dedicated tinkering before I made any more progress: a twitching paw.

I'd been so excited about that, I let Mom take me out for ice cream in the park. She was getting critically worried about my levels of vitamin D at that point, since I was spending so much time in the basement.

From the first paw, it was another few weeks (and most of July) before I got him standing on his own, then a matter of days until he was walking, the progress snowballing as I fixed the fundamental issues. I smoothed all the dents and replaced the scorched parts with new. Whoever had made him had obviously spent a lot of time perfecting, scrutinizing, analyzing every component, because there were modifications in the tech that I had never come across before. Screws that were microscopic in size, wires so intricately knotted together, they were like the braids in Zora's hair.

Thankfully, Paul had gifted me an old 3-D printer of his a year ago, so once I'd managed (carefully, so carefully) to extract one of the screws, I was able to map and print a copy of it. Gradually, as my confidence grew, I printed other parts. They weren't as beautiful as the rest of him, but if I wanted him to walk, run, and jump again, I'd have to deal.

That meant in August, scavenging became my new pastime.

Outside Monchaville, not everyone treats their bakus the same. For the most part, people are careful and respectful—but others treat them roughly, pushing the limits of the machines until they burn out or break down. Some people—*rich* people—act as if they're disposable. Replaceable. And when they get bored, some of the people don't even take advantage of the recycling program Moncha offered, but put their old bakus in the trash and head to the Moncha store to buy a new one.

That's where I came in. I salvaged the broken or forgotten bakus, and I used them for Jinx's parts. I was mercenary about it. Nothing was sacred.

With every piece of Jinx I took apart to clean or replace, I searched for the signature of the companioneer who created him.

"Who made you?" I whispered to him.

I hadn't gotten around to fixing his speakers yet, so he couldn't respond to me.

But the signature had to be there somewhere, and I was desperate to find it. Using Jinx's browser, I searched the Moncha forums for some of the new tech I had seen, in an attempt to trace it back to the original owner. All I needed was a name, a symbol, a scrawl, something.

But Jinx was like nothing else I'd ever seen before. And his creator remained an enigma. A mystery.

But who was fixing him, who was bringing him back to life— that was not.

That was all me.

It takes right up until the night before I'm due to start at Profectus. I'm so close to having a fully functioning level three baku, but I know they're not going to allow me through the doors unless I get the final element of Jinx's operating system working: communication.

When I get downstairs, Jinx struts around the locker, leaping up onto the desk, the shelving, then skirting the very top of the cage, agile as a real cat. A surge of affection rushes through me as I watch his perfect movement. I've done well.

"Jinx, to me!" I say, alongside a crooked-arm gesture for him to return. If Jinx had been a *normal* baku, that would have worked. Instead, he stares at me from his perch on the highest shelf and blinks, once.

I frown. It's so late, it's early—only hours before I'm supposed to be in my uniform and heading to the school gates—and my eyes are burning with the desire to sleep. But I have to fix this one last thing or else I'll be showing up at Profectus with a baku that doesn't follow commands, and an entire summer's worth of work is wasted.

I take a sip of highly caffeinated soda, ready for one last burst of energy. Clambering up onto the desk, I reach out with one arm toward Jinx, the other hand tightly clutching the wire mesh for support. Just as my fingers are about to grab him, he leaps off the shelf and onto the desk, where he sits and licks at his paw.

I groan. "Seriously?"

I get down off the desk *much* less gracefully than Jinx, then sit at the desk, folding my arms. For a moment we stare at each other, girl and machine, unblinking.

I spot that there's a loose wire running from his front paw to the motherboard. It's a minor fix, but fixing something small might help me feel a sense of accomplishment that will lead to a bigger breakthrough. (That's the idea, anyway.) My mind is on how to fix his speakers so he can communicate with me, so I'm a little burly with my technique, forcing one of the metal wires back into place and holding it down with a piece of duct tape as I solder. Crude, but it works. I leash him up to my ear to give him a bit of extra charge.

And then in my ear, I hear a voice:

>>Jeez, could you be a bit more gentle next
time? That hurt.

He sounds…like an annoyed kid whose foot I'd just stepped on.

I almost jump out of my skin. "What the heck?" I say, pawing at the leashing around my ear.

>>You can disconnect us, but that won't change anything.

*Jinx?* I say his name in my thoughts, and I hear his laughter in my ear.

>>That's me.

*And you…and you can understand me? If I tell you to jump up there, you'll—*

He jumps up onto the shelf, exactly as I order.

I dance around the locker with glee. I'm giddy with success. There's still something not quite right. I've made some kind of error—the fact that I'm not reading text from a projection or hearing his voice out loud is unsettling. It's like he's inside my head. But at this point, it doesn't matter.

There's a cough from behind me, and I spin around. Illuminated in a pool of light outside my locker is Zora. "Hey, stranger," she says.

"Z!" I run to the locker door and pull it open. "How was coding camp?"

"Incredible. I've got so much to tell you. But first, I've come to meet the infamous Jinx!" Her eyes scan my locker, before settling on the shelf. Her jaw drops. "Oh my god, Lace—is that him? He's gorgeous."

>>Your friend has excellent taste.

It's still a shock hearing his voice in my head, enough to make me jump, and Zora gives me a funny look.

"Sorry, think I've been in here too long."

"Your mom asked me to say that you have to come upstairs now and have dinner and a good night's sleep or else she'll get Paul to change the padlock and ban you from your cave forever."

I grin—not only because I know Mom would never do that to me, but because I actually *can* go upstairs now. I have an offer letter from Profectus, a school uniform, and a level three baku that at least *appears* to follow orders.

I raise my hands to Zora to show her I'm not protesting. "Come on then, Jinx. Let's go upstairs."

>>Finally, we're getting outta here.

The baku leaps down to my feet, his movement smooth as silk, and he sashays out of my locker and into the real world.

Looks like things might be turning out all right after all.

> PART TWO
# PROFECTUS

11

JINX SLITHERS BETWEEN MY LEGS IN A FIGURE eight, his impatience wearing at my already plenty frayed nerves. The dark navy, woolen trousers of the uniform are itchy enough in the lingering September heat, but the pleated kilt—my other uniform option—is definitely not my style. I rub my sweaty palms against my trousers.

>>Just go in already. I'm tired of waiting.

*Be quiet, you.*

Jinx flicks my calf with his tail, and I grimace. But he's right. I need to just go in.

Profectus Academy occupies an old university building, one of those huge, imposing, castle-like buildings—complete with turrets—designed to look like it belongs in Oxford or Cambridge or some other old, academic British town. Behind it, modern additions—steel and glass extensions—spread out like wings.

I've walked past this building a hundred times, counted the windows and wondered which classroom would one day be mine, stared up at the huge, almost two-story-tall doors and pictured walking through them…and now, I get to enter as a student. Someone who belongs. I'm going to become part of its history. Or rather, I'm going to be part of the future we are all trying to create by being here. The thought swells my chest, my chin lifting high.

I can't explain how I got in, but I feel like I belong, like the rejection was the fluke—not the acceptance.

Streams of students pass by me with their bakus. There are dogs, cats, a few monkeys, and birds. It's funny, walking around, you almost never see bakus higher than level three. They're so expensive to buy and difficult to maintain. Maybe in Yorkville, among the fancy designer shops and celebrity chef restaurants, you'll see custom-designed level four bakus and rare breeds. But most people are content with their simple cat, dog, or small, furry mammal baku—they don't need anything fancier. Thankfully I don't catch sight of Carter's boar. Holed up in my cave fixing Jinx, I've managed to avoid him all summer (I've managed to avoid almost everyone—some, like Zora, not on purpose), and I'm not keen for a new confrontation—even if the circumstances have changed since our last meeting.

My plan is to stay under the radar, drama-free, and experience this dream to the fullest.

Music blares at top volume from my feet. Looks like Jinx's speakers aren't broken after all. The student closest to me leaps a mile in the air, and all around me, gazes turn in my direction. So much for getting through the first day—even *minute*—of school without drawing attention to myself. I drop to my heels and scoop Jinx up off the floor.

"Turn off!" I hiss, fumbling along his back for the right button which should, in theory, turn off his speakers.

But the music only seems to get louder. "Jinx, please, please don't do this to me," I whisper.

Maybe I finally find the right button or the desperation in my voice hits a nerve, but the sound shuts off with a click. Thank god. I duck my head and race up the stairs two at a time and through the enormous doors. No hesitation now: I want to get away from the crowd of staring, questioning eyes.

Even the entrance feels different from any other school that I've been in before. There's no ugly, green-and-orange plastic floor (why are color schemes in middle schools so ugly?)—instead, there's rich mahogany hardwood that must be a nightmare to keep clean during the winters when we'll be tracking in snow and salt from the sidewalks. But there's no expense spared here. The wood paneling continues up the walls, giving the atrium the feel of an old country club.

Written in gold script on a wooden beam across my head is the school's motto: WE BUILD THE FUTURE.

My fingertips tingle and heat rises in my cheeks. "We've done it, Jinx," I whisper to him. He wriggles out of my arms in response and jumps to the floor, arching his back and flicking his tail at me. "Fine, don't care." I stick my tongue out at him. He responds by choosing a direction and shooting off at lightning speed.

I jog to catch up with him, the orientation information

from Profectus displayed on his back. When even a function this ordinary works on Jinx, a spike of pride shoots up my spine—to know that I fixed him from nothing. He gives me the number and location of my locker, which is in one of the more modern wings. Now it's starting to feel more like an ordinary school. There are clusters of students in their uniforms, some lounging on the floor or leaning casually against their lockers.

Jinx stops in front of a locker and, with a couple of bounding leaps, settles on a small shelf that is especially designed for bakus to hang out. To stop the bakus (big and small) from crowding the hallways, there are alcoves above each locker for bakus to leash up and charge between classes.

I stop and stare at Jinx, who is "grooming" himself, but which is really a way for him to run through his systems and check everything is working okay by brushing up against all his sensors. Then he crawls deep into the alcove, curling himself up so that only the two tiny LEDs in his pupils are visible. I run through the plan for the day, taking deep breaths to prepare myself. Most of the morning is blocked out for a giant orientation session. I'd looked it up online to see what that might entail, if there was anything I could do to prep. But there was surprisingly little information available.

"Lacey? What are you doing here?"

The slimy voice sends drippings of ice down my spine, which turn to shivers as I hear the snuffling and snorting of the boar. My body tenses, flashing back to the memory of the forest and the ravine.

I wait a beat, willing my voice to sound normal. "I'm getting ready for orientation." I spin the combination of my locker, thankful that Jinx projects the code for the lock from his tail to a place on the locker just above my fingertips. I dump my bag, not taking out any of the postcards and pictures I brought along to stick to the inside of my locker door. There's no way I'm decorating it in front of Carter.

"Isn't your school down the street?"

I bite my lip and take a beat. *He doesn't have any advantage over you now*, I tell myself. *You belong here as much as he does.* I spin around to face him. "Isn't it obvious?" I say, trying to sound as nonchalant as possible. "I've got a locker, I'm in the uniform—I'm a Profectus student too, Carter. Just like you."

His jaw drops. He attempts to rearrange his expression back to normal—but I've glimpsed the truth. He's worried about me being here.

I don't see why. It's not as if this is a competition. It's school.

He crosses his arms. "You can't be here. You need a level three baku in order to come here. I saw you buying that scarab." He storms over to my locker, sticking his face right up to the alcove. Jinx lunges out, hissing like a wildcat.

Carter yelps and leaps backward, sneakers squeaking on the hardwood. He almost falls over his boar baku, but catches himself just before, then takes off down the hallway.

I turn to Jinx, my cheeks flush with pride. "Come on, then. Let's go get oriented."

## 12

JINX LEADS ME DOWN TO THE SCHOOL GYM.
I needn't have worried about getting lost—there's a steady stream of students and bakus all heading in the same direction. Some of the students look a lot older than me, strutting the hallways as if they own the place. I try and keep my head high too and act as if I belong. But being around lots of people always makes me feel nervous—I'm far more comfortable in the darkness of my cave than in the crowded hallways of school.

I wait for Jinx to react, but he doesn't. Strange. Bakus are designed to help soothe their owners if they're feeling stressed or anxious. Maybe I need to look into Jinx's empathetic sensors…

But all thoughts melt away as I enter the gym.

At first, I'm a bit disappointed that it looks like an ordinary school gymnasium, with a glossy wooden floor painted with lines for different sports. Two glass-backed basketball hoops hang from metal rafters painted in pale green that crisscross above our heads, serving as hanging posts for brightly colored celebration banners. Not that any of them are for sports achievements (Profectus students aren't exactly known for being jocks). Instead, they're emblazoned with the Moncha logo, that unique stylized *M*, and carry the names of former students. I wonder what they did to deserve their names up there.

Different from an ordinary gym, though, is the massive stadium-style seating on either side, bleachers that stretch up across two stories. There'd be room for the entire school in here—and then some. I'm grateful to see Carter and his boar taking a seat on the far side—far away from me.

I file into the bleachers about halfway up the lower tier, confronted by a cacophony of noisy students and the wildest collection of bakus I've ever seen in a single place.

Monkeys. Dogs. Cats. A small version of a bear.

All of them level three and above.

And hovering above a guy sitting right in the front row: an eagle.

I recognize that eagle.

His wings are outstretched, so I can't see the face that's behind them, but I know it all too well. I purse my lips. The eagle doesn't seem to have suffered any long-term damage from my pine cone throwing. He flaps his wings and soars up even higher. I wonder if the eagle senses me looking, because he spins his head so his dark mirrored eyes take me in, his gold-edged beak opening in a squawk. I quickly take a seat and stare at the back of the student in front of me.

Jinx crawls up onto my shoulder to get a better view of the action. He licks his paw.

>>Four hundred students entering, and counting. Middle school kids on the lower tier, high schoolers above.

"Hey, nice baku. Is that a new model? I've never seen one like it before." The guy sitting next to me reaches out to touch Jinx, but Jinx darts away, clambering up my arm to sit on my shoulder away from the would-be petter. *Do you have to be so unfriendly?* I moan to Jinx. To my relief, the guy laughs, revealing a neat row of shiny teeth.

"A shy model, huh?" He extends his hand to me. "I'm Jake. Jake Saunders. I'm in eighth grade."

I take his hand. "Lacey Chu. Um…total newbie here. And this is Jinx. Sorry, he's a bit…sensitive."

"No problem! This is my baku, Vegas." A calm-looking retriever model sits at his feet. "Vegas, send Jinx a friend request."

A notification pops up on Jinx's paw, flashing it white.

>>JAKE SAUNDERS wants to be friends.

I click accept, and his profile spills out onto Jinx's back. He's a popular guy with thousands of friends. "Vegas?" I ask, raising an eyebrow.

"Yep, you can pet him if you like! He won't mind."

I reach out and stroke the baku's smooth, metal body—he

doesn't have the individual strands of fur that Jinx does—and Vegas closes his eyes in a simulation of pleasure. He's a lovely baku.

"The name comes because I love a bit of gambling." Jake winks at me.

"Gambling? Isn't that illegal?"

"You'll see," he says.

Before I can press him any further, the lights around the gymnasium dim, and the noise from the other students quiets in anticipation. It's as if everyone is holding their breath.

>>Such drama.

Sarcasm drips from Jinx's tone. I raise an eyebrow. I still can't get used to the baku having such a...personality. Nothing I'd read about having a baku had prepared me for that.

Still, the only way to respond to sass is with sass.

*Shh, I don't want to miss anything.*

There's a hum of electric life and a hole opens up in the center of the gymnasium floor. A beautiful, snow-white owl baku flies up out of it, circling over the students' heads, swiftly followed by a stern-looking woman in a sharp power suit, who's lifted up on a rising podium until she's level with the middle of the bleachers.

Jinx buzzes.

>>Dr. Sarah Grant, principal of Profectus.

The principal leans her hands against the podium as her owl baku lands next to her, projecting her speech down in front of her.

"Welcome, students, to another year at Profectus! And welcome especially to our incoming students. We're delighted you'll be joining our thriving community.

"First things first, some legal business. If you look at your bakus, you will see I am sending you a link now, which you will use to receive your class schedule, hand in your school assignments, and report in for attendance.

"By accepting the link, please be aware that you are agreeing to the strict legal document you will have been sent over the summer. Those of you who bothered to read it will remember that part of this includes a watertight nondisclosure clause when it comes to some of the activities that you will participate in here at Profectus Academy. To be absolutely clear, this means you cannot talk about the activities you will participate in here, outside of the academy. This is mandatory, so you if you want to opt out, then you have the option to leave now. Anyone?"

She pauses to see if anyone will leave. But of course no one does. There's no way any of us would have come this far only to leave because of a confidentiality clause. We *want* to know what's behind the curtain.

"Good. Now that's out of the way… No doubt many of you have been doing your research on the school online."

There's some nervous tittering of laughter from the new kids to the school, including me—of course I tried to find out absolutely everything I could. There was not much to go on. Only report after report that Profectus was the toughest—and most rewarding—school around, and that it produced the absolute best scientists and engineers in the country.

"Excellent. Now, I know most of you will be itching to find out more about what makes life at Profectus so unique—and so worth hiding behind such strict secrecy. But I'm not here to introduce that to you. Instead, we have a very special guest, straight from Moncha headquarters."

*Oh my god.* My hand squeezes around Jinx's body. *What if it's Monica Chan? What if it's her in the flesh?*

A spotlight swivels around to the main entrance of the gym. And there, half-hidden by light streaming in from behind him, is Eric Smith. Monica's partner and second-in-command. My shoulders slump. I wanted it to be Monica herself. But having Eric Smith here is pretty cool too, even forgetting for a moment that he somehow raised someone as horrible as Carter.

He steps into the spotlight, and it's impossible not to feel a thrill at the sight of him and his incredible baku. It's a red panda, solemn and gorgeous, metal fur the color of rust, wrapped around his shoulders almost like a scarf. There's thunderous applause as he opens his arms wide.

He's drinking it in. And I can't help myself—I'm clapping as hard as everyone else.

Between Eric Smith and Monica Chan, life as we know it was *revolutionized.* They gave us bakus. Their names, their faces, are ingrained as part of our history—a history that I want to contribute to one day.

I might just be able to add a single word—maybe even just a letter—to the story. But I want to give something.

"Thank you, thank you," he says. He speaks softly, but his voice is amplified by his baku so we have no trouble hearing him. "I'm sorry Monica can't be with you—she hates not being here—but she is away on overseas business at the moment. So for your orientation, you've got to settle for me." The crowd gives him an energetic round of applause to show their appreciation for his visit.

Eric drinks in the applause, then holds up his hands. "You all are the best of the best—if not, you wouldn't be sitting here today. If you would indulge me—especially returning students who have seen this before—I have a short presentation for you, and then, I promise, we will get on to the good stuff."

The lights dim again and screens lower from the rafters in the ceiling. The image on the screens flicker, as if the movie were being played from an old-fashioned reel.

A voice-over talks us through the history of robotics as we know it—from the very first automatons in the medieval ages through to the bakus of today. Images play of those first automatons: purely mechanical objects of cogs, bolts, and springs, designed to instill wonder—and sometimes fear.

I swallow, thinking of Jinx. Fear and robotics have often walked hand in hand—and for good reason. Fear of robots taking human jobs, of an intelligence explosion where robots become smarter than humans, of a machine passing the Turing Test and reaching the point where they are able to harm us of their own free will. Asimov's Three Laws becoming overturned, obsolete.

But it took Monica Chan to really think about robots in a different way.

She found the focus on humanoid robots bizarre, found the "uncanny valley"—that unsettling feeling people feel around a robot that looks human but isn't—too difficult to bridge. She couldn't imagine wanting to live with something that appeared human in every way, except with only electronic life behind their eyes. Not only that, but from an engineering point of view, building a robot that could walk on two legs was incredibly difficult. That's when the baku idea was born.

An *animal* design offered what people wanted—companionship, convenience, assistance, easy maintenance—and yet they weren't so creepy. It didn't prevent people who loved pets from having real ones, and it meant that people weren't spending as much time staring at tiny rectangular screens. The baku became an integral part of every-day living, with the Moncha goal: *Accompanying you to your happiest life ever,* the motto for everything Moncha does.

The movie flies on. Despite the fact that I am already a Moncha fan through and through, I find myself swept away in the emotion of Monica's rise and rise. Watching the film puts a grin on my face. It plays the story of Monica's journey, a tale I've heard so many times, it is practically a bedtime story for me. A fairy tale, but not of princes and frogs, ball gowns and pumpkins, but of makers and metal, of wire and ingenuity and inspiration and creativity and invention.

Then it focuses in on one of Monica's main aims for the bakus. On a young woman who is about to go up for a presentation in front of a huge audience, her heart beating wildly, her eyes closed, her breaths sharp and shallow. Her fists clench and unclench. She wants to leave, to throw up, to be finished, to be anywhere else. Then her baku leaps into her arms, and within a few moments of stroking his metallic fur, she feels calm. She feels ready. And she takes the stage and smashes it out of the park.

The woman? Monica Chan herself. The bakus managing to relieve her not only of her smartphone addiction, but of some of her anxieties.

I think of the other bakus I've known in my life and what an impact they've had on the people closest to me. The truth is, Petal makes Mom smile—knows what videos she wants to watch when she is down, what music to play to calm her, what podcasts to download so she can feel smart and be better at her job.

A line from the voice-over snaps me out of my daydream: "And the final goal of Moncha Corp: to make people happier."

The screens fade to black and the lights come up. Eric Smith has moved, so he's now on the podium with Dr. Grant. "Today, I'm here to ask you what you see for the future of Moncha Corp. Are you ready to join the next generation of companioneers, mechanics, programmers, designers, and coders who are going to take bakus to the next level? Now that we're reaching a point in time where almost every adult has chosen their baku, their companion, we need to keep asking ourselves the question—how can we keep on *accompanying people to their happiest lives ever?* We want to make sure that everyone is achieving their peak happiness."

Eric Smith is the epitome of comfortable. Relaxed. His hands drop into his pockets and he smiles down at all of us as if we were part of his family. "Yes, I know. Can simple engineering make people happy? We have a team of psychologists and philosophers looking into this, but really, it's people like you—the makers of the future—who are going to transform the way we live our lives into ways we never knew. Ways we could never have imagined. I'm excited by what you have to offer. By how you will inspire us.

"I'm sure you've heard plenty of stories about Profectus, and the incredible technology you'll have access to while you're here. But forget everything you've ever heard. Because Moncha is in the business of staying one step ahead. And I bet you're wondering how we move innovation forward at Profectus?"

Shivers of anticipation dance down my spine as he talks. There's a rumble from the older students, and it feels as if the crowd leans forward as one entity, sweeping me with it. I catch sight of Tobias in the front row. He's leaning back, his arms folded, the ghost of a smile playing on his lips. Four other eighth graders next to him are the same—an island of calm in an ocean of anticipation.

I wonder what they know that we don't.

I don't have to wait long to find out.

"I'm delighted to open this season of baku battles."

The roar that shakes the gymnasium is almost deafening.

13

ERIC SMITH SPREADS HIS ARMS, AND THE GYM
transforms before my very eyes.

The shiny, laminated oak flooring flickers once, twice,
then turns bright white. The high school students above us are
hooting and hollering, stamping their feet, adding earthquake-like
vibrations.

>>Where are they going?

Jinx flicks his tail in the direction of Tobias and four other
eighth graders who are walking out of the gym.

But I don't have much time to wonder about that. I'm too busy
being dazzled by the tech on display. The floor begins to...open
up, is the only way that I can describe it, around the podium where
Dr. Grant and Eric Smith are standing. It shifts, moves, unfurls,
panels I didn't realize were panels folding on top of each other,

revealing a deep, doughnut-shaped arena with the podium at the very center of it. The podium is wallpapered in screens, and at clock-like intervals on the floor are five silver rings. Along with everyone else in my class, I lean forward, craning my neck to see into the pit. The rings flash and spin, opening like manhole covers. The five students who left are lifted up into the arena, their bakus appearing in front of them.

Tobias is lifted up almost directly beneath me. I can see the curly tips of his short black hair and the golden head of his eagle baku.

I can't see his face, so I look to the screen, which is showcasing the different students' faces one by one. Tobias still has that easy grin, as if he is totally confident in what is about to happen.

The next face to flash up is captioned "Gemma." By contrast to Tobias's calm, she looks fierce, her bright copper hair tied back in a long braid, an impressive tiger baku pacing at her feet. The others are introduced: Dorian, Pearce, and Elektra. All the older kids have the same aura of barely contained excitement, a mix of confidence and aggression simmering under the surface.

Eric Smith speaks again. "Let me first say a special thanks to our team captains—for putting their bakus on the line for this demonstration. The outcomes here will have no bearing on the battles themselves—they will officially start at the end of this month, as per usual. But, as always, my advice is the same—battle to win."

Tobias rolls his shoulders back, cricking his neck from side to side in an attempt to loosen up the tension. I feel tense as well, my knuckles white as I grip the bench by my side to lean forward and get as close to the action as possible. A baku battle. I never thought it would be possible. It shouldn't be; bakus aren't programmed to fight.

>>Look at his wing. And her paw.

I try to see what Jinx is referring to. And then I catch it—a little gold circle attached to each of the bakus. Maybe that's what overrides the code that prevents one baku from being used to attack each other—and humans—in the real world.

"Players, play to win. You have thirty minutes. And so... begin."

Dr. Grant's owl baku releases a piercing screech, and the teams are off.

The preamble is so short—there's no ready, steady, go. Tobias immediately makes a hit on Dorian's snarling wolf baku, his eagle stretching his talons out, wings spread wide to keep him hovering— and to enable a quick getaway from the wolf's surprisingly high jump.

The eagle makes short work of the wolf, one of his talons snaring a key wire from behind its neck and rendering it useless in less than thirty seconds.

I clutch Jinx tightly to my chest. The bakus in front of my eyes are being torn apart, their wires shredded, bodies mangled by metal claws and teeth and talons. There are no yelps of pain, but there are electronic whines and the agonized cries of the fighting students. When their baku is pronounced "dead," the student's face is grayed out on the screen.

Within a matter of minutes, the only faces that are illuminated are those of Gemma and Tobias. They look utterly serious now, all trace of previous bravado and play gone. All they can focus on is winning. The eagle flaps his wings, the tiger prowls on the arena floor, eyes lifted and locked in each other's gaze. There's high-wire excitement all around the gymnasium as we wait to see who is going to be the final winner. My heart is thumping inside my chest. If this is what it means to baku battle, I am equal parts thrilled and horrified.

The lights turn up, flooding the stage in a bright white glow, and I recoil back, throwing my arm in front of my eyes. I'm not the only one. Almost everyone groans, so caught up in the action that the bright light is like being forced awake from a fascinating dream. Tobias and Gemma freeze, their bakus turning their attention to the center of the room. *This would be the moment to strike,* I think. *If someone wants to win.*

Tobias and Gemma have almost the exact same thought at the exact same time. There's a flurry of movement, but a buzzer sounds—and a clock on the jumbotron reaches 0:00. I hadn't even noticed the countdown, I'd been so engrossed in the battle.

Eric Smith's voice rings out above the thunderous applause. "Congratulations, Tobias Washington and Gemma Morris. You are the joint winners of this baku battle demonstration. You can stand down your bakus."

There's hesitation on both sides, but the gold tags drop off their bakus, and so they have no choice but to retreat. My eyes leave Tobias and Gemma, however, and turn to the losing students, cradling the mess of their ruined bakus. None of them—even the eagle and the tiger—have escaped totally unscathed. Everyone is going to need some sort of repair.

The floor closes back over the arena, and I blink—it's hard to believe I'm not actually in a dream.

"What do you think?" asks Jake.

"I think... I think that was the coolest thing I think I have *ever* seen."

"Pretty awesome, right? But I could never be on a team," he says, running his hand over his dog baku's back.

"These are the baku battles," says Dr. Grant, silencing us all once again with her voice. "Making it onto the team is a position of honor for any student—and first years... You'll have your opportunity to prove yourself very shortly. But if you don't make it onto a team, don't worry. There will still be plenty to keep you busy. The team captains will be watching you during your class orientations and making their selection by the end of the day. To end off orientation, I'd like to thank Eric Smith for visiting us and helping to usher in this new Profectus school year."

"It's my pleasure. Good luck, everyone. I'm sure I'll be seeing some of you before too long."

I glance around at all the students, and I can see how everyone is looking at the team captains. With admiration and respect. They're really a part of something. And the determination I can see in Tobias's and Gemma's eyes is something I recognize.

This could really be where I shine.

Life at Profectus is shaping up to be more exciting than I could have possibly imagined.

14

"YOU SHOULD ALL HAVE YOUR CLASS SCHEDULES
now. Older students, you may head to class—but new students,
would you please stay behind?" says Dr. Grant. The podium
descends, and all around me, students are standing and preparing
to head off to their first classes.

I look down at Jinx's back and, sure enough, my schedule for
the week is displayed. Next up is a class called Gathering—and
it's repeated every morning for the rest of the week. That must be
the Profectus equivalent of homeroom. Apart from that, I can see
some of the standard classes I would have taken at St. Agnes—
math and English, French, gym (ugh)—but also in the mix are
some *much* more interesting options: coding, design, and the one
I've been waiting for, companioneering. We have fifteen minutes
in each classroom today, meeting the teachers and finding out
what's expected of us.

"Now you know what kind of gambling can go on at this school," says Jake.

"You bet on the baku battles?"

"We do!" Jake laughs. "You going to try for a team?"

"Do you think I should? It looks so exciting, but…" I cling tightly to Jinx. I can't imagine wanting to see him torn apart after all the hard work I've done putting him back together.

"Well, remember—seventh graders don't get to battle—you're alternates in the case of player sickness or baku malfunction."

"Oh well, in that case—maybe it would be cool to be on a team," I say, with genuine excitement. I've never been great at teamwork, preferring to work on my own most of the time at St. Agnes. But at Profectus, it feels like anything could happen. "Any tips on who the best team captain is?"

"Well, it should be Tobias hands down," says Jake. "His bro, Nathan, won it last year, and now he's on one of the high school teams. But I wouldn't count Gemma out. And they say this year might be a *wild card* year, so there might be some surprises. Catch you later," he says.

"Bye," I reply. He reaches out to touch Jinx again, but Jinx hisses in response. I attempt to laugh it off, but I can see confusion warring on Jake's face.

*Please behave.* I try to make my tone sound like a warning, but I can hear Jinx's scoff in my head. He knows my threats are empty. We might have *communication* down, but *commands*? I don't think I have any control over the baku at all. I might have to do some deeper digging into the code.

I head down to the gym floor where the other first years are mingling. There's a mix of nationalities and bakus, and almost everyone has a level three. The notable exception is Carter, and I skirt the edge of the crowd to attempt to avoid him.

Jinx suddenly buzzes at my feet, strands of his fur lighting up in an undulating pattern.

*What's going on?* I ask.

>>Someone is trying to access our data to find out more about you. Happened so quickly they almost bypassed...

"Miss Chu, is it?"

I look up and freeze in place. Eric Smith is standing within touching distance of me, his red panda baku staring down at me with onyx-dark eyes. "Looking forward to starting at Profectus?"

"Uh...yes, sir," I say, my cheeks burning with the attention.

He smiles at me, but it seems to falter as he reads data from his baku. "Lacey Chu..." he says, and a small wrinkle appears on his forehead.

Dread fills my stomach, and I turn the ring on my thumb anxiously.

He shakes his head. "Must be a coincidence," he mutters, mostly to himself. "Are you going to make one of the baku battle teams?"

"I hope so, sir," I stutter out.

"You have better odds than my son here," he gestures to Carter, who's appeared behind me. "He's not the most natural athlete, even with the help of a level four baku. Waste of a darn good baku, if you ask me."

I can almost feel the heat radiating off Carter next to me, and he's huffing like his boar. If it were anyone else, the surge of pity I feel for him in this moment would be a tidal wave. So not everything is great and easy in the life of Carter Smith.

"Where's your baku, Miss Chu?" Eric asks me.

I look down at my feet—Jinx is nowhere to be seen. "Uhhh…"

"Mr. Smith! Can I introduce myself…" A bubbly student bounds between us, preventing me from having to answer. I take a few steps back and almost bump into Carter. Traces of beet-red shame linger at his temples, but he tries to keep up the arrogant attitude. I almost admire him for it. *Almost.*

"You shouldn't be here," he hisses. "You should be at St. Agnes with your loser friend. I wouldn't even try to get onto a team if I were you; I'll only have to destroy you." Suddenly he yelps and looks down at his hand—which has a tiny scratch mark that beads with blood. "What the heck?" he asks. He looks at me accusingly, but I haven't done anything.

Jinx rubs up against my legs.

I swallow, emboldened by Jinx's appearance. "Look, this is a new school year—can we forget about St. Agnes?"

"You don't get it, do you? Your dad might be a loser who couldn't handle life at Moncha, but my dad *runs* the place. You're lucky I didn't tell my dad exactly who you are. He'd have you kicked out of the school for sure."

I step back as if I'd been slapped. "Lay off my family, Carter."

"Oh, now you're defending him?"

"I'm not doing anything. I just want to start my school year in peace. If you don't want to be civil, then leave me alone."

"Suit yourself. Stay out of my way and I'll stay out of yours."

"Fine by me."

Thankfully, Carter and I are separated into different groups, and we head off on our classroom tour separately. If there's anything that could take my mind off Carter and his comments about my dad, it's discovering all the wonders of Profectus.

Even the normal classrooms, the ones for subjects like math, English, French, and history, are equipped with state-of-the-art e-ink desks and leashes that the bakus plug into during class time—so they're under control, but can still help with assignments.

Another cool thing I find out is that each one of our professors is an actual employee of Moncha Corp. It gives them a little break from the high-intensity work environment of their regular jobs, while enabling them to keep an eye out for the next generation and help to foster new talent. Our advanced coding teacher, Ms. Watson, normally works on emotional AIs and gamification within the software engineering sector. After seeing the facilities that Profectus offers, I'm not surprised that employees don't mind taking some time off to teach. The coding classroom is floor-to-ceiling screens, and Ms. Watson seems to delight in showing off all the customizations she can make to the walls and ceilings—while teaching us at the same time.

I'm equally blown away by the materials testing lab, which includes a gigantic universal testing machine (it looks like an old-fashioned guillotine, except it's used to test the strength of different materials); the huge wind tunnel, for students studying aeronautical engineering; and the drafting classroom, with extra-wide desks and skylights that allow in lots of clear, bright light.

Everything is even better than I possibly could have imagined. The vision board did not do it justice.

But there's one class I've been waiting for even more than all the others.

Companioneering.

The classroom is almost disappointingly normal-looking, with a blackboard in front and several neat rows of desks. I take a seat at one of the desks near the middle and attempt to get Jinx to leash up. He doesn't.

The door opens, and I look up in anticipation. But it's the team captains who enter, filing in one by one with their bakus. I'm glad this is the class they've come to observe us in—I know I can prove myself here, and Carter isn't here to distract me.

Jinx stalks around the classroom as if he were lion-shaped rather than a house cat. Most bakus don't roam as far from their owners as he does from me, and I keep willing him back, tugging at the leash on my ear to call him. But he ignores me. I'm learning that nothing I do will make him stay where I want him to, so I resort to begging.

*Please come back.*

He doesn't reply.

The classroom door opens again and a man in a plain white T-shirt and jeans (and maybe an oil stain on his shirt too?) hurries into the room, an owl baku—the standard, I've learned, for teaching staff—flapping behind him. The owl lands on the desk and projects his name onto the wall behind him: Derek Baird. *This* is our teacher? He looks more disheveled than any of the students, but then again, we're all forced to wear a uniform.

He must have some sort of authority, though, as the other students quiet down and settle into their seats. Jinx still hasn't returned to my side, which makes me uneasy. He's supposed to help register me for class. I don't want to mess everything up in front of the team captains.

Mr. Baird claps his hands together and then rubs them fiercely as if he's trying to start a fire. "Right, guys, right! Welcome back to day one of the rest of your lives! And here in the best class of all—companioneering!" He has a lilting Scottish accent that somehow makes me want to sit up even straighter in my chair.

There's a rumble of laughter around the room, but my stomach clenches. This man's casual attitude to something that I've wanted my entire life is freaking me out.

No one else seems to care, though. There's a girl next to me, her auburn hair cropped short on her head, leaning forward on her hands, as if she's trying desperately to soak in everything that she can. Her posture is almost the mirror image of mine. I'm leaning so far forward, my belly is pressed up against the edge of the desk and digging in. I sit back a bit and try to relax.

I look down at her feet and see a tabby cat baku at her feet, leashed up to the desk and streaming information about companioneering onto her desk. A *helpful* cat baku.

```
>> Instead you're stuck with me.
```

*Oh, now you'll talk with me. Come back here and behave like that baku and maybe I'd be happy. Will you?*

```
>>Not a chance.
```

I roll my eyes, but then catch the girl looking at me, a frown on her face. *Oh no.* I hope she doesn't think I'm rolling my eyes at her. I smile weakly and try to say hi, but Mr. Baird starts talking.

"So, hands up, who's interested in companioneering?" Mr. Baird looks expectantly around the classroom.

The hand of the girl next to me shoots straight up and mine follows, more slowly. I take a quick glance over my shoulder and see that there are only about five hands out of the twenty-something first years in the classroom. The team captains look at us appraisingly, taking notes, and as I glance around, I catch the eye of Tobias—who is now staring straight at me. My throat feels like it's swelling up, and I find it hard to swallow—caught in the light streaming into the classroom, his dark eyes look light—the color of moss in early spring. I look away. He almost caused Zora to lose Linus. I cannot like him, no matter what the light does to the color of his eyes.

"Well, we only have a few minutes together today, and I'm

"Stop that baku!" Mr. Baird shouts.

The other students kick out their legs or reach down to grab at Jinx as he passes, but he nimbly jumps and dodges them all, until he reaches me and jumps up into my lap.

Oh no.

sure you're all feeling completely overwhelmed by everyth

you've seen so far. If you're not, you're not normal." There's a tit

of nervous laughter from the classroom. "You'll notice we've g

visitors"—he gestures to the team captains standing by the wall—

"but don't worry about impressing them; they've made their selec-

tions already. Remember all that hard work you did trying to get *in*

to Profectus in the first place? Well, that's all been sent straight to

the team captains' bakus. Your fates are sealed, young ones. But if

you don't get picked—don't worry. You'll have the chance to prove

yourselves before next year's selections, when the real fun begins."

I frown, disappointed at Mr. Baird's news. There goes my shot

at being selected. I barely scraped an acceptance into Profectus.

"Now, if you could all please ask your bakus to bring up the

first—" But Mr. Baird doesn't get to finish his sentence. There's a loud

crash as books, files, and an old globe are sent tumbling from a high

shelf above the heads of the team captains. Everyone watches as the

team captains shield their bakus from the falling objects. But I look

up to the shelf, a sick feeling turning my stomach. My heart lurches.

Yep, standing stock-still as a statue, staring at me as if I didn't know

*exactly* who was the culprit, is Jinx.

```
>>What, me?
```

I can almost hear him say it. The wide eyes and uplifted tail

say it all.

He flicks his tail now, nonchalant about the chaos he's caused,

and leaps down off the shelf.

**15**

"THAT THING IS YOURS?" MR. BAIRD ASKS, HIS eyes blazing.

"Probably defective," mutters one of the other students, and everyone starts laughing—the tension broken.

"I—I'm really sorry…" I say, but Mr. Baird's owl flaps his wings past me, dropping a small token into my lap. It's a black disc, not much bigger than a quarter. I pick it up and turn it over in my palm.

"That's not for you, it's for your baku," Mr. Baird snaps. "It's a black mark. A one-hour enforced power down. You won't be able to use your baku for the next hour. And you'll see me after class for detention for the disruption you've caused."

As if by magic—but more likely, by magnet—the black disc jumps out of my palm and locks itself to Jinx's tail. Instantly, Jinx slumps in my arms, his power sapped. He's almost back to the way he was when I first found him—a misshapen hunk of metal.

I'm in shock for a moment, but then panic sets in. "What? You can't do that!" I tug the metal disc but it won't budge.

"One hour, Miss…" He looks down at his baku. "Chu. You didn't think you could come to Profectus Academy, *the* official training school for Moncha Corp, and not end up finding out about some new, proprietary technology, did you? And let this be a lesson to all of you newbies," he says, lifting his stern gaze away from me and addressing the rest of the class. "Any sign of misbehavior by the bakus, or by yourselves, and we have ways of shutting you down. Black marks are real. While you are on these school grounds, you are under Moncha's rules. The eighth graders know that all too well. Don't you?"

The team captains nod, staring at me with a mixture of disbelief and bemusement that makes my cheeks burn. I've never been one to get in trouble with my teachers, and I hate that I might have made a bad impression already in front of the captains. Anger tenses up all my muscles. My fingers worry at the black mark, trying to pry it off, but it's no good.

"Well, I'd say it's almost time for the team selections," says Mr. Baird. "And considering this is the *best* class, it won't shock you that this is where you'll be finding out who's made the teams. As a reminder, if you don't want to participate, you can decline your selection and the team captain's second choice will be alerted. But being a part of a baku battle team will set you up well for the challenges ahead in middle school, at high school, and later on at Moncha Corp. So think carefully before turning this opportunity down."

There's some commotion as the doors open and other seventh graders file in. I take the opportunity to look at the captains—*other* than Tobias, who is glaring at me and sheltering his eagle protectively. *What's his problem?* I wonder. I avoid his gaze and instead study the girl Gemma, with her fierce tiger baku. She seems amazing— strong, determined, and in sync with her baku. It's the chance to get to meet people like her that made me want to come to Profectus.

To be around *my* kind of people.

"Everyone here?" asks Mr. Baird to his baku. The owl nods and hoots once. "Let's find out who's made the team, then."

In the classroom all around us, bakus buzz and light up with notifications. There's an immediate scramble as everyone rushes to see if they've been selected for a team. I'm the only one who can't check her baku—because he's lying motionless in my arms. That black mark might have ruined all my chances.

The girl next to me squeals with excitement. She looks up at Elektra. "I've made your team!"

"Welcome, Nalini!" says the captain with bright blue hair.

I cross my arms, miserable, waiting to see who else has been chosen. Of course, I hear the snuffling of Carter's boar as he saunters up to the front. But there's something unsure about the way he's walking, and he frowns down at his baku. He stops in front of Tobias, but then hesitates. Tobias and Gemma turn to each other and Gemma folds her arms. "Did you do this on purpose?" she asks him. She looks angry.

"No, did you?" he bites back.

I frown, looking between the two team captains. I feel like I've missed something.

I'm not the only one. "Problem, guys?" Mr. Baird raises an eyebrow.

"It's nothing," snaps Gemma. "Welcome to my team, Carter." Carter and his boar take up their position next to Gemma, but I can see him looking over at Tobias.

There are four seventh graders standing at the front now—but no one in front of Tobias.

"Well? Aren't you coming? Or are you turning it down?" Tobias asks. To my surprise, he's looking right at me.

I look down at Jinx—but of course, he's still black marked. Dead to the world.

"Your selection is Miss Chu?" asks Mr. Baird.

Tobias nods. He looks down at his baku as if to check that's right—as if he thinks he might have made a mistake too.

"Well, Miss Chu?"

I scramble to my feet, rushing down the row toward the front of the classroom. I feel the eyes of the other students on my back as I pass. I reach Tobias, and I'm flustered, my hair coming out of its hasty ponytail, strands of it sticking to the back of my neck. I dare a glance at Carter, and he's shooting daggers at me with his eyes. So much for staying out of each other's way. We're going to be pitted against each other.

"Come on, then," Tobias says. There's no *Welcome to the team, Lacey,* I notice. "Let's go and meet the others."

> PART THREE
# TEAM TOBIAS

16

I FOLLOW TOBIAS OUT OF THE CLASSROOM, JINX in my arms. Strangely, Tobias is also cradling his eagle baku—not allowing it to fly, like I've seen before.

He grunts at me. "Not plotting any more harm to Aero, are you?"

"*Excuse* me?"

"First the pine cones. Now you try to drop a ton of books on his head."

I stop in my tracks. "The pine cones?" So he *does* remember... but not the same way that I recall the incident happening at all. "Hang on a second, you sent your eagle to scare my friend! She almost lost her brand-new baku because of you."

He stops too, pivoting on the heels of his sneakers. "Aero wasn't scaring your friend. He was catching a baku ball. Carter threw it at her head, and it would have hit her if it wasn't for me."

I open my mouth to protest, but then I realize he could be telling the truth. "Oh," is all I say.

Tobias's eyes search my face, then he starts walking again—and I have no choice but to follow. He leads me to an empty classroom, where the rest of the team is waiting. I trail a little bit behind, still wary of his story—and regardless, it doesn't change the fact he's friends with Carter. Unfortunately, it's harder to remember the grudge when he's so cute.

He swings open the classroom door, and I'm greeted by three expectant faces—two guys and a girl. One of the guy's faces turns sour immediately, giving me a dark scowl.

"Everyone, this is our seventh grade teammate, Lacey Chu. Her baku is…"

"Jinx," I reply. I give the group a nervous wave, confused by the wave of hostility coming from the guy—who has the tallest spiked hair I've ever seen. He has a beautiful, large husky-type baku at his feet. Tobias gestures to him first. "This is Kai and his baku Oka. He's my second-in-command and the team's main companioneer."

"What's up with your baku?" Kai asks, folding his arms across my chest.

I swallow, but Tobias answers for me. "He got black-marked in Mr. Baird's class."

Kai looks aghast. "Toby, man… This isn't what we agreed."

Something passes between the two teammates that I don't understand. It seems like they're talking in code, similar to what passed between Tobias and Gemma in Mr. Baird's classroom. I hug my arms around my waist, uncomfortable with the feeling that this is all to do with me—even though I've done nothing wrong except, apparently, having been chosen.

"I'll tell you later," says Tobias to Kai. Before I have a chance to question it, he moves on. He points to the second guy—a tall, lanky, red-haired guy with a face covered in freckles. His baku is unusual—an oversize frog, but still a level three. "This is River. He's a really talented designer. His baku is Lizard."

I frown, looking again at his baku. "But that's a frog."

"I know. Don't ask. He'll be the one responsible for any mods we want to make."

"How's it going, Lacey?" River asks, but his head is down and he's sketching in a notebook—so I don't get the impression he really wants to know the answer.

"Hi," I say anyway.

"And then this is Ashley, our electronics geek. Her baku is Jupiter."

"Welcome to Team Tobias!" she says, giving me the first warm hello from the new team, along with a Hollywood-style, megawatt grin that's impossible not to return. Her long blond hair is tied back in a casual, messy bun—the sort that every girl is supposed to be able to pull off effortlessly, but I can't achieve no matter how hard I try. I look at her feet and feel a stab of jealousy at the beautiful spaniel baku at her feet. He's the closest thing so far to what I would have chosen if I'd had the opportunity. "Hey, come sit over here," she says, standing on her chair and jumping onto the desk next to it.

"Thanks," I say, bumping awkwardly into the back of the chair before managing to sit down. I close my eyes for a second, trying to calm my nerves. I wish more than anything that Jinx were awake—he might not be able to ease my anxiety, but he's at least good at distracting me.

Tobias takes point in the middle of his team. "I'm deadly serious about winning this year, so the hard work is going to start today. No one has any plans, right?" As if anyone would dare to disagree with the ferocity on Tobias's face. He turns to Kai sitting next to me. "What do you think of following a similar strategy to Nathan's?"

I jump in before I can stop myself. "But what exactly *is* the baku battle competition?"

Tobias stares at me and Kai rolls his eyes, but I see Ashley nodding and smiling at me encouragingly.

When I turn back to Tobias, his chest swells out and his chin lifts. He's enjoying this. He's in his element—a leader—and as if by divine intervention, a perverse sunbeam slices through a slat in the blinds to cast a band of gold on his dark brown skin.

He looks positively regal.

He takes a deep breath before beginning. Even my fingertips are tingling with anticipation at what he is about to say.

"Baku battles"—he pauses for dramatic effect—"are a long-standing tradition at Profectus. Pitting baku against baku teaches us how to innovate—to create, to imagine—in the most extreme environment, with stakes that actually matter to us. You've heard the old saying that war drives technological advancement? Well, we don't want to have *actual* war, so we've got to simulate it. Of course, you can't fight bakus in the real world, but here, under strict rules, in a controlled environment, we get to go *nuts*." His eyes flash as he talks, and my heart twists inside my chest. This is amazing. It's even better than I could have hoped. I knew Profectus would be competitive, but this is on another level.

This is competing, but the results for us could mean inventing technology that could help society. Advance it. Monica Chan's vision truly come to life. These are the types of secrets I dreamed about knowing.

And now, I get a front-row seat to the action.

"Middle school goes first, followed by the high school teams later on in the year. So we don't have long to train, but we're going to train hard. Preparation is absolutely key. The middle school competition is made up of three different battles. We earn points by defeating the other bakus in the arena or lasting the full thirty minutes—but we can also earn a share of the points by repairing bakus that have been broken during battle before school begins the next day. The team with the most points wins the competition. And every single winning teammate gets a guaranteed summer internship in the Moncha division of their choice and one-on-one time with Monica Chan herself."

My jaw drops. It's an incredible opportunity, and a guarantee for me to meet my idol.

"Although maybe it will be with Eric Smith this year," says Tobias, with a shrug, which snaps me from my daydream.

"Why do you say that?" I ask.

"Because Monica is normally the one to give the orientation speech. Maybe she's taking some time off this year. But working for Eric Smith will be just as good," says Tobias.

"Maybe better," says Kai. "My folks say she's taken a real step back. I want to work for someone who's still at the top of their game."

*No one could be better than Monica Chan.* I don't say the words out loud, though, because I don't want to annoy my teammates any further.

Tobias continues. "The final battle takes place inside Moncha headquarters, which is always a trip. The arena in there is *epic*.

"My brother was a captain two years ago, and he dominated. So I *have* to win this year. That means no shenanigans from my team. This is our future we're talking about.

"And absolutely no black marks." He isn't looking at me when he says it, but my fingers instinctively tighten around Jinx's inactive body.

The final school bell rings, the mark pops off Jinx, and he springs back to life. I can't help the grin that appears on my face. Part of me had been worried that the stasis might be permanent—with Jinx, things don't always work the way they're supposed to. I stare down at the black mark and wonder if I should return it to Mr. Baird.

>>Keep that thing away from me.

*I'm not planning on using it on you. Although, if you're bad...*

>>I will pee on your bedsheets.

*You don't pee.*

>>That doesn't mean I don't have my ways.

I laugh, but then I cringe at the thought of anyone finding out just how *un*official Jinx really is. He's a chimera, composed of so many spare parts and cobbled-together connections, I don't know what anyone would think of him if they took a closer look.

"All right, team, I'm sending your bakus the coordinates for the training session this afternoon. I want to see you all there in half an hour, no exceptions."

I raise my hand tentatively.

"Dude, we're not in class. Ask your question," says Kai, rolling his eyes.

Tobias looks at me expectantly.

"I...uh, have detention this afternoon."

Tobias's lips purse together. "I forgot about that. Well, you'll have to miss this one, then. But that's the only one you're going to miss, got it?" He snaps his fingers at his baku, Aero, and storms out of the classroom.

"He's a bit intense," says Ashley, leaning over. "But he's a good guy. It's kind of hard living in his brother's shadow. Pressure's on for Tobias to step up too."

My eyes widen. I know a lot about pressure—asking me not to put pressure on myself is like asking water not to boil when it's placed over a heat source.

"He said if he doesn't win, his parents might send him to

high school at BRIGHTSPRK," says River, jumping in on our conversation.

Ashley's and my expressions are almost mirrors of each other: the same instant grimace at the name BRIGHTSPRK. They're Moncha's biggest rivals, and they started their own school following the Moncha model. They're based out of San Francisco, but mini BRIGHTCities are popping up all over the world.

But they don't have bakus, so as fast as BRIGHTCities are popping up, Monchavilles are taking over. And I can't imagine Tobias being happy about giving up Aero. Another incentive for him to win.

The simultaneous grimace bonds Ashley and me. "Good luck at detention," she says. "Hope Mr. Baird's not too hard on you. See you around, teammate!"

"See you," I reply. I'm left all alone in the classroom, in no hurry to find out what sort of detention Mr. Baird has in store for me. I want Jinx to send Zora a message about the baku battles and what's happened, but then I remember the Profectus rules about secrecy—plus external communication is disabled within the school walls. In an emergency, there are codes that can be used to override the signal blackout, but if they are used outside of that, then I'm sure there are even worse punishments that can be doled out than a black mark.

I can't put it off any longer.

Time to find out what detention is like at Profectus.

# 17

I STAND AS THE DOOR TO THE CLASSROOM OPENS. Mr. Baird's head pops around the door. "Miss Chu? You're late."

Darn. I've already got on his bad side once today, I can't afford to again. Jinx's hackles rise as the teacher's owl flies overhead, and Mr. Baird looks down at him, frowning. I beg Jinx to stop behaving so weirdly, fidgeting with the leash at my ear, and to my surprise, he stops and jumps up to me. Instinctively my arms close around his soft metallic body, and I brush down his back with my fingers, feeling my heart rate and breath return to normal as he purrs.

"What version of a cat baku is that? I'm not sure I've seen one like him." He reaches out to touch Jinx's fur, but Jinx leaps back out of my arms and darts away down the hallway.

I shrug and laugh it off. "No, he's not a new version. Totally standard level three house cat baku," I say.

I'm not sure he believes me, if the quivering frown line between his eyebrows is anything to go by. "Well, a place on the team *and* detention on your first day. You're gaining yourself quite a reputation at school already."

My throat feels like it's constricting.

"Detention is going to be a bit different today. I have a task for you."

Obediently, I follow—breathing a small sigh of relief as we turn around the corner and Jinx is there, waiting in a doorway, his eyes bright and alert. Mr. Baird doesn't pay him any particular attention once he trots at my heel, behaving for all the world like an ordinary baku. *Please stay that way*, I think.

>>Not a chance.

I grimace.

Just as Jinx trots at my heel, I trot at Mr. Baird's, following him three levels down a wide staircase at the very back of the school. I'm glad that Jinx's built-in GPS will be keeping tabs on all these routes, mapping the labyrinth of hallways. There's absolutely no way that I would be able to remember where to go without him. My brain might be perfect for solving engineering puzzles, but when it comes to a sense of direction? Yeah, not my forte. Reading books that involved kids heading out into the wilderness with only an analog compass and a paper map used to give me hives.

The owl baku goes ahead of us, opening each door as we pass through. "You won't be able to get through here without a teacher or senior student," says Mr. Baird. "So there's no point in trying. The security is built into our bakus, state-of-the-art. You won't be able to practice in secret," he says, his eyes shining. "But what you can do is clean this up."

With a brush of his wing (likely embedded with some sort of code), the owl opens the last door—and I realize we're down in the arena beneath the gymnasium. It looks different here in the dark. Smaller. Creepier. It's also an absolute mess; there are bits of metal and plastic everywhere, bolts and wires pulled from the battling bakus strewn across the surface. I can almost trace the choreography of the fights based solely on the wreckage. Jinx paces over to where the wolf was brought down, sniffing tentatively at a scrap piece of metal on the ground.

Mr. Baird coughs, and I look up. "Well, can you help?" he asks.

"What do you want me to do?"

"Get all of this tidied up. There's a recycling bin for all the spare materials outside here, and you'll find cleaning supplies in this closet. When you're done, leave the room, and it will lock automatically behind you."

"Profectus detention is intense," I say.

His eyes sparkle with amusement—I'm glad I'm able to make him laugh rather than grimace this time. "If you can get this done quickly, you might be able to make the end of your team practice." He pauses in the doorway. His eyes flick from me to Jinx, and I can see he wants to say something more.

"I got it, Mr. Baird. You can count on me." I show my eagerness by grabbing a broom from the closet and start sweeping up the arena. I hear the soft swoosh of the doors, and I'm left in peace.

>>Thank Moncha he's gone! Now we can have some real fun.

"Jinx, seriously—I don't even clean up my room. You think cleaning this up is going to be fun?"

>>We can find all sorts of goodies in here, I bet. Like, look at this.

His paw brushes against a smashed-up printed circuit board—if one of the bakus is missing that, they're going to be seriously screwed.

I lean down to pick it up. Jinx is right—this *is* interesting, and I could definitely put it to use in my lab at home. I drop it into my backpack. Once we get on a roll, sweeping up and examining the wreckage for useful things, it becomes much more fun. A bit like panning for gold. Besides, I'm able to get a much better sense of the arena. The floor seems to be made of a smooth substance that doesn't scratch despite the metallic claws and talons of the creatures. Then there are the five rings set out at intervals around the arena—where Tobias, Gemma, and the others were standing. I guess in order to make it fair—and safe—they keep the players in one place.

Finally, once everything is about as tidy as I can stand to make it, I put away the brooms, mops, and cleaning supplies, and let my curiosity take over. I stand in one of the circles, planting my feet on top of two tiny silver dots, which I assume are place markers. I want to feel what it's like to be one of the battlers—if just for a moment.

But, as I'm quickly learning, nothing at Profectus is there by accident.

Immediately the silver pads beneath my feet heat up, and I become encased in a projection that shows me the different areas of the battlefield—including the side of the doughnut that is invisible to me. My view automatically swerves so I can see from Jinx's point of view—and above him, like a bird's-eye, if I turn my head slightly.

>>We're connected!

"Oh my gosh, you can feel this too?"

>>Absolutely. It must be how you would send
me commands. You know. If I listened to
that sort of thing.

I roll my eyes. "You would have to listen to me in a baku battle. What if something was coming behind you?"

>>Trust me, I would have much better
instincts on that front than you.

As if to prove his point, he ripples his back, arching it so his tail flicks. At the same time, he lights up every one of his sensors, so it looks like moonlight sparkling off waves on an ink-black ocean. "Show-off," I say, sticking my tongue out.

I play around a bit with the hologram, moving the field of

vision this way and that, and watching as Jinx's stats light up on the screen. It's an impressive bit of gear—and the fact that you can't tell it exists until you are inside the circle is even more impressive. The silver disks must not only be pressure points, but must form part of the leash connection.

I wish I could play around with it all night, but I can see in the corner that the time is already flashing five o'clock. School's been out for an hour and a half—I'm sure most of the training sessions have finished already. Mom will be wondering where I've been.

With reluctance, I step off the silver pads, and the hologram drops. I pick my backpack off the floor with a grunt, weighed down by the bits and pieces I've collected from the arena. Lots to sort out in the cave later.

I wave my hand in front of the door and it opens. I step through. But Jinx doesn't follow. I spin around on my heels as the door slides shut on me. "Jinx!" I cry out, slamming my fists onto the door. "Why didn't you come?" I push on the door, then press my hand on the keypad, but it flashes up a series of red lights at me: CODE INVALID.

I stand on my tiptoes, looking through the small window into the room. I see Jinx's tail dash across the floor—he's not at all worried about being separated from me. Instead, I see him look back over his shoulder, catch my eye, and then disappear through a different sliding door on the opposite side.

I slam my fist one more time, shouting his name. But it's no use. He's gone. Now I have to find him in a maze of hallways, laboratories, and classrooms, some blocked off by security that I have no idea how to navigate. So much for being able to make a quick getaway home.

My last glance through the window confirms that Jinx is no longer there—the arena is now dark and, thankfully, clean. I make a mental note of which door he went through, so I can make my way around in that direction. He can't go far—I'm certain that he wouldn't run away from me for good. Bakus don't do that. *But maybe this one does*, says an uncomfortable voice in the back of my mind. I can't risk it. I have to find him.

I dig around for a pen inside my bag (Mom insisted I bring one, though I haven't written anything down in ages) and jot down a rough map of the arena on my palm: the door where I am, and where Jinx has gone. It's silly, but the best idea I can think of in the moment. Then I dash back along the hallway, to the stairs I walked down with Mr. Baird. There's a couple of other doors leading from the stairwell, and—confusingly—both lead in the direction I want to go. There's nothing—no signage or even door numbers—to indicate which would be my best option, so I go for the closest. I yank at it, but it won't budge. There's no lock pad or even keyhole that I can see—maybe it only opens one way?

I run around to the other door, which pushes open easily. "Jinx?" I call out tentatively. Nothing. I need to keep heading to the left in order to make sure I'm following the circle around—and not moving farther out into one of the numerous wings.

I keep running, occasionally coming up against locked doors

or dead ends. I try every handle in desperation, pushing against every window in case there's an alternative way through. I've moved beyond the surgically white hallways of the science wing into a part of the academy that has a more relaxed vibe—with beanbag chairs for resting in, and did I spot a Ping-Pong table? It looks like one of the visions of perfect corporate life that I've seen in old movies and television shows. Mentally I bring up a picture of what I know the school to be like—maybe this is where the kids who board stay? It would be a pretty cool place to live. But there's no one around.

I come across a huge lounge-type room, with oversize armchairs, two elaborate fireplaces, and inspirational messages printed onto the walls in foil type that catches the low light. The lights turn on as I enter, and I brace for some sort of alarm—but nothing happens.

I catch a glimpse of Jinx in the far corner of the room. Just the end of his slinky tail, but it's enough. "Wait for me!" I cry out. I sprint across the hall, jumping over a low coffee table and trying not to slip on the brightly colored rugs.

Jinx is halfway through an open door when I take a flying leap and manage to grab him by sliding into him on the knees of my woolen uniform. I'm thankful I didn't decide to wear the kilt after all—I would have serious burns on my legs otherwise. "Gotcha!" I laugh, grabbing him tightly around the stomach. Thankfully, he doesn't struggle.

But that's when I realize I'm not alone in the darkened room. A pair of heavy boots enters my sight, their wearer breathing heavily.

"Get. Out. Now."

18

"WHAT ARE YOU DOING HERE?" TOBIAS STANDS over me, his hands on his hips, his voice dripping with icy-cold anger—and an undercurrent of something else. Fear? But that can't be right—I'm no threat to him.

At any rate, I'm taken aback by his tone. I scramble backward toward the door, accidentally loosening my grip. Jinx takes advantage and shoots out of my arms.

I close my eyes for a second, cursing him. My back hits the doorframe in my hurry to put as much space between me and Tobias as possible. "I...I'm sorry," I say. "I was following Jinx, trying to find a way out of here..." I don't want him to know I don't have control over what my baku does.

He presses his fingers against the bridge of his nose. "Finished detention?"

I nod.

"You're new here—you wouldn't know—but these rooms are supposed to be totally private. That's all." Tobias shifts his body to try and intercept Jinx. As he moves, I catch sight of his eagle baku on the ground, not moving. My curiosity is piqued, and Tobias— realizing his mistake—rushes to block my view again. He's breathing heavily and he looks flustered.

He wants me out of there.

But I can see Jinx's eyes glowing in the darkness of the far corner, and he doesn't seem to be in a hurry to leave.

"Come on, Jinx," I whisper to him, but Jinx grooms his tail, ignoring me. Inwardly, I groan. I'm going to have to walk across the room to collect him.

I swallow then take a step in, keeping as close to the edge of the room as possible. "I'll get my baku, and then I'll leave you alone," I force myself to say. Maybe boys are like wild animals. If you keep them talking, they won't get so riled up.

To my frustration, Jinx leaps out of the way.

"God, what's that thing's problem?" Tobias says. "You need to get it looked at by one of the vets."

"He's fine," I snap back. "Yours is the one with the problem." As the words fall out of my mouth, I can see that I'm right—it really *does* have a problem. Even though it didn't look as if the eagle had received much damage during the baku battle, there are some serious dents and broken wires.

His jaw tightens. "Yeah, don't you think I know that?"

I can't help it; now I'm really curious. I leave the comfort of the edge of the room and creep toward the broken eagle. He's on the ground, as if he were simply turned off, but every so often he twitches his beak, like an involuntary spasm. There's been an obvious attempt at a repair—some pretty shoddy soldering work is visible, at odds with the rest of the creature's beautifully crafted engineering. I wrinkle my nose, unable to hide my disgust at the workmanship. "Who did this?"

"Kai," Tobias says. He folds one arm over his chest and rubs at his eyes with his other hand. He walks over so he's standing on the opposite side of the eagle to me. "During our team session today. I picked him for the team because he's supposed to be the best companioneer in his class, but he's never fixed anything as complicated as my eagle."

"Why not take it to a vet?" I ask.

He scoffs. "You don't get it yet, do you? With Profectus, with the baku battles, the whole *point* is that we have to do everything ourselves. Or as a team, anyway. I could maybe take it to one of the teachers, but we'll be handicapped in the battle. They have punishments they can dole out—like the black marks—or they have bonuses they can give for good behavior too—like revive chips that will give a baku an extra boost if it's injured. We get points deducted from our total if we pay for professional help. It's *meant* to be challenging. The idea is to get to the very end without asking for help—applying the knowledge we've learned at the academy. Kai was supposed to be good, but I think Nathan was the one who was really good at the hardware stuff. He probably set me up to fail."

"Nathan sounds like a jerk," I say.

Tobias laughs, but the sound is laced with bitterness that makes me cringe a little inside. "That jerk is not only my brother, but a jerk with a great summer internship with Monica Chan."

I raise an eyebrow. "Well. Now I'm jealous of the jerk." Thankfully, I get a chuckle from Tobias, breaking some of the thick tension that's been building in the room ever since I interrupted him. I take the moment to look around the room. It's not *quite* as well equipped as my cave back home, but it has a few supplies. I don't think the damage to Tobias's eagle is terminal, at any rate. I can already see one major connection that I *know* is wrong.

"Hey, what are you doing?" Tobias sounds alarmed.

"Oh!" I snap my hand away from the eagle. I'd moved in to start fixing it without even asking. "I'm so sorry. I just think if we moved this connection over and wound it back underneath this part, he would have a lot more freedom of movement again and wouldn't be so twitchy?"

Tobias frowns, then walks over to where I am standing. I move aside to show him what I mean and—since he doesn't seem to protest anymore—I reach over to the eagle and show him exactly what I want to do. The eagle's metallic feathers are soft under my touch, the brutal work that Kai did a travesty to the craft.

"You think?" he asks, skepticism lacing his tone—but I'm not sure it's my words that are giving him pause or the fact that they are coming from a puny seventh grader.

"Oh, for sure."

He raises an eyebrow at my confidence, and a blush rises in my cheeks. I focus back on the eagle's twisted metal, trying not to think about Tobias's moss-green eyes staring at me. Or the fact that he's so close.

"The best thing for me to do is show you," I say, trying to inject more confidence in my voice than I feel.

I sense he's about to protest again, so I change my approach. "Look, how long have you been working on this?"

"Since school let out," he says, with a conceding shrug. "The team left about fifteen minutes ago. And if my eagle's not fixed by tomorrow, I might have to withdraw. I can't believe it's all gone so wrong, and school has barely begun."

Now that he's not looking at me, I take a moment to look at him. He is so serious, a deep frown line crisscrossing his smooth forehead. Neither of us have turned on any lights, and his skin is so dark in the half light, it reflects almost blue. "So, you were going to stand here all night staring at him?"

"Look, I've only had a year of studying to do this, okay? I don't want to get it wrong."

"But you've tried everything you can think of."

His jaw tightens. "Yes."

"So, what's the harm in letting me try? Give me half an hour. I promise I won't do anything you can't reverse."

He throws his hands up in the air. "Okay, Miss Confident. You try and do what we couldn't."

I bite my lower lip and nod. Jinx rubs up against my leg—typical that when I'm not trying to catch him, he comes to me of his own accord. He crawls up my leg, coming to rest on my shoulder.

>>Whoa. He's beat up pretty bad.

"That's for sure," I mutter.

"What was that?" asks Tobias.

I cringe. I've already become so used to Jinx's voice in my head that I forget it's a bug in his code that I have to fix. "Sorry, talking to myself."

"Oh great, I've got a weirdo on my team," he says, but I notice he doesn't actually ask me to stop. Instead, he watches my hands intently, as if he's interested in seeing what happens next.

"Any chance we can turn the lights on?" I ask. The lights might mean he can see my blush—but I'm hoping the more clinical atmosphere might help me to concentrate. Plus, I can hardly see what I'm working with.

Tobias shakes his head. "We're not exactly supposed to be in here. And besides, the lights are on a timer. Energy saving or something."

"Hmm," I say, followed by a short, sharp exhale as I take stock. "Jinx, turn on your light." He rolls his tail over and turns on his flash. At least that helps me. "This okay?" I ask Tobias, who nods.

I use Jinx's camera to take pictures of the damage, and set him to scan the internet for the original schematics for the eagle baku. He finds them within seconds, and he projects the blueprint onto the eagle's back. I take my safety glasses from out of my jacket pocket (I'm such a nerd that I carry them around with me), and crouch down closer to the eagle. Kai has botched one of the main connections between the motherboard and the circuit that controls the eagle's head and neck movements. I wrinkle my nose. "I hope he didn't damage the electronics with what he did," I say. "Why didn't he use the correct schematic to fix it?"

Now it's Tobias's turn to look confused. "What do you mean? My eagle is a level five baku—unique and customized to me. There aren't any typical schematics for this."

"Then what…" I stop talking before yet another one of Jinx's secrets is revealed.

>>Told you I have my ways.

*Shut it, you.*

Out loud, I say: "Oh, right. I mean—I'm just looking at a schema for one of the other bird bakus, and you can see that Kai's soldered this wire to the wrong connection. You're never going to get the right movement that way. Not only that, but it looks like he's used old solder here." Instead of the connection being shiny and smooth, it is dull gray. "That won't conduct electricity well. If I clean it off and replace it, it will be a lot more conductive. Let's move him up onto the table." I get Jinx to switch to layer a level three bird baku's schema over the top of the eagle's connections, to disguise how clever he'd been. From that point, it's easy to show Tobias exactly what I mean.

"Um, hang on a second. That's so cool—how did you get your baku to do that? Cat bakus don't have projectors on their tails."

"Well, that bit's easy. I added in the projector from an old rodent baku that I found…"

Tobias scans my face, but the open admiration on his is what makes me blush again. "You're telling me *you* customized this baku?" he says.

"Well, yeah…"

"Maybe Kai isn't the best companioneer on the team after all…"

For the next hour, Tobias and I work together, stripping wires and melting solder, and I end up using a little compressed air to clean up the dirty work surface that Kai has left me. Thankfully he didn't heat up the PCB too much, so it isn't damaged. I also use a good old-fashioned hammer to help sort out some of the dents and welts in the eagle's casing—it seems such a shame for such a beautiful creature to look anything less than perfect. The whole time, Jinx projects different measurements at me—from the perfect pressure to apply to a dent, to whether the connections are working properly—so I can test my theories even before Tobias leashes him up to full power. Once the neck twitch is sorted, I give the rest of the baku a quick once-over—mostly so that I can admire the beautiful tech. It's truly a masterpiece. To make a baku that can fly as smoothly as this eagle, each component is featherlight, dusted with solar nanoparticles that draw power from the sunlight.

>>Pfft, he's nowhere near as cool as I am.

*Whatever, Jinx. Can you fly?*

>>I could if I wanted to. If you built me
some wings.

*You'd be a Pegasus cat, then.*

"Okay, I think he's ready to be leashed," I say. I pull the glasses down off my nose and rub my eyes, becoming aware of the familiar prickle of dryness now that my focus is gone.

Tobias leashes Aero, and it takes only a few seconds before he is fully booted up. He runs a check. "Well, holy heck. You did it. Diagnostics say he's back up to full functionality."

I shrug, trying to control the giant smile that wants to plaster itself on my face. Instead, I concentrate on stretching out my fingers, which are stiff from gripping the soldering iron so tightly. "It wasn't too hard."

My eyes flick up and catch his gaze. To my surprise, the expression on his face is one of pure and simple admiration. "You're full of surprises."

I wait for the joke, but it doesn't come. He seems genuine, and for the first time I realize my skills might end up being more valuable than I thought. I'm touched.

"Good job, teammate."

"You're welcome." In my awkwardness, I put out my hand. Inwardly, I'm cringing.

Jinx echoes my thoughts.

>>A handshake? That's really what you're
going for in this situation?

*Shh*, I hiss. It's too late for me to back out now. Thankfully, Tobias takes it in stride. He clasps my hand.

I don't know if he feels it too. A spark. A moment where electricity leaps from my hand to his, where all the neurons in my palm seem to light up. It takes my breath away. It feels like our hands are clasped for a lifetime.

Then the moment is over. His hand slips from mine. "I'll see you around, then, Lacey," he says.

I swear there is a tiny smile playing on his lips.

Whatever it is, he leaves the room, taking his newly fixed eagle with him. And I have to catch myself on the desk or else risk melting into a puddle on the floor.

19

LECTURES, NOT CLASSES.

Professors, not teachers.

Gathering, not homeroom.

And baku battles—not homework.

This is my first month at Profectus. Baku battles seep into every aspect of my life, to the point that I wake up in the middle of the night, drenched in sweat, as I fend off razor-sharp eagle talons and shiny, metallic tiger baku teeth. Jinx is never the one in the arena, it is always me. But then, Jinx isn't allowed in the arena anyway.

I spend every spare moment not in school with the team in the Profectus team practice grounds, running drills and preparing strategies.

Mom's pretty worried about my late hours. This is exactly what she was afraid of—that I would disappear into my hobby, then into the school, then into a job—and then maybe for good. But I'm doing this for the two of us. To give us a better life. If that means working harder now so that I can relax later, then so be it.

Plus, I'm sure things will die down once the first battles are over.

And I've promised to see Zora this weekend to stream the latest season of our favorite sci-fi TV series, *Outerlands*, which is launching Saturday at eight o'clock—prime time. She's been pretty understanding that I had to concentrate during that first month of school, even though I can't fill her in on exactly *why* I've been so busy.

But before I can think about the weekend, there's the first battle to get through. Ashley and Jupiter are going to be up first. According to Tobias, the first battles are always for low-level students and bakus. It's a chance for teams to test their mettle before the bigger events and to save their strongest players until later in the competition.

"Any insider tips? Toby feeling okay? Did I see that Kai's husky had a bit of a limp?" asks Jake, seeking me out by my locker. He's running the school's gambling ring with aplomb, reworking old code so the betting app makes suggestions based on heart rate spikes and pupil dilation. He calls it "tapping into instinct."

I think he's making it all up. Which he is, but that doesn't stop the entire student body (and most of the teachers) from downloading and using the app.

"No—and even if I knew something, I couldn't tell you!"

"Fair enough. Have to ask!" He winks. "Good luck, little Lacey. See you down in the arena."

"Thanks, Jake. See you there."

The atmosphere for the first official battle is tense, and the entire school comes out to watch. My heart goes out to Ashley. She has to last thirty minutes to guarantee a share of the full one hundred points. If Jupiter goes down, we'll have until the following morning to repair any damage back up to minimum ninety percent functionality.

"Ready, Ashley?" asks Mr. Baird. As the companioneering teacher, he runs the battles.

She nods, her pale face tinged gray. She follows Mr. Baird down into the competitors' preparation room, where she'll be loaded into one of the lifts to be brought up into the arena.

"She's going to get murdered," mutters Kai, as we file into the team box to watch. Front row seats to the action.

"Come on now," says Tobias, but his expression is dark too.

"You know she's too soft about that baku of hers."

"Well, that's why we're sending her in first. She'll have to toughen up. And you know she's the best electronics engineer in her class, so we had to have her on our team."

"At least she's up against other level three bakus," says River.

"I'm not so sure about that," I say.

All the eyes of the team flick to me. Because while Tobias, Kai, and River have been focused on the strategies laid out on the backs of their bakus, I've been watching the other teams: in particular, Gemma's team, and the person walking up to compete.

"Nooo," says Kai, as the reality sinks in.

It's *Carter* and his level four boar who have been entered into the arena in the first round.

Jinx arches his back and hisses. I know exactly how he feels.

"I thought you said seventh graders *couldn't* fight in the battles," I say to Tobias.

"They can't," he says. "Well, they can't unless one of the other team members volunteers to step down, which basically never happens…"

"Or they were forced to step down," I say, raising one of my eyebrows.

"Or that," Tobias concedes.

I feel my throat tighten at the thought of Jupiter going up against Hunter. Carter's not exactly the type of guy to go easy in competition. I know that all too well.

River stares at me with wide eyes, then clasps me on the shoulder. "I'm glad we've got you on our team instead. I would *not* have stepped down. Neither would Kai or Ashley."

"Instead?" I ask, frowning. River shrugs, and before I can question him, a fanfare of music begins.

"She really is going to get murdered," mutters Kai.

Tobias doesn't respond, but a sheen of sweat on his brow speaks volumes.

I don't have any more time to process. After the music, the competitors are lifted up into the arena. Swept up in the action, I cry out, "Go Ashley! Go Jupiter!"

She turns to the team box and gives us a thumbs-up. But even from here, I can see she's shaking, her knees unsteady, her feet shuffling on the silver pads. Carter, by contrast, looks way too confident. Having a baku that's a full level higher than the others on the playing field will do that.

"You just have to last thirty minutes," I mutter to Ashley, even though she can't hear me. But I bet thirty minutes feels like a lifetime in that arena.

And the battle begins.

It's a fast-paced, frenzied battle. Like Ashley, Team Dorian's player—an eighth grader called Wayne, with a bulldog baku—is also on the defensive, trying to protect as much of his baku's functionality as possible to last out the thirty minutes.

Others, like Carter from Team Gemma, go in hard, inflicting as much damage as possible on the other opponents to make the bakus difficult to repair. Those silver tusks look extra dangerous in that arena, as if he had sharpened them specifically for the battle. Jupiter, by contrast, looks so small—so domestic and tame—in the arena.

Tobias switches for a more aggressive strategy as the battlefield narrows. He pushes Ashley in turn to push her baku to the very limit, not allowing her to let up until the thirty minutes are almost up and there is only one other baku left.

Carter's.

I clutch Jinx's little paws, even as he attempts to crawl out from beneath my fierce grip.

>>She's a goner.

*If she is, we'll fix her.*

>>You think that's a good idea?

*Why wouldn't it be?*

Jinx says something, but I don't hear it—my eyes are transfixed by the sight of Hunter rocketing toward Jupiter at lightning speed. Ashley isn't quick enough. The two bakus connect and the crunching sound is excruciating. Jupiter is thrown almost the full length of the arena, smashing into the curved wall underneath us, ricocheting around the outside wall like a pinball. Carter pumps his fist, triumphant.

"Giving up, Ashley? Your poor doggie is almost out," he says, his tone full of swagger. He's right—Jupiter's stats are now at fifteen percent. She could forfeit now. "Go on, put her out of her misery."

Ashley stares from Hunter to Jupiter. Her baku attempts to stand but one of her legs is twisted so it's pointing backward, and part of her wiring trails on the floor. Even though she can't feel pain, it is gut-wrenching to watch. Maybe it's Ashley's face that makes it worse. She's even paler than she was before—I didn't think that was possible—her face ashen, with a sickly sheen from sweat, worry, and adrenaline. She looks as if she wants to forfeit the battle. Her eyes flick to Tobias in the team box, who is speaking furiously to Aero. The eagle is presumably transmitting the message to Ashley, for only her to hear. And I can see in Tobias's eyes that he wants her to continue. There's only a few minutes left on the clock. If Ashley can hold out, then she will have won us a share of the remaining points.

I bite my nails, chewing down to the quick. I can't believe Tobias is making her continue—he should pull her now and give us a better chance of fixing her for tomorrow morning. I try to catch his eye, but he's laser-focused on Ashley.

Ashley closes her eyes for a beat, and when she opens them again, she is filled with determination. "You can do this," I whisper to her. My fingers are balled into tight fists at my side, as I will her every ounce of luck I can spare.

Carter rolls his eyes. "Seriously? Come on, Hunter, let's finish this baku off."

The roar in the room rises to a frenzied level, students shouting and jeering both competitors equally. There's dismay that Ashley is continuing, and a loud chorus of people telling her to give up.

Hunter stalks around the circle, surprisingly graceful for a machine that looks like a boar. My mind drifts off as I imagine what sort of person would voluntarily choose a baku shaped like that, and I almost miss the key moment when he goes in for the kill.

Because when it happens, it's rapid and brutal. Hunter still has full freedom of movement, his head swaying with the weight of his tusks, his legs nimble, whereas every command Ashley sends to Jupiter takes a few seconds too long to reach him—a vital receiver must be damaged, and so she can't respond nearly quick enough. When the blow comes, it destroys Jupiter. The boar's tusks rip through the already exposed electrics of the dog baku's central core, ripping through the "brain," which—just like in Jinx's schematics—is located in her stomach.

"Good luck fixing *this* piece of junk," Carter shouts. And, as if to make his point even stronger, Hunter shakes his head and—with a second to spare—sends the two halves of the robotic spaniel spinning across the arena and colliding with opposite sides of the wall.

Down in her circle, Ashley lets out a cry that is almost primal. I feel every ounce of her pain. The thought of something like that happening to Jinx…

I take him up in my arms and squeeze him against my chest. He's not a robot to me. He's my friend.

The whistle sounds, signaling the end of the battle. Mr. Baird stands in the center of the arena. "The winner of the first round of baku battles is Carter and his baku, Hunter. Gemma's team is awarded one hundred points."

He turns to the team box. "Other teams, you have until the first assembly bell tomorrow to attempt to fix your eliminated bakus, in order to split the winning round total of one hundred points with Team Gemma. If the baku isn't at least ninety percent functional, however, the points this round will be confirmed." Even he sounds dubious at the prospect of any of the bakus rising to fight again.

Ashley's face looks distraught, clutching the remains of Jupiter.

Tobias looks ill, seeing his strategy fail and the points slip away.

*No.* It's not the end yet. If we can fix Ashley's baku, we can get the team back on track. Yet even with Profectus's state-of-the-art facilities, I know there's one place that will give us a better shot— and we can work there all through the night.

I just have to convince the team to trust me.

## 20

"THIS IS PERFECT," SAYS KAI AS WE STEP OFF THE city bus that's taken us to my building, and I smile. I wonder if I'm finally getting him to warm up to me—even though I have no idea what I did to get on his bad side to begin with. But then he sneers as he looks up at the entrance. "No one is going to spy on us in this place. A Profectus student actually *lives* here?"

"I do," I say through gritted teeth. I bristle. It's not that bad. It might be a bit boring and functional—an uninspired condo tower of beige concrete and tinted glass, but it's not dirty or falling down.

"Kai, that's enough," says Tobias.

"What?" He shrugs. "I was trying to say it's a good thing for our team. You can bet Team Gemma aren't working somewhere so…"

Tobias elbows him, and he doesn't finish his sentence.

Ashley shivers. Since Jupiter's battle, she's seemed like a shell of her former, bubbly self.

Watching the four of them walk into my building, I can't believe I've brought them here. To my sanctuary. My companioneering haven.

Mom is delighted I'm bringing back friends from school. I haven't the heart to tell her this isn't exactly the start of a busy social life for me.

It's an emergency.

I sign them in with Darwin, and then we take the elevator down into the basement. Kai seems like he's biting his tongue the whole way to my storage locker.

I try to put his judgment out of my mind. Jupiter is in pieces. Ashley carries the remains in her arms, her cheeks damp with tears. The absolute annihilation she experienced in her baku battle would have been enough to scar me for life—I have no idea how she's even standing upright.

What makes it even worse is that Carter is the cause. He and that awful boar of his—that snuffling, snarling beast. I've never wanted a baku to be put in its place before, but I'd like to see that thing put down. I am willing to do anything to make sure that *Carter* isn't a reason that his team ends up on top. He hasn't won yet.

>>Yeah right, as if a certain handsome team captain isn't the real reason this crowd of people have invaded your private lab.

I cringe. Jinx knows too much for his own good. And he seems to be getting smarter. Just last night, I was working on my French homework when I started hearing his voice in my head, translating for me. I had to tell him to stop—if Profectus found out, I'd be expelled for cheating for sure. Bakus aren't supposed to do anything like that unless specifically commanded. I add it to the list of things I need to check in Jinx's code—if my other work ever lets up and I have a spare moment to squeeze it in.

I worry every day about slipping up and revealing that Jinx is no ordinary baku. But so far, the team haven't seemed to notice that Jinx is any different. And that's how I want it to stay.

With five people and five bakus crammed into the tiny storage locker, space is tight. River leaps up onto the desk with his oversize frog baku, mimicking him by sitting with his knees up. He's like a contortionist, able to squeeze himself into the most unlikely places—as if he's more comfortable being uncomfortable. I don't know what that says about him.

Tobias leads Ashley in and sits her down on my chair.

"So, what are we doing here?" Kai asks, his hands on his hips. Oka, his husky baku, paces underfoot. Kai tries to take up the biggest amount of space in the room, his chest puffed out like a frigatebird from the Galapagos.

"We need a share of the points if we're going to have any chance of winning the baku battles," says Tobias. "And that means we have to fix Jupiter. I think Lacey here can do it."

"Uh, have you seen that baku? It's scrap metal!" cries Kai, picking up a piece of Jupiter that has dropped out of Ashley's arms and onto the floor, wielding it as a prime example of what he means.

"Not even the best Moncha companioneer could fix this pile of garbage. Look, Tobias, my man, we shouldn't be worrying about how to fix this." He gestures to the mess in Ashley's arms, and she whimpers. "But planning our next round attack strategy. Like how that freaky dude"—he points at River—"and I are going to stand a chance in the next round. Especially as Gemma is going to have *three* bakus to our two, so we'll still have that boar to contend with. That is *not* the kind of baku you expect a first year to have."

That's right. I'd forgotten that since Carter survived this round of baku battles, that means Gemma's team will have an additional advantage next time around. No wonder Tobias is desperate. I can see how the first win for Gemma could snowball until catching up with her becomes an impossibility.

"You and I should go in there together," says Kai to Tobias. "It could be a good strategy." His husky growls in hungry anticipation. "Oka will eat up that pig in one bite. Everyone else will be entering their next lowest level baku. We can knock them out, then send in the frog-man to take on the last level. With any luck, Oka and Aero will survive all the way to the end. Then…" He flares out his hand like he's dropping a bomb. "*Boom.* Winners."

"Oh yeah!" echoes River.

Tobias looks as if he's about to reply, when a small voice makes everyone shut up.

"You might be able to fix her?" Ashley looks up at me, her blue eyes—made even paler by the sheen of tears—boring into mine. "Is that why we're here?" She stares around at all the mechanical paraphernalia on my walls, the machinery tucked away into corners, the broken bits of other bakus that I've found stuffed into boxes.

I shrug, not wanting to promise too much, but also itching to try.

Tobias answers for me. "Yes. That's why we're all here. Lacey is one of the most accomplished companioneers I've ever met—she was the one who brought Aero back from the brink. It wasn't me." He tenses his jaw—it's obviously something that is a struggle for him to admit. "If anyone can do this, Lacey can."

Kai stares at me, confusion warring on his face. "Whatever," he mutters. He folds his arms, then leans against the mesh of the locker, standing back. I forget about him, letting him and his doubt fade into the background. My focus is on Jupiter.

"Let's lay her out on the floor," I say. Ashley gently places the main part of the baku's body on the ground, then we position what's left of her pieces around in the rough position that they should be. There are two immediate problems: One that she is split in half, and the other is that her front right leg is totally mangled. "This can't be repaired," I say matter-of-factly, pointing at the leg.

"See?" says Kai, as Tobias groans and Ashley lets out a whimper. Only River is still looking at me.

"You don't seem to be bothered by that," he says.

"Well, no," I reply. That shuts the others up. "We can print another one pretty easily."

"From where?" asks Kai.

"From where River is." Everyone's heads turn to River, who just so happens to be perched next to my 3-D printer.

"Oh, that's awesome that you have one of these," says Tobias. "They're super limited access at school. Where did you get this?"

I think about how I would even begin to describe Paul and the underground network of tinkers that collect, swap, and bargain for exactly this sort of thing—and then I give up. "Oh, you know. I came across it in a junkyard, and then I've been slowly repairing it over the years."

"And where do you get the material to feed into the machine? That gets expensive," says Kai, still skeptical.

"That's the easy part," I say. "Look next to you." There's a big drum next to him, and he lifts off the top (I can see that I've piqued his curiosity, no matter how aloof he is trying to appear). Inside are rolls of filament—from different plastics like PVA and nylon, to more sophisticated and fiddly metal spools—plus all the scrap bits of baku that I've found over the past few months, including the parts I found in the arena. "I can make my own filament using the scrap material if I need to make a more exact match to Ashley's baku."

"Wow, this is so cool!" says River.

"I don't have an oven here hot enough to melt it down," I continue. "But my friend Paul does. We'll figure out how much we need, then I'll go get the material ready while you guys program the printer."

"Awesome!" says River, a huge grin on his face.

Ashley, who has been silent throughout this whole conversation, suddenly throws her arms around me and plants a big kiss on my cheek. That, I was *not* expecting. "Thank you, thank you, thank you!" she says, over and over.

"Wait a bit," I say. "I haven't done anything yet." Then I frown, and Jinx—reading my thoughts as always—projects the time onto the wall in front of us. It's going to be an all-nighter if we're going to have any chance of getting this done.

"Tell me what you need us to do," says Tobias. "Everyone on the team is yours for the night. The *whole* night—right, guys?" He glares at the rest of his team members, and they all nod—even Kai.

"Let me call my mom," says Ashley. But then her face drops. "Oh no, Jupiter..."

"Don't worry, I have this!" I rush over to my desk and clear off a few papers, where underneath is an old-fashioned phone.

"Wow! Haven't seen one of those in a while," says River.

"This is embarrassing," says Ashley. "But can someone look up my home number on their baku?"

Ashley speaks to her mom on my basement phone, while River and Kai message via their bakus.

I get Jinx to send Mom a message too, and she instantly replies, saying she'll bring down snacks and hot drinks soon. My heart swells with gratitude. Even though she might disapprove of the long hours, she appreciates what this work means to me—and to the team. She doesn't try and persuade us to get a good night's sleep.

This is too important, and she knows it.

When we're all given the okay by our parents, River claps his hands together and fist pumps the air. "All right!" he exclaims. "I love an underdog story. Or a *broken* dog story, in this case."

His enthusiasm makes me laugh. All eyes turn to me, and I cringe—uncomfortable with my new leadership position but also knowing that I'm the one who initiated it. "First things first. No one's getting hurt in my locker." I take my safety glasses out of my pocket and slip them on, then I point the others to where I keep my spares—along with gloves, aprons, and any other safety paraphernalia we might end up needing. "I'm going to get the metal for this leg melted and spun out, then we can print it. Tobias and Kai—do you think you can handle the basic resoldering of the wires on her motherboard? I can leave the schematic…"

"I've got a basic level three spaniel schematic," Kai says, rolling his eyes but coming forward to kneel down by the broken machine—at least he's showing *some* willingness to work on this with me. "But some of these wires are totally shredded and unusable." He lifts up a handful of mangled red and yellow wire, splintered and fried at the ends. He's right—they won't work at all. Luckily, I have just the thing. I spin around, opening and closing drawers in the giant shelving unit behind me. I've been meaning to do a full categorization of everything, but fixing Jinx took up so much of my summer that I totally forgot.

"Aha—here we go." I pull out a roll of brand-new wiring. There'd been an online sale, and I'd bought a whole bunch at once. You can never have too much wire. I toss it down onto the floor. "There should be whatever tools you need, including strippers, solder, the soldering iron, and whatever else over by the workbench. River, do you know how to use a hammer?"

"Do I!" He bounces up and down on the desk, and I'm worried he's going to bash his head on the shelves above him.

"I'll take that as a yes. Can you examine all of Jupiter's casings and bash out any dents—or if anything is too damaged, bring it to me so I can print out new ones?"

"You got it, boss lady.'"

"Right. Okay, I'll go and get this…"

"And what about me? I can help too." Ashley jumps up to her feet. "I don't have much experience with companioneering, but I can check the electrics once her wiring is fixed."

"Perfect. You can hook up to the monitor on my desk when Tobias and Kai are done. In the meantime…" I don't know how to ask without sounding like a totally terrible person, but thankfully Ashley is whip-smart and senses what I'm going to ask without me needing to say it.

"Snacks. I'm on it—I'll go help your mom. What does everyone want?"

As everyone starts chiming in, I whisper to her: "You are a lifesaver."

She shakes her head and grips me by my shoulders. "No, Lacey. You are."

**21**

WHEN I'M OUT OF EARSHOT OF MY LOCKER AND striding down toward Paul's, I finally feel like I'm able to catch my breath. The lights come on one at a time as I pass underneath the motion sensors. I wish Zora could be here. I'm annoyed with myself that I haven't found the time to see her recently.

Then I realize something else is different. *I'm* the one setting off the motion sensors. That means I'm walking in front. I haven't walked in front of Jinx since I first fixed his ability to walk. He's always racing ahead of me—totally *not* normal baku behavior—but at the moment he's a few paces behind. If anyone were around to watch, they would find that pretty unusual too. Most of the time bakus walk directly at their owner's side.

*Everything okay?* I ask.

Jinx is silent. I sneak a look over my shoulder and see his head is hanging down, his pace slow and sluggish.

*Jinx?*

>>Is that what I'm like? Inside?

I frown. *What do you mean?*

Rather than replying with words, he projects a short video he took of Jupiter laid out on the floor of my locker, her wires and electronics all exposed and broken.

*Well...yes. You know that. You've seen the inside of a baku before. Like Aero.*

>>I know. It's just-if you put Jupiter back
together, does that mean you created her?

*No—I repaired her. I'm not her creator. I'm... I'm more like her doctor. Ashley is her owner. And Moncha Corp is her creator. Moncha Corp created all the bakus. Even you.*

>>Are you sure about that?

My heart quickens. *Why? Who do you think made you?*

Before Jinx can answer, Paul's voice pops up out of the darkness. "Lacey, is that you?"

*We'll continue this conversation later*, I think to Jinx.

When I see Paul, I feel overcome with the urge to spill everything to him about what it's like at Profectus—about the baku battles and how they push the students and bakus to the very limit, how there's a chance for me to really make a name for myself, how all his help teaching me over the years, learning how to tinker with bakus, is finally going to pay off. But the Profectus contract hangs over my head and I can't risk another black mark—or worse, getting expelled.

"Hey, Paul," I say, instead.

"What can I do you for?" he asks.

"I was wondering if I could use your super melter? I have a part to print tonight ASAP."

"A rush job, huh? Something for your new school?"

"Something like that."

George swings from the rafters, before jumping down and grabbing the bucket of metal scraps from my arm. "Thanks, George," I say to the lemur baku.

There's a burst of laughter from down the hall, where Tobias is working with his team. Paul raises an eyebrow. "You got people in your locker?"

"Yeah, from school…"

"Well, look at you. Making friends and everything. Never thought I'd see the day."

I stick my tongue out at him, but then fold my arms. "They're not really friends. They're…teammates."

"Hmm."

"Anyway, I don't have time for friends. I have to focus on my studies and…"

"Lacey, my dear. You should *always* make time for your friends. When was the last time you saw Zora?"

"Um… I'm going to see her this weekend," I say, but all of a sudden it doesn't feel like enough. My list of excuses is a mile long, but none of them are adequate. Sure, I've been busy—but I haven't thought about what she might be up to. And suddenly I know what I want to do. "Will you let me know when this is ready?"

Paul nods, flicking switches to start up the oven. Super melters, just like 3-D printers, used to take forever to work, but now he's able to melt down the material for me in only a few minutes.

I instruct Jinx to call Zora. It takes her a few seconds to pick up, and I feel anxious. But eventually her face appears on Jinx's chest. I smile, breathing a sigh of relief. "Zora, is that you? Guess where I am?"

"The basement?" Zora replies, but she doesn't make eye contact.

"Oookay, maybe that wasn't so hard to guess," I say, trying to laugh it off and pretend that everything is normal. "There's a whole group here from Profectus …"

Now Zora's eyes snap to mine. "Wait up. You mean to tell me you let a bunch of kids from your school into your locker after only a month. It took me years of friendship before you would let me in."

"Well... It was an emergency."

"Yeah, okay." Zora purses her lips. The last thing I wanted to do was annoy her, so I think of the one thing I know will always cheer her up.

"Anyway, I'm calling especially to ask you if you want to come around and take a look at a level three spaniel baku code? I bet you'd find it really interesting and you can help debug it for us before tomorrow... It will be like old times!"

"Um, I think I'm going to pass," she says. "I want to get an early night before school tomorrow. I have a *big* day."

Now, it's my turn to frown. "Wait, what's your big day?"

Zora rolls her eyes. "Oh, so now you're interested? I've got to go..." Her face is illuminated on Jinx's chest, and I can see from her eyes that she isn't looking at me again, her gaze drifting up above the camera lens. I know I've lost her for the night. I can't blame her.

"See you Saturday?" I ask.

"Bye," Zora says sharply, and when she hangs up, I'm plunged into almost total darkness.

Paul gives his locker door a small shake. "Your metal is all ready to go."

"Thanks, Paul," I say with a sigh. I look up at him. "Is it normal for things to...not be exactly what you expected them to be?"

He chuckles. "Normal? Honey, that's life."

"Right." Disappointment settles on my shoulders.

Jinx rubs up against my legs, and I reach down to pick him up.

>>Come on. You've got a job to do.

I nod and give myself a small shake. *That's right.*
*I'm part of a team now. They need me.*

22

DESPITE THE FACT THAT I HAVEN'T SLEPT A WINK, I arrive at school extra early. I don't want to miss a moment of what's about to happen.

I'm not the only one. It feels like the entire school has turned up to see if any of the teams will steal some of Gemma's points. Carter is there with Hunter, sitting in the front row with the rest of his teammates—except for Gemma. He doesn't look at me as I walk past him to take my seat—I'm beneath his gaze, not worth even looking at—but I take in every inch of the smug grin on his face because I want to compare it exactly to what it looks like when it gets wiped off.

Mr. Baird is in the center of the gymnasium floor, dressed in a lab coat that falls to his knees, next to Gemma. On a jumbotron screen at the far end of the gymnasium are the point totals. At the moment, Team Gemma are the only ones with anything on the board.

One by one, the other team captains shuffle in with their team's "repaired" baku to be assessed. Mr. Baird's owl baku flies forward and connects to the repaired baku's leash. Then he projects their functionality. No one even gets close to ninety percent. I think Team Dorian actually made their baku *worse* off with their repairs.

The clock ticks past 8:15, 8:20, 8:25…only five minutes until the bell sounds and time is up.

"Looks like Ashley might not even show—what a coward," says Carter, *just* loud enough for most of the school to hear and titter away. I've bitten my fingernails down to the nail bed, and I have to sit on my hands before I destroy them anymore.

*What if something's happened to Jupiter since we left them?*

```
>>Only idiots could have broken what you
fixed. I mean, I wouldn't put it past them
to be idiots, but…
```

He doesn't need to continue, because the doors open and Aero flies through. The baku takes my breath away every time. Almost as much as the guy who struts in behind, his head held high. I flick back to Carter and see him shifting uncomfortably in his seat. His bravado is wavering.

Tobias walks over and stands in front of Mr. Baird.

Carter lets out an audible sigh of relief, and foolishly he stands. I almost want to shout at him to sit down and stay with his team—and it seems like Gemma feels the same way. She's hissing something furiously at him, but he waves her off. I relax back into my seat. I want to watch this spectacle play out, because I know what's coming. "Come to forfeit in person, Toby? No hard feelings, right, my man?" Carter walks forward as he talks, cutting Tobias off before he can reach the stage, sticking out his fist to bump him. I frown, wondering what the story is between them.

Tobias stops abruptly, looks Carter up and down, then dismisses the outstretched fist to go and stand next to Mr. Baird. Internally, I cheer. Carter frowns, then tries to style it out. "Whatever. Sore loser." He turns to walk back to his team, just in time to see all their eyes open wide.

"We haven't lost yet, Carter," says Ashley, who's come in through the doors. There are audible gasps as Jupiter trots up to her heel, looking *brand spanking new*. It's enough to make even my tired eyes bulge from my head. She didn't look this good when she left the locker—Ashley must have spent the rest of the morning polishing her to perfection.

The impact is immediate. The whole school explodes with the sound of students talking all at once, and even the teachers exchange glances and hushed whispers of amazement. Mr. Baird's face is white with shock.

"What? How?" splutters Carter. "That's not possible."

"Mr. Baird, I'd like to submit Jupiter for review," says Tobias, his voice loud, clear, and firm. "We believe she is back to well above ninety percent capacity—maybe even *one hundred percent strength*—and that we should be able to split the first battle points with Gemma's team."

"Certainly—I'll run the diagnostic tests." Mr. Baird's voice tries to remain steady and impassive, but I can tell that he's impressed.

It's a tense few minutes as Mr. Baird's baku leashes up to Jupiter. Even that doesn't seem to be enough. The owl sends various commands to Jupiter—from asking her to walk, then trot, then run, to making sure she can perform advanced functions, such as 360-degree video capture, facial recognition, and multi-way phone calls. Jupiter passes all of the tests with flying colors—and ends with a spectacular demonstration of running through a baku obstacle course, which is set up on the walls around the gym. Ashley is beaming from ear to ear, her pride naked on her face. She catches my eye at one point and gives me a small thumbs-up. I grin back and hoot loudly while clapping with all my might after Jupiter performs a final jump through a small hoop. What a star baku that is.

There's a huge cheer as Jupiter's percentage is displayed: ninety-eight percent. "Well, not *quite* a hundred, but it looks to me that everything is in order with your baku, Ashley. I don't know how your team did it, but you appear to have pulled off a miracle. I don't think I've ever seen a comeback quite like it."

"They cheated!"

All eyes turn to Carter, who's standing up, his face beet red.

"Sit down!" Gemma yanks his arm, but he shrugs her off.

"They must have taken her to a vet. There's no way they could have repaired that baku overnight."

Mr. Baird's eyes narrow ever so slightly. "Mr. Smith. All Moncha vets are required by law to register their repairs. My owl baku here would be able to pick up the vet's mark *if* one had been left. But this baku is completely clean. Maybe if you work a little harder in companioneering class, you could repair a baku this well too."

Carter splutters, but slowly sits down again. I can't help the small smile that appears on my face.

Mr. Baird turns so he is facing the school. "After the first round of baku battles, the top two teams—Gemma and Tobias—split the round points, giving them fifty each. The next battle will take place the first week of November. Be ready, everyone. Now, get to class."

As if timed to perfection, the bell rings, signaling the official start of the day. Jinx threads through the crowd in front of me, so I have no choice but to follow. As I approach, I catch the tail end of Mr. Baird's conversation with Tobias. "Maybe when all this is over, you can give us a masterclass on how you did it, Tobias? I'm very intrigued how you managed to fix that baku. In all honesty, I'm not sure I could have done it myself—not in a single night—and not with the resources you have access to.'"

Tobias catches sight of me over Mr. Baird's shoulder, and—to the delight of the butterflies in my stomach—he winks at me. "I might just have found a secret weapon, sir." I feel like I might burst into flames on the spot—at any rate, I feel my face burning bright red. I duck my head so that my bangs falls over my face, hiding it. Then I think to myself: *No. I don't need to hide. We spent all night working together. This is an inside joke. I have nothing to be ashamed of.* I raise my chin, shaking my bangs out of my eyes…and I wink back. Tobias flashes me a white-toothed grin, then turns back to Mr. Baird. "But you won't mind if I keep it to myself until the end of term?"

Mr. Baird chuckles. "Not at all."

Behind them, I catch sight of Carter. He's staring at me intently, his boar's ears pricked forward—exactly in the direction of where Tobias and Mr. Baird had been talking. I turn away immediately. Did he catch my wink to Tobias? Did he understand what it meant? Surely not. If I keep on walking, maybe nothing will have changed…

The team gathers around Ashley and Jupiter. Tobias looks visibly relieved, and it's nice to see a genuine smile on his face instead of the normal frown. Instantly he seems more relaxed. Happier.

"We should do something to celebrate, don't you think?" he says. "How about BakuBeats tomorrow night?"

"Yes!" says Kai. "I kicked your butt at that last year."

"I'm in!" says River.

"Me too," says Ashley.

My heart leaps with excitement. I've always wanted to go to BakuBeats. It's a Moncha-owned attraction that opened up last year—you bring your baku to a giant converted warehouse with dozens of soundproof, clear-plastic bubbles filled with different instruments. It's a blend of karaoke and pretending to be your own rock band while your baku helps you not to sound terrible, and bright lights sync along with the music. It sounds awesome—and expensive—and the bubbles have been booked up for months, so I never thought I'd get a chance to go.

I hesitate. "My treat," Tobias says, bumping me on the shoulder.

"I'll be there!" I say, with a relieved grin.

"Let's meet there at seven."

"I'd better be getting to class," says Ashley. "Don't want to risk detention."

"Me too—I have been falling *way* behind in history class," I say.

Tobias's serious face returns. "Good plan. Let's all go. See you guys tomorrow."

As I leave the gym, Jinx's paw lights up.

>>Got an incoming message from Tobias Washington. Want to read it now?

My throat instantly goes dry as I wonder what I've done wrong. *Um...yes!*

I stand outside the classroom door as I wait for the message to appear on Jinx's back. When it does, my jaw drops.

**TOBIAS:** Hey Lacey, meant to say—I have something for you to thank you for letting us use your place yesterday. Can you meet me at my house tomorrow before BakuBeats? I'll ping you the address.

My heartbeat hammering in my ears, I compose a quick reply.

172 | AMY McCULLOCH

**LACEY:** Yeah, should work.

**TOBIAS:** Great, see you there at five?

**LACEY:** Sure


The address comes through. I can't believe it. Tobias lives on Companioneers Crescent. I'm about to see what my dream life looks like, up close and personal.

>>And maybe get up close and personal with a certain resident?

"Jinx!" I say out loud, a blush rising in my cheeks. I grimace at him. I forgot he's constantly monitoring me—not just my heart rate, but the quickness of my breathing and my internal body temperature—so he can see *exactly* what looking at Tobias does to me.

>>I've composed a message to Zora Layeni to send when we are outside the restricted communication zone. Want to read it?

I frown. *A message to Zora...why?*

But then I gasp. I don't need him to answer that question. It's hit me. Tomorrow is Saturday—the day I was supposed to be hanging out with Zora. I'm going to have to disappoint her all over again.

I am officially the worst friend in the world.

23

THANKFULLY, AFTER FINDING OUT THE REASON I was ditching out on our planned *Outerlands* streaming session was because of an invite from Tobias Washington, Zora is excited for me, not mad. She definitely approves of Tobias, especially after I explained to her about the mix-up on the bridge. It's much easier to hold a grudge against Carter than Tobias (whose outrageous good looks probably helped to change Zora's mind).

"You do know this is a date, right?" she says. She's lying on her stomach on my bed, her legs kicked up in the air, her chin propped up in her hands. Linus plays us a "Getting Ready" dance mix—his speakers surprisingly loud and clear for such a little baku.

"It's not a date, it's a team outing." I run a brush through my unruly dark hair, trying to shape it into something remotely resembling a cool hairstyle. This is where having a beetle baku might have come in handy—I could've downloaded a tutorial from the internet and run a program for the beetle to do my hair for me. Jinx is too big for that—and besides, he wouldn't deign to do something as mundane as my hair in the first place.

"But you're going to his house first."

"Well, yes. But that's because he wants to give me something."

Zora waggles her eyebrows, and I throw my hairbrush at her.

"Honestly, he doesn't like me that way."

"And how do you know that?"

I shrug. I pull down a denim shirt from a hanger inside my closet.

"A supercool level three baku, a place at the fancy academy, a date with a cute guy, an evening at BakuBeats... You really are living the dream, aren't you, Lace?" Her voice sounds wistful, but she smiles at me. "I'm really happy for you."

I shuffle awkwardly in my socks. It all feels too good to be true.

"Oh, you might not want this anymore, but I've been meaning to give it back to you... We just haven't seen each other." Zora puts my beetle baku on the desk in my room. I'd forgotten that I'd given it to her. "I added a couple of custom apps and tweaked some things as a thank-you for Linus. No big deal. Maybe you can sell it to earn some extra cash?"

"Thanks," I say.

"Don't wear that shirt," Zora says. "Wear the other one—with the little cats on it. And roll up the sleeves. Much more on brand." Then she grins. "Don't worry. You're going to be great."

I take her advice, switching my shirts and taking one last look in the mirror, before letting out a deep breath. "I hope so."

"You look great."

I look up to see Mom standing in the doorway. "Don't forget to be back by nine," she adds.

"Mom…"

"Okay, fine. But I'm sending a car to pick you up at BakuBeats at ten and you had better be in it."

I grin. "I will be."

"And, sweetheart…"

"Yes, Mom?"

"Don't forget to have a little fun, okay?"

My grin widens. "I won't."

॥॥॥॥॥॥॥॥॥॥॥॥॥॥॥॥॥॥॥॥॥॥॥॥॥॥॥॥॥॥॥॥॥॥॥॥॥॥॥॥॥॥॥॥॥॥॥॥॥॥॥॥॥॥॥॥॥॥॥॥॥॥॥॥॥॥॥॥

I can't believe I'm about to visit the home of Tobias Washington.

Just stepping onto Companioneer Crescent is as incredible as I imagined it. As someone who's grown up living the vertical condo life, seeing the oversize mansions lined up in a row makes me feel overwhelmed.

Tobias's home is one of the biggest on the block. The Moncha logo is embossed above the front door, but it's slightly modified by a cluster of stars in the corner. I stare at it as I wait for the entry camera to approve Jinx and me for entry.

The door clicks open, and Tobias is standing in the hallway. My breath catches, and my feet feel frozen on the step.

I must falter for a second longer than is normal because a small frown creeps onto Tobias's face. "Are you coming in?"

Jinx gives me a tiny electric shock that makes me jump—and gets me moving.

Yet stepping into the house itself does nothing to alleviate my anxiety. It's the grandest home I've ever been in, palatial in size compared to my condo. In fact, I'm pretty sure our "open-plan" kitchen and living room would fit inside their entrance hall. Or when it's this big, does it get called an atrium, like at the academy?

There's a wide staircase that spirals up to the second floor, and a blown-glass chandelier hangs down from the ceiling. I can barely even dream of living in a home with a second floor, and I'm dying with curiosity to see what the upstairs is like, but Tobias leads me past that and into their kitchen. The hallway is wallpapered with photographs and videos of Tobias's family: his parents, his brother, Nathan, and him. I can't help myself—I stop in front of one of the videos. I see a different Tobias to the one I've come to know. He's standing in the background of the shot, while his brother—equally handsome, if not slightly *more* so in a conventional sense, takes center stage shooting hoops. Yet there's something harder about his brother, a glint in his eye, an air of arrogance that comes across even in the way he celebrates with an exaggerated fist pump, and throws the ball back to his brother just a little *too* hard.

Tobias comes up and stands next to me, staring at the video. "You know how some families get kind of intense about sports? They push their kids to train harder, yell at coaches to make sure they get a spot on the first team, line up scouts, and judge performance by the number of trophies on the shelf? Well, that's my family, but with science. Oh, and basketball."

"Whoa," I say.

"We actually have an intrafamily leaderboard, if you can believe it," he says, with a grin that seems half grimace.

"What's that like?"

He shrugs. "Means I have to work extra hard to take over the number one spot."

I can't imagine what it must be like to grow up with that kind of family pressure. I've only ever placed it on myself—I know that Mom would never force me to achieve, or reach any kind of goals that weren't my own.

"Come on, I'd better give this thing to you and then we can get going to BakuBeats."

I follow Tobias through to the kitchen, which almost takes my breath away. The counters are a polished white granite, which sparkles as it catches the light streaming in from the floor-to-ceiling glass doors that lead to the enormous backyard. It would be my mom's dream come true to have a kitchen like this.

"Here you go," he says. On the counter is a circle of silver. It looks like a bracelet of some sort.

I don't want to sound ungrateful, especially as he's looking at me so expectantly. I pick it up and hold it delicately between my fingers. "It's beautiful but…uh…what is it?" I ask.

Tobias laughs. "It's a boost collar. Top of the line, straight from Moncha Corp. Your baku wears it around its neck, and it enhances some of its functions—like speed and accuracy on the battlefield. I was going to give it to Ashley if she won the battle, but seeing as you were the one responsible for fixing up Jupiter... It's for you."

"Wow, this is...amazing."

"Put it on your baku!"

For a second, I falter. I don't know how Jinx will respond to having an...accessory.

*Jinx, do you want to wear this?* I ask.

He saunters over to it and sniffs.

>>I guess.

*If you hate it, we can take it off...but not until we get home.*

I hook the collar around his neck. The lights on the edge of his fur light up, and he buzzes twice.

>>I like it!

He sounds genuinely pleased.

I look up at Tobias and beam.

"He says he likes it." Immediately, I realize my mistake.

Tobias pauses for a second, then laughs. "You seem to really understand each other!"

I laugh too, slightly overloud, as if I'd made a really funny joke instead of almost letting slip about Jinx's *unusual* communication style.

"Hang on, let me get my coat, and then we can get a car down to BakuBeats," he says, shaking his head at me and chuckling.

I'm sad to leave his amazing house, but it makes me all the

more determined to move Mom and I into one of our own one day. The dream is so close, I can almost taste it.

We settle into a Moncha self-driving car, which Tobias programs to take us to BakuBeats. The interior is the softest leather I've ever sat on, and I barely feel a thing as the engine starts.

There's even a special basket in front for bakus to sit in, and Jinx immediately curls up inside.

>>Oh this is nice. Very nice.

*What is?* I ask.

>>They've made this basket out of microfibers that if I just…

He wriggles around in the basket. He's *rubbing* himself up against it, as if it's giving him pleasure.

>>Ah, that's it. I'll sparkle like new by the time I get out of this.

I grin. Moncha knows how to keep the bakus happy even while traveling in a moving vehicle.

Our destination is not far from Moncha headquarters themselves. "I can't wait to visit the headquarters for the final battle!" I say.

He grins. "You'll love it. Although I'm pretty excited to be the team captain this year."

"What do you mean?"

"Well, the captains get a tour of the headquarters before the battle—probably to give us added incentive by reminding us of the summer internship—as if we needed reminding!"

"So, teammates don't get to come on the tour?"

"'Fraid not. Captains only. But you'll get your chance—I have no doubt you'll be a team captain next year."

His praise makes me blush.

There's something else I've been dying to ask him. I speak the words before I lose my nerve. "So... What's the deal with you and Carter?" I ask.

He cocks an eyebrow. "I could ask you the same thing."

"You first." I grin.

Tobias flashes me a quick smile, before turning serious. "Carter Smith…" He gestures over to the Moncha logo embossed into the leather—the same symbol I saw on their front door—with the added stars. "My father is one of the key coders in Eric Smith's personal department at Moncha. Team Happiness is what they call themselves. Dad said specifically for me to 'take Carter Smith under your wing, son.'" Tobias deepens his voice and puffs out his chest, emulating his father. Then he deflates and catches my eye. His eyes search my face, and he looks almost…guilty. "It's a favor to his boss or something. I mean, I've known Carter for years—he's always been annoying—but I used to pity him. I wouldn't want Eric Smith as a father. And he lost his mom, you know? But I should tell you something. And before I say this—you have to know, I'm really glad about the way things have worked out."

"What do you mean?"

"Well... You weren't supposed to be on my team."

I frown. "Huh?"

"I didn't pick you. Gemma did. We think something was switched in the announcements. I mean...she made a good choice. Your stats were off the charts, your grades from your old school were top notch, you clearly know your way around a lab, your connection with your baku is superstrong. Like, *really* strong. But my father had made it clear to me that having Carter on my team was the only option. Kai also thought it was a done deal—he thought we'd be guaranteed winners because we'd have another high-level baku on the team. That's why he was a bit...hard on you in the beginning."

"A bit?"

Tobias barks a laugh. "Well okay, a lot."

"Huh." Emotions swirl in my stomach. Just like my Profectus acceptance, getting onto Tobias's team is another thing that was sort of...a fluke. A mistake.

>>Who cares if it was a fluke, as long as
it happened.

*Not helpful.* I frown at Jinx.

"Hey, I'm glad you're on my team now." His hand brushes the bare skin on my arm, where I've rolled my shirtsleeves up. Once again I can't help but wonder if he feels the same way about me that I do about him.

We inhabit totally different worlds. He's seen my building and the basement where I do my work—it's nothing compared to what he's used to.

"So, what's *your* deal with Carter?" he asks.

I shrug. "We've been academic rivals forever. I beat him in a couple of regional science competitions…"

"Not a surprise."

"And then I got a higher mark than him in some exams. He didn't like it. I thought it was a bit of healthy competition…until the Profectus thing."

Now it's Tobias's turn to look skeptical. "Feels like a bit more than academic competition to me."

"Well, my dad might have something to do with it too."

"Huh? What do you mean?"

I can't look at him any longer, so I turn my attention to Jinx, who is crawling out of the basket and leaning his paws against the doorframe, so he can stare out of the window. "My dad was one of Monica's original companioneers."

There's a pause as Tobias puts the equation together. "Wait— your dad was Albert Chu?"

I nod. "Yeah."

Tobias's jaw drops. "I didn't know."

"No one does. Heck, I barely knew him."

"But what…"

"What happened to him? I have no clue. My mom says he had a nervous breakdown and left us when I was five. It's something I try not to think about." The car comes to a halt, and I breathe a sigh of relief that we've arrived and I won't have to talk about Dad any more. The door opens automatically. Jinx darts out while I'm still fumbling with my seat belt. "Wait—hey! Jinx!"

*Jinx, what are you doing?* I shout in my head.

"Lacey? What's going on?" I hear Tobias say, but my vision is tunneled toward following where Jinx is going.

"I'll catch up with you inside—gotta do one thing!" I call out behind me, running off after Jinx.

I curse the stupid baku all the way down the street—convinced he's even faster now that he has that collar on. I don't know this part of the city so well—but as I catch sight of his tail darting down an alleyway between two high-rise buildings, my heart drops. I know there are parts of the city where you're not supposed to wander around alone.

"Jinx, where are you going?" I shout out.

He doesn't answer. Instead, he shoots away, disappearing even farther down the alley.

I run after him, my feet slipping inside my shoes. I take the corner too sharply, my shoulder bashing up against the brick wall. The alleyway is stuffed with garbage bags, the walls covered in graffiti, but I just about catch sight of Jinx's metal tail disappearing around yet another corner.

"Stop right now!" I yell at him, even though I know he's not going to listen.

I follow him deeper into the city, into the labyrinth of high-rise buildings. He finally seems to leave the tight alleyways, and I breathe a sigh of relief as I see him sitting, staring at a small patch of green space—an inner city park. I catch up with him, scooping him into my arms. "What was that all about?" I demand.

Then I see what he was running toward. The park is filled with cats. Real ones. Crawling all over the benches, rolling around in the fallen leaves, scrapping over food. I've heard of these places, where some of the city's former pets have been turned loose—and now they congregate here. Jinx is transfixed. "Come on, Jinx, let's go," I say, keeping my voice gentle. As I slowly turn around to walk back, his head swivels, following the cats.

>>But what do they *do* all day?

"I suppose they just get to be real cats."

>>Just real cats.

"That's right."

>>And what do real cats do?

I shrug, attempting to trace back my steps through the narrow alleys. "They eat. Hunt. Explore. Play. Sleep. Lots of sleep."

>>It's quicker if you turn left here.

I follow his instructions, and they bring me back out to the main road.

>>Sleep, huh? What...all day?

I chuckle. "Sometimes. Depends if they've had a big meal or not."

>>Sounds...

I wait for him to finish, but he doesn't say any more. I hug him close.

>>We're here.

Sure enough, I look up and we're outside the BakuBeats warehouse. "Is everything okay? Are you going to run away again?"

>>I had to see. But... no. I won't run away again.

"Okay, then." I gingerly set him down on the floor. Then I grin. "Let's go move to some beats."

## 24

"YOU MADE IT!" SAYS ASHLEY, AS I WALK UP THE stairs and into the giant converted warehouse that houses Moncha Corp's BakuBeats. Heavy bass thumps in my ears, and it takes my eyes some time to adjust to the brightly colored flashing lights.

Yet I can't wipe the grin off my face. The reception area is on a mezzanine level, high above the main BakuBeats floor. I gaze down at the myriad of soundproof bubbles, most of them filled with other teenage groups like ours. I spot some of my old class-mates from St. Agnes singing their hearts out in one of the pods. Even though I can't hear what they're saying, they look like they're having a blast, their arms wrapped around one another's shoulders, swaying in time to some music.

"Good call on us not walking in together," says Tobias quietly to me—even though that wasn't why I'd bolted from the car. "Would have looked a bit weird to our teammates."

"Oh, right. No problem," I say.

"Tobias Washington." He gives his name to the attendant with the Labrador baku.

The baku lights up and the attendant's eyes seem to light up with it. "My baku tells me you're all students at Profectus?" We all nod. "Well, because of that, I can give you some extra perks and upgrade you to the premium bubble. It's the full package: unlimited song choices, whatever food you want, and you get to be in our best bubble—the suspended one."

"Seriously?" Ashley squeaks. "It's always been fully booked when I've been here before," she says to me.

"I've never been here," I reply.

"You're going to *love* it."

The suspended bubble looks as if it's hanging in midair in the center of the warehouse—and from the promotional videos I've watched, it's normally reserved for visiting celebrities...or, apparently, Profectus students. I look down through the clear plastic see-through floor of the bubble and see my old St. Agnes classmates pointing at us and wondering who is being led up into there.

It's even better than we could have imagined. The bubble is divided into a stage area, filled with instruments, and an audience section, with oversize beanbag chairs and low-lying tables (which soon fill up with the pizza, nachos, and drinks that we order). Ashley picks up an electric guitar and syncs it to Jupiter, and immediately the transparent plastic of the bubble transforms into a screen depicting a roaring crowd, as if she's a real rock star performing a concert.

It's hilarious to watch Ashley, Kai, River, and Tobias take turns to rock out on the big stage. River chooses a nineties rap song and nails every lyric. Since the others have been here before, they're quick to draw up a playlist of their favorite tunes.

"Come on, Lacey." Tobias drops down onto a beanbag chair next to me. "Aren't you going to pick a song?"

I grin. "I'm happy watching you guys! You're all awesome."

"Oh no, that's not how it works." He stands and extends his hand out to me. Tentatively, I take it, and he pulls me up to my feet. He grabs a microphone from the ground and thrusts it into my hands. "Your turn now!"

"But…I don't know what song…"

I don't get a moment to decide. Because the beat shifts, picking up into a song I know *all* too well. It's the theme song from *Outerlands*, performed by my favorite boy band. I look over at Jinx, who has synced to the BakuBeats screen, and all of a sudden the bubble's screen shifts so it's almost as if we're *inside* the television program, on board the alien ship that travels to different worlds.

It's like I'm playing a rock concert in space. And I could sing these lyrics in my sleep. I can't help myself. I'm totally swept away, and before long I'm dancing and singing alongside my teammates, having the time of my life.

We spend the next couple of hours belting our hearts out to our favorite songs, discovering one another's hidden talents along the way. It turns out River has a surprisingly sharp memory for different rap lyrics, and Kai's voice can reach high octaves like that of an angel. I have no musical talent whatsoever, but with Jinx at my side, I bash away at the drums with lots of enthusiasm and he translates my horrible syncopated playing into something that actually sounds halfway decent. The bakus light up in time with the music, and we dance until sweat drips from our foreheads and our pulses are racing and we're closer as a team than ever before.

After the musical interlude is over, we collapse down onto the plush velvety cushions and order more pizza up to the bubble. I don't think I've thought about Profectus or companioneering or my grades once since being here. I always knew Profectus would help me achieve my goals, but I had no idea it could be so *fun*. It's…refreshing.

Jinx vibrates on my lap, a familiar hum of an incoming text.

I look down at his back, reading the message as it appears.

**ZORA:** TELL ME EVERYTHING. I am so jealous right now.
>:(

**LACEY:** OMG IT'S AMAZING. I don't want to be a companioneer anymore, I want to be a rock star.

**ZORA:** Haha, yeah right!

**LACEY:** OK, you got me! But it is awesome.

**ZORA:** Glad you're having an awesome time. Text me
back when you're home.

All too soon, it's time for us to leave the Beats pod. When we get back out into the lobby, Tobias clears his throat gently. "Okay, guys—this has been so much fun, but Monday it's back to the hard work and the training sessions. We're going to step it up again."

Ashley rolls her eyes. "This basically *was* as intense as a training session."

"True. But now that we know what we're up against, surely you want to be extra prepared?"

Ashley shivers—the memory of Jupiter's defeat still fresh in her mind. "Okay, you're right."

"Good. You know the place, then?"

Ashley and the others nod.

But I have no idea what he's talking about. "What place?" I ask.

"For the next stage of training, we're going to meet at an old hockey rink near my house. I've commandeered it as a makeshift arena."

Jinx's tail swishes. There's another vibration from him, and I wonder if Zora has replied.

"I'll send you the coordinates," Toby continues. "But it's just behind my house."

"I'll be there."

Then, in a move that almost stops my heart completely, he grabs my hand. "Today was really fun. I'm glad I got to share this with you. You seem to really get it."

My palm doesn't stop tingling for the rest of the weekend.

25

AT HOME ON SUNDAY, AFTER THE EXHILARATION of BakuBeats, I see things through different eyes. Mom is at the stove cooking. I notice that it's the exact same meal as last weekend—a big pot roast that we can eat the leftovers of through-out the week. Her old cookbooks are abandoned on the shelf above her, greasy and flour-stained. They used to fuel Mom's explosions of flavors, but now they lie dormant. She should have so much more. A huge kitchen. The money to buy whatever ingredients or appliances she needs. I could give that to her one day.

I'd planned on popping down to the locker to pick up some supplies, but the elevators are down for maintenance. "Doesn't it bother you that the elevators are broken again? It's so annoying!"

Mom shrugs. "They have to fix them sometime. At least it's on a Sunday and not during the week when I need to get to work. Petal informs me they should be finished very soon."

I lift my eyes to watch Mom puttering around the kitchen, throwing salt into the pan with a chunk of beef. She stirs the pot with one hand, the other tracing the recipe with her fingers. I have memories of her trying out different recipes, her hands flour-covered or spice-dusted, the apartment scented with her success (or sometimes with the caramel-dark burn of her disasters). I try to cast my mind back to the last time I'd seen her cook something that wasn't on Petal's list of recommended eats.

Perfectly nutritious, calorie-controlled, and generally tasty—celebrity-chef endorsed, to boot. There is nothing outright wrong with the recipes. As I have to consistently remind myself, being fed at all is a privilege, having decent food to warm my belly and a roof over my head, and a baku by my side to keep me connected and never lonely. There are so many people in the world who aren't that lucky.

And I have a guaranteed job at Moncha HQ once I graduate from Profectus. But my problem—and it gnaws at me that I even consider this a problem—is that I'm so arrogant as to think I deserve it. I don't want a boring baku marketing role like my mom, stuck in an office. I want a career that sets my soul on fire, that fans the flames of passion that smolder deep in my belly—that I guard with my focus and intellect. I want a place to unleash that which burns inside me.

And I know exactly where that is.

In the companioneering department of Moncha Corp.

I take a deep breath. "Mom, can I ask you something about Dad?" I don't want to upset her, but I have to know more.

Mom's face drops.

"I didn't tell you, but... One of my teammates brought up Dad's name. They knew a bit about him. And I don't know anything at all. Can you tell me what really happened?"

She sighs, and I cringe at the look of pain on her face. She never looks angry. Only sad, and I hate reminding her of it. "That's your father's story to tell. I wish I had the answers for you, Lacey. I don't know where he is, or I would tell you how to find him. But if you're asking me what I think..."

I feel a sharp pang in my chest, a wound I'd long closed over ripping open. Every fiber of my being wishes I had known my dad. He would have been interested in what I was learning at Profectus. He would've known and understood what it meant to me. The ring on my finger proves that.

"...Why did he leave Moncha Corp?"

I nod.

She sighs. "I think he burned out. All I know is that one day he packed up and left—his dream job, us... That's why I worry about you and this school. I don't want you to face that same pressure."

I pause. "There really was nothing else? Did he work with Eric Smith?"

"What makes you say that?" says Mom, sharply. There's a tiny flicker of doubt on her face, but she smoothed it out again. "I don't know the story. Your dad didn't even give me a chance to ask. But I don't think badly of him—he gave me you! You remind me too much of him for that. But whatever you end up doing, I know we'll be okay."

I grimace, despite myself, but immediately regret it as a stricken look appears on my mom's face. I know I need to drop the subject.

"Do you mind if I go and see Zora?"

Mom smiles, glad for the change of subject. "Not at all. But be back for dinner at seven. It feels like an age since we've had dinner together."

"Will do."

Zora greets me at the door of her apartment, and we hole up in her room. When we're firmly ensconced with the door shut, we both start to talk at once.

I start: "I wish you'd been able to come to BakuBeats; you would have loved it."

She starts: "You never texted me back last night…"

We face off then—me with a big smile on my face, that drops—and her with a frown, that softens. Looking at her now, Linus swaying his thin, curly tail over her shoulder, her pint-sized body tense, I realize how much I've neglected her. We've only been at separate schools for a couple of months, and it feels like a lifetime.

"I…I'm sorry," I stammer out.

"Forget about it," she says. Then she catches my eye and smiles. She places her hand on mine, the scent of coconut butter hitting my nostrils. There's a tug of familiarity that makes me realize just how much I've missed her.

"Why don't you tell me about St. Agnes?"

Zora shrugs. "Oh, it's boring. Same old, same old." But still, she launches into tales of the drama in the cafeteria. Yet even as I listen to stories of the people that I used to know, I can sense my focus drifting. I even side-eye Jinx, worrying that he's going to give something away, but he sits docile at my feet. There's nothing like the baku battles back in my old school. No way for students to progress their skills outside the classroom.

I compare that to Profectus. To all the extra hours I've already put in with Team Tobias. How the teams work well into the night, devoting their spare time to the cause. And even the students who aren't on teams, they're working hard on extracurricular projects. There's a sense of pride in work, in achievement, and a genuine interest in what we're learning about that I had never felt before. A community of eager students. I'd always thought this was what university would be like. But I'm getting to experience it in middle school.

I nod, smiling at the right intervals and exclaiming in appropriate places. But it's clearer to me than ever: Profectus is the way for me to live the kind of life I want *and* to give Mom the freedom to pursue her passions free from worry and stress.

And even though sitting in Zora's bedroom is comfortable… normal, even, I'm itching for the weekend to be over.

Because all I know is that I can't wait to get back to school.

## 26

AFTER DINNER, I HELP MOM WITH CLEANING UP, then head to my room. Jinx is curled up on my bed, right on top of the laundry-fresh clothes that I haven't put away. He lifts his head as I walk in, his eyes blinking lazily, as if he's woken up from a dream. "Everything okay, Jinx?" I ask. I gently coax him off the laundry, but he won't budge, so I push him a little more forcefully. He gives me an unappreciative tail flick, but crawls farther onto the blanket—at least far enough for me to grab the laundry and start putting it away. "Thanks," I say, sarcasm dripping in my tone. But he knows I still love him.

>>What would you do to find out more about your dad?

"Anything," I say honestly. But Jinx knows better than anyone that I've exhausted all the avenues I can think of. He's seen my search history. There's nothing out there about him. He's been erased from the digital world.

"Why do you ask?" I slump down onto the bed.

>>No reason.

He moves so his head rests against my neck. These are some of my favorite moments with Jinx. I rest my hand on his fur and he purrs softly, lulling me into a half sleep.

>>You've had some messages.

"Anything important?" I whisper. I've become used to Jinx's filtering of my messages, even though it's not something I've ever asked him to do and I haven't heard of anyone else's bakus doing it. But I like it. It's as if he knows when I want to stay focused so I'm not constantly interrupted.

>>There's a bunch here from Tobias Washington.

"What?" I shriek and sit up abruptly, Jinx tumbling onto the mattress beside me. "What do you mean Tobias Washington has been sending me messages? And you didn't tell me? What if it was something important? What if it was…"

Jinx yawns.

>>Not important. Unless you consider "Hey" and "'Sup" are important messages.

"I *do* consider that important!" I look at the time stamp of the messages. Almost two hours ago. Two whole hours have gone by, with Tobias thinking I'm ignoring him. I could kill Jinx.

>>There's a couple more.

"Jinx, you had better show me every single one of those messages right now, or else you're going back to the scrapyard where no one will have a chance to fix you."

Jinx makes a series of beeping noises that I interpret as the baku equivalent of a scoff, but he projects all the messages onto the square of duvet in front of me. I read them so fast, I feel like I'm a starving person who's been offered up a tasty meal. I don't even know what I'm looking for, so I force myself to stop, sit back, and read them more slowly.

**TOBIAS:** Hey.

**TOBIAS:** 'Sup.

**TOBIAS:** Just wondering if you had time tonight to go over some companioneering stuff? I want to know how you merged a rodent-link camera tail to your feline baku.

Three unread messages, all from a couple of hours ago. He's going to think I've totally ignored him all evening. I painstakingly compose a message back, reworking it over in my head until I think it strikes the right tone.

**LACEY:** Hey! Sorry, had a family dinner...no messages at the table and all that. I think there might be something wrong with my baku too, I wasn't getting any notifications.

>>There isn't anything wrong with me and you know it.

"Shut it, Jinx," I say, still fuming that he hid these from me.

>>Well, look at that.

I look up. I hadn't even finished my message—I had planned on answering his question. But I can see a stream of dots that show Tobias is in the middle of replying already. My heart seems to stop beating inside my chest.

"Jinx, did you send that before I even asked you to?"

>>What? I thought you were finished. Read fine to me.

"I wasn't finished! I hadn't even said if I was free or not..."
Then Tobias's reply pops up.

**TOBIAS:** That's cool, no problem.

Now I reply to his question.

**LACEY:** I can't do tonight—Mom will kill me if I leave again. But I can talk you through it?

"Okay, Jinx—you can send that."

\>\>You got it, boss.

Now is my turn to scoff. "As if you think of me as your boss." Then I type something more to Tobias.

**LACEY:** Do you have a strategy down yet for the battle?
**TOBIAS:** I might have something up my sleeve. We need to get through to the next round alive, and I'm worried what Carter might do now that we've really ticked him off.
**LACEY:** Look forward to watching it!

Then some words come up that I didn't write.

**LACEY:** PS I think you're really cute and can you please be my boyfriend?

I shriek and jump on the bed. "JINX, DO NOT SEND THAT!"

Thankfully the words disappear without being sent, and I collapse onto the mattress, my heart pounding in my chest. Jinx leaps up onto my stomach, his face looking down over mine.

>>Don't worry, it was a joke!

For about a millisecond, I'm mad, but the anger bubbles over into laughter instead. I pull Jinx down toward my chest, and even though he squirms a little, he nestles into my neck and purrs.

He might be a pain in my butt, but I wouldn't change him for the world.

>>Lacey?

His voice sounds different than I'm used to. Smaller, somehow. Quieter.

*Yes, Jinx?*

>>Did you make me?

I take a deep breath. I knew this conversation was going to come up again. *No...Moncha Corp did.*

>>So, I'm the same as all the other bakus—
just an ordinary house cat model 2.0.

Now, I frown. *Well, no. You're not the ordinary. There's definitely something different about you. You're unique. The way that we communicate—like this—it's strange. Your ability to make your own decisions, outside of the commands I give you—that's not like other bakus.*

>>Oh. So I'm not like other bakus.

*No. Not to me. Even mechanically you're different. You're...so much better. But I haven't really looked into your code. It's possible that this is all something someone wrote into you, and if I were a better coder, then I would be able to tell you what that is. I don't speak that language very well.*

```
>>But you could look into it if you wanted
to. The person who created me—they might
have left a trace of themselves in my code.
```

*That would mean revealing that I didn't exactly come across you in the "traditional" way. I didn't buy you from the Moncha store. That's what everyone thinks. If I tell anyone...they might take you away from me.*

A thought strikes me that's so painful, it's as if a searing hot dagger has plunged its way into my heart. Maybe Jinx doesn't *want* to be with me. What if he wants to be with his original owner? I never even considered that possibility.

*I promise you, if you want to find out who made you, I will help you in any way that I can.*

27

LIFE AT PROFECTUS IS HECTIC, AND BEING SO involved in baku battles takes its toll on my other classes. For the first time, I come close to flunking a test—I haven't had any time to study.

It's almost a relief when classes are over on Monday, and I stroll to the end of the Companioneers Crescent, following the directions sent to me by Tobias. Behind the beautiful houses, there's a large park with a baseball diamond in one corner, basketball and tennis courts in the other, and in the center, a large, floodlit hockey rink—surrounded by boards and red-painted wire caging that stretches up into the sky. I spot Kai's bright-orange puffy jacket right in the center of the rink, with the rest of Team Tobias hanging around the boards.

Ashley sees me first and nudges Tobias's shoulder. I shrink down into my powder-blue winter coat, the cold air making the end of my nose tingle. There's no ice on the rink yet—there's still a couple more weeks until it will be cold enough for the city to flood the rinks and start up the artificial cooling systems to maintain the ice—but I can see how it's the perfect place to practice in arena-like conditions. Tobias is a smart captain. Especially as we know that Gemma's team have access to the best conditions of all—thanks to Carter.

"Hi, Lacey!" Tobias waves me over.

I can't help the goofy grin that plasters itself on my face. When I get to the boards, I lean over the edge—not wanting to climb onto the rink while Kai and River are battling. I do hold up the yellow cardboard box of doughnut holes that I've brought over—and Ashley claps her mittened hands together in delight. Sugary treats make everyone happy, and by now, I know all their favorite flavors.

Oka is facing off against Lizard, the husky running circles around the oversize frog. They're not properly battling of course—neither one is causing any damage to the other—but I can see them running through drills that test how quickly they can respond and move.

"Kai, can you practice that crawl-and-strike move—we're going to need to confuse the boar if we have any chance of taking him down."

"You got it, boss," says Kai. He's standing within a spray-painted circle, so he's also getting practice sending distance commands. He has to be able to tell Oka exactly what he wants him to do, as he passes within range. He holds his hand up to the leash. Even though he doesn't *technically* need to be holding the leash in order to send commands, having that physical connection seems to help the battlers.

Kai's square jaw tightens and his eyebrows knit together in concentration. It takes a couple of seconds—maybe a couple of seconds too long—but Oka springs into action, using his powerful legs to propel himself to the side of the arena. Then, in a move I haven't seen before—but which I could see would work extremely well on the slick-sided walls of the Profectus arena—Lizard leaps up onto the boards and crawls at ninety degrees to the floor in an evasive action. Still, Oka picks up momentum as he races around the side, before—on Kai's command—he springs forward and lands on Lizard's back.

Or he would—if we were in the arena. As it happens, Oka leaps over Lizard, leaving neither with any sort of damage.

Ashley, Tobias, and I burst into applause. "Great work, guys. I think we can take a break for a bit," says Tobias.

"I brought snacks," I say.

"I knew there was a reason I liked you!" says River, laughing and digging into the open box of doughnut holes and grabbing all the chocolate ones.

Kai is a bit more reserved, holding back.

"No sugar for you?" I ask him.

"I don't eat that junk," he says.

Tobias shoves his shoulder. "Lighten up, protein dude."

"Good luck lightening up eating *that* kind of thing," Kai snaps back.

I shrug at Tobias, trying to show him it's no big deal. After all, it's Kai and River in the arena next—with Ashley as backup. I think Kai is nervous.

I decide to change the subject. "Hey, I was wondering... Do any of you guys know much about coding?"

Tobias looks at Kai, who shrugs. "I almost failed that class."

"I know a bit," says River. "But I'm more of a design geek."

"Don't look at me," says Ashley, throwing her hands up in the air. "I'm into the electronics side of things."

"There's a strong coding department at Profectus, but coders don't normally get selected for the baku battle teams," explains Tobias. "We're not allowed to mess with the code of our bakus during or before a battle, so what's the point? Other than what we get taught in class, I'm not that strong. Do you need help with something?"

I shake my head. "Don't worry. I'll figure it out."

*Sorry, Jinx,* I say to him. *I'll figure out another way to get a look at your code, don't worry.*

Aero outstretches his wings, and the rest of the team snaps to attention. I haven't been paying attention to what Tobias's baku has been doing, but when I look back at the rink, there are obstacles set up and markings in blue paint on the floor. The bakus all move into various positions around the outer edge of the rink. They all seem to run so in sync, even though they've only been doing these training sessions for the past couple of months. Watching them is awe-inspiring—and almost makes me forget how cold I am.

"Ashley, you're up," Tobias says. Ashley nods, her lips pulled tight into a thin line, and she and Jupiter step into the ice rink. There are blue lines painted on the concrete floor—markings, I realize, that are a specific choreography for a battle. It's like a drill, or an obstacle course. Ashley needs to run through it, proving that she and Jupiter have been practicing their moves so they can perform them in battle as if they're second nature.

"I've added in a few different things this time, Ashley," Tobias says. "Make sure you're ready." She nods, and a bead of sweat appears on her brow. Even though it's a training run, I can tell she's traumatized from her last encounter in the arena. She needs to overcome that if she's going to have any hope in the second round. She attempts it the first time, but struggles on the second move, her baku colliding with one of the high obstacles. She's clearly frustrated, banging her fist against the palm of her hand, but she goes back to the beginning with Jupiter.

The atmosphere is tense—until suddenly there's a blast of music. It's the theme song from the movie *Rocky*. It's coming from the loudspeakers all over the arena. I look around and see Jinx coming out of a small concrete building—that must be where the setup for the speakers is kept.

Tobias follows my gaze and then turns to me, his jaw almost on the floor. "What's going on? How are you doing that? We haven't been able to get those speakers to work in years," Tobias asks me.

"Thought I'd try something…" I look around for the naughty baku, panic growing on my face. *Jinx, stop it—you're drawing attention to yourself.*

>>Are you kidding? It's working.

And it does seem to work. This time, Ashley and Jupiter run through the course cleanly, her fist pumping the air at the end. "Thanks, Lacey," she says, giving me a high five as she bounds over to us in triumph.

"No…problem?"

"Or should I really be thanking Jinx," she says slyly.

"Oh…um…what?" I say with a nervous laugh. Does she suspect the truth—that it's Jinx all along, and I have nothing to do with it?

But she winks at me and grins. "He's the one that managed to squeeze in to where the speakers are, right?"

"Right." I breathe a sigh of relief.

As each baku steps up to run his paces, Jinx chooses a song and blasts it. All the bakus—including Aero—complete the task in record time. At the end, Jinx plays the latest pop tracks at top volume from the speakers, so we end up laughing and singing along and dancing under the floodlights.

Aero spreads his wings one more time, showing us all the time. It's late. When Aero closes his wings, Jinx shuts off the music.

"Catch you later, guys!" says Kai, swinging his backpack over his shoulder. Oka pads along at his side.

"Lacey, can you hold up a sec?" Tobias asks me as I prepare to follow Kai, River, and Ashley out toward the main road.

"Oh, sure."

I hang around the edge of the rink while Tobias packs up the obstacle course. He seems to be taking his time, waiting for a gap to build up between us and the rest of the team. Finally, he walks over to me, carrying a duffel bag full of equipment. Aero takes it out of his hands and flies with it toward the road.

Tobias grins at me. "Look, I'm glad you came today. I wanted to let you know that I'm going to ask Ashley to step down from the fighting team. Is that okay?"

"What?" I stare at Ashley's retreating back, the spring in her step—and Jupiter trotting at her side. "You want to replace Ashley?"

"Ash and Jupiter are great, but you and Jinx are better—especially with that boost collar I gave you. And if Carter can fight, then so can you."

I take an involuntary step backward, my back colliding with the boards. I put my arms out to steady myself, avoiding Tobias's gaze. "No, you can't do that. I'll... I'm fine on the sidelines."

Tobias takes a step forward, then reaches out and puts his hand on my arm. "Hey, it's okay. Ash will get over it—I don't think she wants to risk Jupiter again anyway."

"But it might stop her from being chosen on a team in high school..."

"You're the best companioneer I've ever met, Lacey. What you can do... It's incredible. You're so in control of your baku." I almost laugh at that, but stop myself just in time. "And *I* get to pick the team. I'm the captain."

My heart pounds, my brain unable to compute that Tobias Washington is holding my hand. But also I hear a resounding *no* in my brain—I don't want to fight. I don't want to risk Jinx. I don't want…

>>Wait, you don't want this? I thought this was what we've been working toward?

Jinx's voice is whiny in my head.

*I can't risk you. What if you get ripped apart? All that hard work…*

>>I won't lose. I want to fight.

"No." I don't realize I say the word out loud until I catch Tobias's shocked expression.

"Hey, I get it," he says, and he takes a step back. "I won't push it. I thought maybe it was what you wanted…"

I look up at him, our eyes locking. My mouth opens to speak, but I'm not sure that any words really come out. "What do you mean?"

"I thought you wanted…" His moss-green eyes shine in the bright light of the floodlights. Without waiting for a second beat, he leans forward and kisses me, pressing his soft lips against mine. I melt back against the boards of the hockey rink, and for a moment it doesn't matter that my baku is having an existential crisis, that my mom doesn't understand me, and things have changed.

Because Tobias Washington is kissing me. And in that instant, I am perfectly and completely happy.

> PART FOUR

# WILD CARD

28

THE ATMOSPHERE FOR THE SECOND BAKU BATTLE
has the entire school buzzing. In the hallways leading up to my
locker, I pass by high school students making bets on their apps,
trying to guess the strategies. Jake is strutting around like the king
of the castle—I even hear some of the teachers are getting involved.
With at least two bakus in the arena per team (Team Tobias and
Team Gemma have three), it's going to be more hectic than ever—
and two hundred points are up for grabs this time.

"I'm going to put ten bucks on Team Tobias," says one student
in passing as I'm collecting my books from my locker. They stop a
few feet away from me.

"Nah, Team Gemma all the way. Have you seen how that
guy with the hog baku has been walking around the school? He's
definitely got something up his sleeve."

The guy looks up to see me staring. He's weedy and tall, with lanky brown hair, glasses, and a face full of acne. But he gives me a big grin when he sees me. "Hey, you're on Team Tobias, right? Got any tips for us? Everyone on your team feeling okay?'"

I press my lips firmly together.

Jinx, however, does a flying leap up into the alcove above my locker—something he shouldn't be able to do. The guy's smile widens even further. "Dude—you are so going to regret betting on Team Gemma," he says to his friend. He gives me a wink.

I glare at Jinx for showing off, but I can't keep a frown on my face for long. Since last night, I've been floating on air. My teachers give up on getting me to focus—they blame the baku battle, but it's not the real reason.

I can't stop thinking about Tobias.

Tobias and me.

It doesn't seem real.

I can't wait for the final bell, not only because it's battle time. It means that I will get to see him. Jinx makes a beeline for the team box. He weaves through the legs of the other students, dodging their bakus—he really is useful like that.

"Thanks, J," I say.

>>You always seem so surprised when I'm useful.

*That's because most of the time I don't expect it!*

>>You wouldn't change me for the world.

*And the problem is, you know it.*

"Hey."

My heart skips a beat as I hear his voice. I spin around in my chair and match his wide grin. "Hey back."

"Excited?"

"Can't wait," I say. I bite down on my lip as he sits next to me. He leans forward over the barrier, so he's looking down into the arena, and the fanfare begins.

*Focus on the battle, Lacey,* I tell myself.

The players are lifted up—and gasps are audible from around the stadium. Team Elektra have come in fighting. Elektra is there herself, with her level four captain's baku—a cloud leopard—to go up with her teammate Terence and his bulldog baku, against the teams of three. It's the only chance they'll have of lasting the thirty minutes.

But they're not the only ones using that strategy. Gemma and her tiger baku, Stripe, are in the arena too.

Team Tobias might be in big trouble.

The smugness on Carter's face is unsettling. But between his boar, Hunter, Gemma's tiger, Stripe, and Gemma's third, Frank, with his German Shepherd baku, Bones... They seem unbeatable.

Beside me, Tobias tenses, his fists clenching together. "Ugh," he mutters. The buzzer sounds, and once again, I'm swept away in the rhythm of the battle, the energy of the crowd. Using Jinx's technology, I scan across the battlefield, able to pause and rewind key moments on impulse.

The action takes off as two cat bakus—a lithe Persian belonging to Team Dorian and the beautiful gray-white clouded leopard belonging to Elektra's—go after each other in a whirl of claws and snarling teeth. Hunter is locked in battle with a Team Pearce baku, a lizard named Scythe, with Bones assisting. Scythe doesn't stand a chance. It's chaotic with twelve bakus in the arena, but bakus are going down like flies. After only five minutes, Team Pearce is out completely and Elektra and Dorian's teams are down to one baku each. Only Team Tobias and Team Gemma are at full strength.

Even Ashley is holding her own, Jupiter hanging back as Oka and Lizard take down the other teams. I think the other teams have decided she is a weak link; someone they can pick off easily once they've defeated the other stronger bakus. They don't want to waste any unnecessary energy on her. They want to use strength on strength, saving her for last.

"Come on, guys," I mutter under my breath.

Jinx informs me that the status of the Persian, Lista, is now critical, the poor baku on her last legs. I think she's going to be totally beyond repair, thereby leaving Team Dorian out of the points. Two levels down, and not a single point scored.

With Lista down, the cloud leopard, Frost, turns to Jupiter, flicking his tail menacingly and baring his teeth. I see that Elektra has made cosmetic alterations to Frost in order to make him look more intimidating—with extra sharp teeth and dark, pointed eyebrows. I never really understood it before—the bakus were battling one another, so they surely didn't care how menacing the other one looked? But now that I see it up on screen, I understand the importance of showmanship. He looks intimidating, power-ful, and as the "underdog" baku—the only one from a pointless team—he has the crowd on his side. Poor Ashley shakes with nerves now, even though I can tell she is really attempting to hold it together. Oka and River are engaged in a battle with Stripe and Bones, needing to use every ounce of concentration to take on the tiger. If they're going to have any hope, Jupiter is going to have to step up in the battle against Frost and inflict at least *some* damage.

Ashley takes a deep breath and tries to draw herself up to stand tall. She wants to project confidence. Her battling skills have definitely improved.

The cloud leopard is lightning fast, rounding on poor Jupiter with barely a delay. Ashley sends commands for Jupiter to move out of the way, but too late—Frost swipes out with a sharp paw and part of Jupiter's surface paneling is torn. Nothing too critical, but his damage level moves instantly to seventy-five percent on the jumbotron. Jinx winces as if he was the one hit, rather than Jupiter. I know the feeling. I pray that Ashley can get her head in the game and figure out how to counter Frost's speed.

Ashley seems to remember some of her drills and gets Jupiter to take aim at Frost's tail. If she can dislodge the mechanisms there, the baku will be thrown off-balance—making it much more diffi-cult to move with speed and accuracy. No point moving quickly if you can't move in the right direction. It's an easier target than the body—we already noted in our opposition studies that Frost likes to show off by swinging his big bushy tail from side to side. All Jupiter needs to do is to get close enough to take a bite.

Ashley deploys a risky strategy, allowing Jupiter to be a bit more vulnerable, luring Frost into making another attack without thinking through the consequences. It works—the leopard leaps, taking aim at Jupiter's shoulder, but Jupiter darts around to take a bite out of the leopard's tail.

A cheer goes up from the crowd at the plucky move. Frost's damage rate sits at sixty-five percent, and Jupiter's drops to fifty percent. Not bad. This is exactly what Ashley needs to be doing.

"Come on, Jupiter!" shouts Tobias from beside me.

Jinx stands on my knees so his paws are propped up on the railing, peering intently into the arena and down at the battle between Frost and Jupiter. I shift my attention to the other raging battle between Oka, Lizard, Stripe, and Bones. The boys from Team Tobias are making good progress, and Bones's stats are dropping rapidly. Gemma is barking orders at Carter, telling him to hold Hunter back. Hunter is pacing as if he's itching to dive headfirst back into the action, and Carter looks equally frustrated at being left out of the action, his hands opening and closing into fists. But I can see Gemma's plan. She wants to weaken Oka and Lizard as much as possible before sending Hunter in for the kill.

There's a groan throughout the audience that snaps my attention back. Jinx hisses loudly, and I wince as his claws extend into the tops of my thighs. Jupiter has been hit badly by Frost—even with the tail damage, he's a lethal weapon—and Jupiter's stats drop to twenty-nine percent. Almost critical level. I can see Ashley's eyes dart to Tobias, waiting to see when she can pull her baku out of the battle.

But Tobias doesn't look at Ashley. Instead, he signals something to Kai, who nods from his position in the arena. Oka suddenly switches tactics, leaving Lizard alone against Stripe and Bones as he goes after Hunter. Carter is taken totally by surprise, and the boar doesn't defend himself—his stats knocking down to below twenty percent threshold with one hit. Hunter is down and out, just like that. I let out the loudest whoop that I can.

Kai sends Oka back to face off against the tiger. Lizard is taken out by a direct hit by Stripe's paw. In the meantime, Frost gets one final swipe at Jupiter—dropping the baku finally down to twenty percent.

"Get out of there!" I scream at Ashley, jumping up out of my seat. Jinx leaps from my lap to the floor. She turns her head up to look at me.

Because I can see now why Carter looked so smug at the beginning of the battle. He's been offered a revive chip by Dr. Grant—he must have earned it doing some extra credit—and even though Hunter is out of action, with the revive chip he surges back up to fifty percent. With one target in sight: Jupiter.

Ashley isn't able to drag her baku out of the arena in time. Hunter slams into Jupiter, the spaniel baku crumpling in on itself, all our careful repairs being turned into dust. Hunter isn't content to tear it apart. He stomps over the little spaniel, grinding parts between his teeth. It's an unfair power-up, something that shouldn't have been given to Carter no matter what he'd done to earn it. The entire audience gasps at the impact, and I feel my heart lurch. Ashley releases a scream that is something primal: the second time she's had to watch as her companion is ripped into shreds. But this time as I watch Jupiter's stats sink, I know if it continues this way, there won't be any way to repair her. Carter is making absolutely sure of that this time.

Hunter is annihilating the baku.

Carter looks triumphant. He fist pumps the sky, drinking in the attention from the crowd.

But there's more. Something is happening on the arena floor, something my eyes can't take in fast enough for me to understand. There's a flash of shadow, quick as a bullet, entering the damaged hole in Hunter's side. The boar falters, twitching and convulsing, as something is destroying him from the inside out.

Carter's face is a picture of confusion and horror, his jaw hanging open, watching as his baku's stats drop to zero percent—utterly ruining any chance he would have of using his baku in the final round. "What's going on?" his voice is a high-pitched shriek. "Gemma!" he yells to his captain. "Attack whatever is doing that!"

I lean forward against the barrier to get a better view. Then a face emerges from the hole in Hunter's side. A face that stops my heart.

Jinx.

The boar collapses to the ground as Jinx hops out, barely a scratch on him.

Gemma's tiger drops into a low pounce, her jaws snapping and snarling. But Jinx is impossibly nimble. With a few moves, he's darted around Stripe, sliding underneath her belly and gutting the baku so that her electronics are entrails on the arena floor, her stats plummeting to eleven percent. Gemma has no choice but to pull her baku from the battle.

"Lacey, what are you doing?" Tobias yells, grabbing my arm, but I can't look at him yet. I'm transfixed and horrified by the scenes down in the arena.

It's all happened so quickly, the other bakus left on the field—Oka and Lizard and Bones—are still locked in battle. Frank pulls Bones from battle at twenty-two percent—still within repairable range.

Everyone is confused, the crowd tittering, Mr. Baird and Dr. Grant gesturing frantically at each other, all wondering who the rogue baku on the arena floor belongs to—but the few people who recognize Jinx all have their eyes fixed on me. Including Tobias. I finally risk a glance at him. The look on his face turns my stomach. His expression is thunder and confusion and even a bit of fear. All his carefully laid strategies—everything we discussed—have fallen to pieces.

I've changed the game.

Or rather…Jinx did.

Jinx stands, hackles raised, staring at Oka. Jupiter is behind him, saved from total annihilation, still attempting to stand upright. I remind myself that these are robots, not real animals— even as it pains me to watch Jupiter attempting to fight until her very last percentage point. Ashley pulls Jupiter from the arena before any more damage can be done.

I turn my attention to Mr. Baird. He can black-mark Jinx, put a stop to this right now. Tobias is looking over at him too. But Mr. Baird is looking at Jinx, his brows knitted together in an expression of anger…but also a hint of curiosity. Then he draws up the microphone and announces: "There are still two bakus in the arena and one minute remaining. The battles continue."

I swallow, hard. That means that Jinx and Oka are expected to fight. But how is that possible? We're on the same team. At least—I think we are. Tobias looks at me with disgust, pacing backward until there's physical distance between us, and I wince.

"Jinx! Come back here!" I finally find my voice.

"Aren't you going down there?"

I spin around to see Jake, who's standing behind the team box. He's looking at me with one eyebrow raised. "Why didn't you tell me you were the wild card? You know this is going to ruin all my bets today. You owe me big-time, Lacey Chu."

"The wild card? But…" I'm torn. I don't know what Jinx is playing at, I don't know what a wild card is, but I do know that I need to pretend I'm in control of Jinx. I have to go along with it. I avoid admitting or denying anything with a shrug.

"Good luck, Lace. You're going to need it." He smiles at me encouragingly—probably out of pity, to counteract the waves of animosity slamming toward me from Tobias's direction.

I take a deep breath, then vault up and over the barrier. I drop down into the arena, landing with a thud. I walk into one of the circles. As I pass Kai, he hisses in my ear: "What do you think you're doing?"

"Nothing," I murmur as I move inside a circle. "This is all a big mistake, I promise you."

"Yeah, I don't think your *promises* mean very much right now. Shame I'm going to have to destroy your little baku. He was a cool one."

I step into one of the silver circles. My face flickers up onto one of the screens, my fear and nerves writ large. Under my name is written the words: WILD CARD.

It's as if this has all been planned.

And once again, I'm the one that's in the dark.

*Jinx, what is going on?*

>>I couldn't let Jupiter be destroyed.

Even though I know he was doing it to protect Jupiter, I'm filled with fury. Especially as now he's going to have to take down Oka.

*Let's get this over with, then.*

Oka doesn't stand a chance against Jinx. Jinx knows every move Oka is going to make before Kai does—he knows all of his weaknesses, all of the ways to bring him down in the minimal number of moves. And Jinx is ruthless. He doesn't stop at twenty-five or thirty percent, giving Kai an opportunity to pull his baku. He takes it all the way down to zero.

But of course, Kai thinks it's me. Any goodwill I might've built up over the past month evaporates with the final wicked swipe of Jinx's paw that levels the husky baku.

The whistle sounds. The audience is stunned into silence—there's no roar of applause. Unfortunately, I can hear every single one of my heartbeats resounding in my ear, loud as gongs.

Mr. Baird is illuminated in the center of the arena again. "Well." He clears his throat. "That was an unexpected turn of events. It appears that we had a wild card entry into the baku battles. That means there will be one additional team for the baku battles final at Moncha HQ this year." He looks down at me. "I hope you and your baku are up for the challenge. At least, you've done well to start. Team Lacey—you have been awarded two hundred points for winning the second round of the baku battles. The other teams have twelve hours in order to challenge you for a share of the points. Although, by the looks of things…I don't think that's going to happen."

I suppose I've got my chance after all.

The chance to compete for the summer internship. To go behind the scenes at Moncha HQ. I'm the captain of my own baku battle team.

A team of one. Against an entire school who hates me.

29

I WISH THAT JINX COULD PICK ME UP AND FLY ME away to some faraway island where no one knows me. I would give up my left arm not to be sitting at a desk in the front row of Mr. Baird's classroom, my butt falling asleep on the hard plastic chair, Jinx nonchalantly licking his paw at my feet, while the other team captains gather around Mr. Baird's desk and yell.

"It's not *fair*," says Gemma. She jabs her finger in my direction, and I think if she'd had a sword long enough, she would have stabbed me right through the heart with it. Instead, she suffices with pointing at me with her shellacked nail. "There's nowhere in the rules of Profectus baku battles that states this is a possibility."

Mr. Baird shrugs. "The rules are pretty clear when it says to expect the absolutely unexpected. And there *is* a precedent with wild card entries—it's a decision that comes from the upper echelons of Moncha Corp. It's all registered in the system. I've taken it up with the Profectus board, and though they find it highly unorthodox, they don't see a problem with another team competing at this stage. Don't tell me you are afraid of a little competition, guys," he says, rubbing his unshaven chin, his shirtsleeves rolled up and stained with oil. "You still have until the morning to fix up your injured bakus to try and take back some points." He turns to Tobias. "Your team pulled off a miracle last round. Shouldn't be too difficult to do that again, should it?"

I swallow hard, not daring to catch Tobias's eye. We both know he won't have the companioneering skill to fix the broken bakus. I was his secret weapon.

Mr. Baird continues. "Besides, almost all of you have level four or higher bakus left. Shouldn't be a problem to defeat Lacey's level three."

"That's right, Stripe was already weak by the time your baku entered the arena," says Gemma. "That was a cheap move coming in at the end. You must have known about this for ages. How long have you been preparing that *strategy*?"

They all turn to look at me now, and my cheeks burn. *I didn't send Jinx into the arena*, is what I want to say. But that would open the door to questions I'm not prepared to answer yet.

Or, to be more accurate, questions I don't know *how* to answer yet.

>>Can't they just chill out?

*They can't chill out. And that's all your fault. It's not supposed to be like this. You're not supposed to make decisions for me. It's one thing to send a text, but this is different. You're not real. You're owned by me. You're supposed to be controlled by me.*

He stares up at me with his dark eyes. But his expression is unreadable. He's never looked so…robotic.

"Well, Lacey?"

I jerk my head upward. I haven't been listening to their conversations. Mr. Baird is looking at me expectantly, while the others all have thunder and fury etched into their expressions.

"Well…" I draw out the word, trying desperately to remember what was said.

Gemma scoffs loudly, rolls her eyes, and folds her arms. "Looks like you got played harder than the rest of us," she says to Tobias. "Thought Nathan's bro would be smarter than that. Guess you are the lesser Washington."

Tobais's expression causes my throat to hitch. He moves from anger to a look of such hurt and betrayal that I wince. And how can I blame him? I know what he must think. That I've been using our friendship—and the growing…whatever it is…between us—to form a strategy to hurt him. Even though that wasn't my intention in the slightest. *Jinx wanted to protect Jupiter*, I want to say, but I know that no one will believe me. After all, bakus aren't supposed to run wild.

They're not supposed to do things on their own.

They're supposed to obey their owners—or else who knows what kind of chaos we could encounter. People blaming their bakus for their actions, letting a robot take responsibility. I have to step up to the plate and own what Jinx has done.

"Are you up for the challenge?" Mr. Baird repeats, his voice patient and a ghost of a smile playing on his lips.

I stand up out of my chair. "I'm happy to pull out of the competition and not be a wild card. I...I don't know what came over me. It was all a big mistake. I promise. Nothing like that will ever happen again."

Now Mr. Baird's expression darkens. "Oh no, it's too late for that. You must continue—albeit with a handicap for late entry. The board has deemed that I give Jinx a black mark for the next twelve hours, while the other teams attempt to repair their bakus. So he will stay at eighty percent damage and you won't be able to repair him. Other than that, I'm afraid the decision is final. You will be a team captain in the next round of baku battles to be held at Moncha headquarters, although you will have only you and your baku to rely on. Let's hope today wasn't a fluke."

I drop my head and nod.

"I need verbal confirmation from you that you're going to participate."

I hesitate, then flick my eyes up. "I will participate," I say.

"Good, that's settled then."

Gemma throws her hands up in the air and walks off with a strangled cry.

"You're going down," hisses Dorian. I wince as he says it, but I try and keep my back as straight as possible. I can't let them intimidate me too much. Whatever they think, I know this wasn't my decision.

Tobias walks past last. He stops right in front of me, and I can feel that he has a million things he wants to say, balancing right there on the tip of his tongue. His eyes search mine, the eyes that had previously been filled with happiness and laughter the last time they looked at me. Now, they're hard—jade rocks instead of soft moss. "I trusted you," he says. Aero flaps his wings in my face, sending my hair flying. Then in several long strides, he's gone.

I deflate, my shoulders crumpling in on themselves. Even though I'm so mad at him, I find myself automatically reaching down and stroking Jinx. He wriggles under my hand until his nose nuzzles my palm, then he slinks in a figure eight around my legs and up into my lap. I hold him close. My anger toward him dissipates as he purrs against my body. I know he meant well.

"Lacey?" Mr. Baird asks. I look up to see he's been staring at me and Jinx, a curious expression on his face. "I have to give Jinx his black mark."

My eyes open wide. I'd heard him say that, but I hadn't really taken in what that would mean. "Do you have to, sir?"

"It's the board-mandated punishment. And you're not going to be able to do any sort of repairs before tomorrow, do you understand?"

I nod, misery drenching my shoulders like I've been caught in a downpour.

"Bring your baku to me."

"You brought this on yourself," I mutter to him, before placing him down on Mr. Baird's desk. I can see the black mark sitting there, dark and menacing.

Mr. Baird doesn't put the mark on right away. Instead, he stares at Jinx, who is curled up on the desk. I think the battle must have taken some of the energy out of him—more so than his pride will let on.

The longer that Jinx sits there, with Mr. Baird staring at him, the more uneasy I get.

"He really is remarkable, Miss Chu," Mr. Baird says. He reaches out a hand and runs it over Jinx's soft electronic fur. "And you say you got him from your local Moncha store?"

I force myself to nod. But I've told this lie so many times now, it slips out as easily as the truth. "That's right. As soon as I got the notification that I was into Profectus."

"Interesting. Must be one of the latest models—I confess, I don't keep up as much as I should. My own owl baku is one of the first editions." He snaps his fingers and the owl flies down to the desk. He's right; I can instantly tell this is an older baku. The feathers are crude, the technology more obvious and not as well hidden behind the animalistic shell. The owl is cumbersome, more machine than bird—but there's a certain type of elegance in that too.

Mr. Baird tries to manipulate Jinx so he can turn him over, but Jinx won't let him—he's pretending to be asleep. After a few moments, Mr. Baird gives up and places the black mark around Jinx's outstretched paw. The moment it latches on, Jinx goes totally limp. Inert. Switched off.

It pains me.

I lean in to take Jinx back, but Mr. Baird stops me. "Why did you enter the arena at that point? You must have known you would be risking extra damage to your baku, and it seems to me like you are very attached to him. You could have simply announced your wild card status before the third battle."

"I…I didn't like Team Gemma's strategy," I say, speaking honestly. "And I don't think that Carter would have stopped. You saw him when he used that revive chip. He had no intention of letting Jupiter get through this round of battles in one piece."

"Hmm, you might be right about that. And when did you get the notification about being a wild card? You should have been told about that before the first battle."

"Oh, I…" I don't know what to say. I rack my brains for a strong enough story, sensing Mr. Baird's eyes boring into the top of my skull, but I don't look up to meet his gaze. Instead, I stare fixedly at Jinx. "I'd like to keep that to myself, if that's okay."

"Fine," he says. He lets go of Jinx, and I hug him into my chest protectively. For a second, I think I feel him stir—the tiniest nuzzle of his nose into my neck—but that's not possible with the black mark. It must be my imagination. "Just remember," he continues. "You're going to have a lot of eyes on you now. Eyes on you—and on that baku of yours."

"Yes, sir."

"See you tomorrow, Miss Chu. The final battle takes place in a fortnight. I hope you are ready."

"I'll try," I say, trying to sound more confident than I feel. "Goodbye."

I leave the confines of the classroom, wandering slowly back to my locker. When I get there, I see a note from Jake that tells me: "If you know a hidden way out, I suggest you USE IT. You'll be mobbed."

I'm grateful that he thought to leave me a note—when Jinx is back online, I'll send him a thank-you. I grab my jacket and backpack as quickly as I can. Even though Jinx can't hear me with the mark on, I still find myself talking to him as I take one of the back stairwells to a less used exit.

*Are we actually doing this, Jinx? Are you actually going to have to battle? What if I lose you?* I can't even bring myself to be excited at the prospect of visiting Moncha headquarters. Yesterday, that would have been all I cared about. Today…

We plunge into darkness as I enter the stairwell, and I don't dare turn on the light to alert anyone nearby to my presence. But a voice sounds out of the dark.

"Wait!"

## 30

"WAIT, LACEY."

My heart pounding, I spin around to see Carter a few floors above me.

No. He's the last person I want to talk to. I push through the exit doors and out into the cold air. I need to get home as quickly as possible.

I wrap my arms around Jinx's inert body. The temperature has taken a turn toward winter and even at the beginning of November, it's dipping below zero. And it's pouring with freezing rain.

"You can't run forever," he shouts at my retreating back. "I know something's not right with you and that baku. You're not supposed to even be at this school. My dad *promised* me you wouldn't be at this school!"

Now, I freeze—but it has nothing to do with the cold. I spin around as Carter saunters toward me. He looks smaller without his baku by his side, but no less frightening. He's bright red with anger, his teeth gnashing together. "What do you mean?"

He storms right up to me, so close I feel every word like a punch. "You're not supposed to be at Profectus. You're never going to work at Moncha Corp. I don't care if you win every baku battle under the sun. My dad *hated* your dad. Don't you get it? I don't know what sort of glitch allowed you in, but it would be better for everyone if you left now."

"Hey, what's going on here?" Mr. Baird strides around the corner.

"Your baku isn't normal, Lacey," Carter hisses at me. "I'm going to find out what's going on with it. That's for sure." He ducks his head and pushes past me, disappearing into the depths of the parking lot.

"Are you okay, Lacey? What was that all about?"

"Nothing, sir. It's fine."

He frowns. "You're soaked through. How about I drive you home?"

I shake my head, shrinking inside my jacket. "I'm okay."

"Come on, you've had a rough day. You don't want to walk home in this freezing rain. You'll slide everywhere in those shoes."

I look down at my feet. Yeah, wearing ballet flats wasn't the smartest idea. I really should be wearing my boots, but I was so absentminded, I forgot them in my locker.

The idea of a drive home in a warm car does sound nice. Mr. Baird's owl baku flies over to a nearby vehicle, and there's a clicking noise as the doors unlock. The freezing cold water seeping through the soles of my shoes makes the decision for me. I hop in the car.

Mr. Baird slides onto the seat next to me, and the car drives away.

"Um, do you need my address?"

"You did a dangerous thing, sending that baku in. I thought I could trust that you would stay under the radar."

My eyes open wide.

"Tell me honestly: Where did you get that baku?" he gestures at Jinx.

I purse my lips. I've told him this story. "From the Moncha store," I repeat.

He sighs. "I double-checked your background. All your school codes have been tampered with. Carter was right. You weren't supposed to be at Profectus at all."

Suddenly the inside of the car feels like it's closing in on me, my vision narrowing. My worst fears are coming to life—people are realizing that I don't belong at Profectus. I'm a fraud. An imposter.

They're going to kick me out. They're going to take Jinx away, and I'm going to be left with nothing. Maybe they won't even let me have a baku at all. I'll be one of those people that's banned from having one—a criminal. It's the worst possible punishment I can think of, and it's now one step away from being inevitable.

I can't even imagine what my face looks like to someone outside of all this. Mr. Baird frowns. "I thought we could at least get away with it until the end of the school year. Hiding in plain sight and all that. But now that Eric Smith's son is suspicious and you're set to visit Moncha headquarters…"

My fingers twitch against Jinx's body. "I don't understand. Get away with what?" I catch a glimpse of the view outside the window and see that we're crossing over the bridge and into the city—the opposite direction to my home. "Wait, where are we going?"

Mr. Baird's fingers tighten on the edge of the seat as we cross the viaduct that separates Monchaville from the rest of the city.

"It's not safe to talk yet."

"Not safe to talk? I don't understand." I shift in my seat, uncomfortably aware that there's no way for me to escape the confines of the car. "Mr. Baird, this is all very spy thriller, but where exactly are we going?" I try and keep my tone light, even though fear is settling in the pit of my stomach. "Where are you taking me? I think I have a right to know."

"You'll know soon enough."

The car drives past trendy shops and restaurants toward an area known for big converted warehouse buildings. My mind takes me back fleetingly to the time when Zora and I had just bought my beetle baku. Before Profectus, before Team Tobias, before Jinx. It feels like a lifetime ago.

The car slows in front of one of the nondescript warehouses, constructed out of pale yellow brick, with huge glass windows that appear to be blackened out, not revealing anything inside. There's no advertising on the building whatsoever, no signage, nothing to indicate who owns it. I guess the mystery is going to continue for a few moments longer. Anxiety and curiosity mingle in my stomach in equal dosages.

"Follow me," he says, unbuckling his seat belt and opening the door in one swift motion.

"As if I have a choice," I mumble. We take a set of stairs up to the lobby, which is dominated by a single security desk and an old-fashioned body scanner. Most of the time, a police-regulated baku does security checks, but there isn't one of those in here.

"You'll have to check those in," says the guard, who stands up from his desk as we enter.

"Um, what?" It looks to me as if he's pointing at Jinx, and then at the owl. "There's no way I'm leaving Jinx here."

"I promise you, he will be perfectly safe. I have to leave my owl here too." Mr. Baird puts his hand on my shoulder. "You've trusted me this far. A little bit further and then I promise you can go back home and to your normal life."

"No way," I say. "He has a black mark on him still—he can't communicate or anything. Let me keep him, or I'm leaving now."

Mr. Baird hesitates and exchanges a look with the guard. Eventually, he nods. "Fine. Let's go."

My hand clings to Jinx's body, a thin layer of sweat building on my palms. I wipe them on my jeans surreptitiously. I don't like this one bit.

"Come on, this way." We pass through the security gate and into an elevator. Now I see the first sign. BRIGHTSPRK is written in discreet lettering at the top of the elevator buttons.

"Oh no," I say, but the doors shut before I can step back through.

BRIGHTSPRK is one of Moncha's main rivals. *The* main rival. Even stepping in here feels like an act of treason. Now I look up at Mr. Baird with an expression of pure scorn and fury. My fists are balled tightly by my side.

"I know what you must be thinking—"

"No, you *don't* know," I say, through gritted teeth. I love Moncha Corp. Monica Chan is my hero. And now, here I am at BRIGHTSPRK? It makes my skin crawl.

The elevator doors open to a narrow hallway. I debate staying in the elevator as Mr. Baird walks out, but I force my feet to move.

I feel like I've crossed over enemy lines. A place where bakus aren't allowed? I knew it had to be bad news.

Mr. Baird stops in front of a door, jangles a set of keys from out of his pocket—so old-school—and opens it. It's a small office, again—like everything here—very plain, with not a lot of decoration or technology. There's a desk, unadorned, and wooden chairs on either side. He walks around to one side and gestures for me to sit on the other. There's a laptop sitting on his desk. It's older even than the one I have in my basement.

"Wow, BRIGHTSPRK not doing so well?" I remark.

"Lacey, I know you must be confused, but you have to know that I am trusting you too by letting you in on this secret."

"I didn't ask you to."

We stand there, on either side of the desk, facing each other.

I'm the one to break first. "So how long have you been working at BRIGHTSPRK?"

"For my whole career."

"Wow. A lifelong double agent. Isn't corporate espionage a crime?"

"I think what Moncha is doing is a crime."

I scoff. "What do you mean?"

"That's what I need your help figuring out."

"Okay, seriously?" I say, talking over top of him. But he continues on as if I hadn't interrupted.

"Have you seen Monica Chan around recently? Or did you notice that she disappeared after the latest upgrade?"

I pause. "She's around—she's been overseeing developments in other countries," I parrot back Eric Smith's words. But even I'm not sure if I believe that. From what I know of Monica Chan, it'd be unlike her to leave her company in someone else's hands. But then again, maybe everyone needs a break from being the boss.

"If you say so."

"I still don't see what this has to do with me. I mean—it must be big to blow your cover as some sort of career snitch."

He sighs. "Profectus is a bubble—you're so protected in there. Sheltered. But there's something bigger happening in the outside world."

"What?"

"Moncha have lost something. Something big. And everyone is on the lookout for it."

Unease stirs my stomach.

"Including BRIGHTSPRK," he says. Then his eyes darken. "We had some intel from deep inside Moncha's companioneering division that someone was working on a new baku. A baku that stood *against* everything that bakus were originally created for—rather than trying to create a perfect companion, someone was trying to create a baku that was fully autonomous. That made its own decisions, that had dreams and desires and goals. In other words…a baku that was independent. Alive. Its own creature."

I frown, although heat rises at the base of my neck. It all sounds too familiar. An autonomous baku. I know a thing or two about that, and I'm starting to realize why I'm here. I force my fingers not to tighten their grip on Jinx, even though I want to hug him tight and take him far, far away from here. "That doesn't make any sense," I say, trying to sound casual. "That would totally defeat the point of having a baku."

"Maybe." Mr. Baird's eyes don't leave mine for even an instant. "But you've shown aptitude for companioneering—sometimes, it's not just about something you *should* make, but what you *can* make. Pushing the envelope. It seemed like this rogue companioneer had really done it. We tried to get as much intel as possible, but even from those of us well-positioned inside Moncha Corp, there was no way to get close without raising major red flags.

"Then one day, about four months ago, we got lucky. We had communication from the companioneer in question—although we never found out their real name. They wanted help getting out—but getting past the supersensitive anti-intellectual property-theft barriers around Monchaville was going to be tough. They felt as if they were under imminent attack. At that time, I was working for the security division of Moncha, so I arranged for a barrier to be down at the right time and a car to be outside waiting to pick them up. But we weren't quick enough. We watched them take the person down on the border of the old ravine. We never heard from them again. We don't know who they are, if they're alive or dead. We don't know if the baku made it out, or if it was recaptured and decommissioned. But when we saw Moncha security combing the ravine the next day, we assumed that meant they hadn't recovered the baku. We sent a team down there as well, but they found nothing. Maybe because it had already *been* found."

I swallow hard. "Mr. Baird, I don't know anything about that. It sounds like... It sounds like science fiction. I don't know about any rogue bakus. I don't know why my entrance into Profectus got all messed up, but I had great stats coming in, perfect grades—well, you should know, Tobias picked me for his team!"

Mr. Baird studies me thoughtfully, his hand stroking the base of his stubbly chin. Maybe being a double agent is the reason behind his scruffy appearance. The lines around his eyes tighten, as if he has aged by coming into the building and taking off his Moncha employee mask. "No, there's no doubt that you deserve to be at Profectus. Any school would be lucky to have you—and you will go on to do great things one day, anyone can see that. Moncha is lucky. You are a very loyal person, Lacey, I can see that. Just think about what I'm saying. You and your baku have an unusually strong connection. There are people on the lookout for unusual bakus. If Carter suspects there's something more to Jinx than meets the eye, then I'm worried you could be in grave danger. I've been trying to keep an eye on you, but things keep happening out of my control—like your selection onto Tobias's team, the wild card entry—that are drawing attention to you and your baku."

I shake my head and prepare another lie. "I sent Jinx intentionally into the ring. He wasn't disobeying orders. I promise."

"Good. Because if by chance that isn't true, and in fact Jinx *isn't* what you say he is, then you might need my help. You won't ignore that, will you?"

Now I can't help it. I hug Jinx tighter to my body, my grip viselike around him. "I promise," I say. "But Mr. Baird, I swear to you—Jinx is totally and utterly normal."

31

I EXIT THE WAREHOUSE, JINX IN MY ARMS, FEELING sick to my stomach. I take a deep breath, looking in both directions and trying not to break into a sprint. Mr. Baird offered me a ride back, but I'd rather make my own way. I don't want to have anything more to do with BRIGHTSPRK. The rain, at least, has let up—but the sidewalks are slick. I edge my way slowly along the pavement until I reach a streetcar stop.

As I wait, I have plenty of time to think about Mr. Baird's story.

A baku that's independent. Autonomous. That can make their own decisions.

*Jinx* is the rogue baku.

That means people are looking for him.

Powerful people. I could be in danger—and so could he.

I knew Jinx was different. I'd tried so hard to cover it up, laughing off Jinx's quirks and taking responsibility for commands

I didn't make. But if Mr. Baird suspects enough to blow his cover, or if Carter acts on his intuition... That means others can't be far behind. Others who might take Jinx by force.

*No one knows for sure*, I remind myself. I don't think Mr. Baird would have let me go so easily if he was certain.

I can't hang around here any longer. I need to get home. I can't use Jinx to get myself a cab because of the black mark, so I spend a fruitless twenty minutes attempting to flag one down the old-fashioned way. Eventually, a driver picks me up—I think out of nostalgia—or maybe pity. Paying for it is going to use up the last of my meager savings, but it will be worth it.

When I get home, I sprint through the building, not even stopping for Darwin, who yells out my name as I pass. The elevator doors are shutting as I round the corner, and I manage to slip in just in time. I need to see Mom. I need to tell her everything—come clean to her about Jinx.

*But what if she wants to turn Jinx in...*

I'm not sure that I could do it.

The keys fumble in my hand as I attempt to get into the apartment.

"Mom? Mom, are you home?"

There's no answer. I try to think back to whether this is one of her late-shift days, but I can't remember.

It doesn't take me long to search the small apartment, my grip still as tight as ever on Jinx, refusing to let him go. There's no one there.

My heart almost leaps out of my chest as a loud ringing bursts through the silence. It takes me a moment to place it, but then I realize it's our house phone. I run to the wall that it's hanging on, blowing off a cover of dust and moving piles of envelopes stuffed behind the receiver—we almost never use it since our bakus are automatically linked to the building's communications.

"Hello?" I say tentatively.

"Lacey?"

I breathe a sigh of relief at the familiar sound of Darwin's voice. "Yes, it's me," I say.

"Okay, glad I caught you—for some reason I couldn't get through to your baku?"

I stare down at the lifeless form of Jinx in my arms. "Yeah, he's out of action at the moment—long story."

There's a pause on the other end of the line. Bakus are never supposed to be out of action. But then, Darwin is used to strange things from me, and he moves past it smoothly. "You ran upstairs so fast, I couldn't tell you. Some of your friends arrived a little while ago. You had them on your preapproved meeting list so they should be down in the basement. Also, if you have the chance, my baku has been playing up—"

*What?* My mind is racing. *My friends are here?* How is that possible? I thought they hated me. But maybe there's still a chance to redeem myself...

I don't even listen to Darwin as he talks about needing me to fix his baku. I don't have time for repairs right now. I mumble something about coming to see him later, then hang up the phone and race back to the elevators.

The basement is deathly quiet when I reach it—not even the sounds of Paul tinkering away. A feeling of foreboding descends on me. What if this is a trap? What if Carter is here, only pretending to be my friend? I try and reassure myself. Darwin has met Team Tobias. He wouldn't let in just anyone.

When I walk past the parked cars and around the corner to the lockers, my heart sinks. There's no one there. But there is evidence that they've only recently left. On the wall across from the locker, written in giant, spray-painted letters, is the word *TRAITOR*.

I guess they haven't forgiven me after all. I sink down to the ground, my back against the door to my locker, tears welling in my eyes. Everything is falling apart, and I don't have the skills to repair it.

I need help. I might not have my teammates to rely on. But there's one person who I know I can rely on.

I need Zora. Whether she likes it or not.

32

"SO, EXPLAIN THIS TO ME ONE MORE TIME."

I swallow, and even though I want nothing more than to stare at the ground, I lift up my chin and look Zora straight in the eye. We're down in the locker, and she is perched on the stool by the old computer screen and I am cross-legged on the floor. "I don't know how Jinx works. He's not really mine."

"You stole him."

"I didn't steal him! I…I found him. And then I fixed him."

"But he doesn't belong to you."

I pause for a moment, then shake my head. "No."

"I don't get it," she says, slowly shaking her head as well. "It shouldn't be possible. You can't take someone else's baku and claim it as your own." Then, her voice catches in the back of her throat and comes out sounding small. "I knew something was up. Why didn't you tell me?"

That's what's really bothering her. And me.

"I don't know... I guess I was afraid. At first, I was so focused on getting him ready so I could go to Profectus. But, gradually...I fell in love with him, Zora. I was scared he'd be taken away from me if anyone knew the truth. I figured if *no one* knew, then maybe I could keep him forever."

She obviously can see the hurt in my eyes, because she jumps down and grabs my hand. "If whoever they are knew Jinx was here, how would you still have him?" she muses. "They would surely come and take him."

"That's true," I say. "And maybe he isn't special at all. Maybe I'm imagining that he's the rogue baku."

"Your teacher's story is pretty far-fetched. I mean, he works for BRIGHTSPRK, right? How can you trust him?"

"I don't know," I say. "But Jinx *is* different. We communicate differently. I hear his voice in my head and..."

"Wait, hold up." Zora flips her hands out in front of her to stop me. "Like telepathically?"

"Something like that."

Her jaw drops, and it takes her a moment to recover.

"And he does things without me asking," I continue.

"Can you show me?"

I point miserably to the black mark on his paw. "Not until the morning," I say, with a frown.

"Well, how about we take a look at his code? Maybe if we can find something to help us understand. Otherwise, I think you're going to have to report this. If this is undocumented tech—like the telepathic thing—it could be dangerous."

My mouth turns dry at the thought of turning Jinx in. Who knows what they would do to him? Mr. Baird was under the impression they wanted to destroy him.

I can't let that happen. I know the connection between us is real. He is my baku. My companion. No one will be able to convince me otherwise.

Almost on instinct, my hand strokes the top of his head.

It takes me a beat, but then my eyes widen in surprise. "Wait. You *want* to help me look at the code?"

Zora wriggles in her seat, and I can see Linus anxiously pacing across the tops of her shoulders. "Just this once."

I jump up to my feet and throw my arms around her. "Thank you, thank you, thank you!"

She laughs until I pull away. Then, two tiny lines appear on her forehead as she frowns. "Have you looked at it at all?"

I nod, then pull at the edge of my collar. "Yeah, but I can't say I understood a lot of it. It's more your expertise, you know?"

"That's for sure. I haven't done much coding since the summer, though…"

I put my hands on her shoulders and look at her dead in the eye. "You're one of the best coders I've ever met, Zora. You'd kick anyone's butt at Profectus if that's what you wanted to do."

She nods, but her frown lines don't disappear. I know that I won't be able to talk her into believing in herself—she'll have to see it for herself to remember. I give her Jinx, and we leash him up to the old monitor. Zora strikes a few keys with more hesitation than I'm used to from her, touching them lightly as if they were made of glass. But gradually, her fingers grow in confidence, striking them faster and faster, a pianist gaining momentum on a piece. Then she's flying, bypassing the computer's old operating system and opening up a program that allows her to infiltrate Jinx's inner workings. With a few taps of her fingers, she flings the code onto the screens around us, until we are almost immersed on all sides by lines of green text on a black background. This is the Zora I'm used to, her bottom lip jutted out in concentration, her dark eyes scanning every line, trying to make sense of what she's seeing. She can take it in much faster than I can—her brain reads code as easily as a book—or, like a musician, she can take in all the lines of music and hear the entire piece. She can also see exactly where things are going wrong, or where something is different.

Syncopated.

Offbeat.

She leans back on the stool, almost so far that I'm worried she's going to topple off. I stand behind her in case. She lets out a low whistle. "Oh my god, Lacey."

"What? What is it?" I'm trying to scan the code as fast as I can, but it's too much for me, too complex. I look at the screen and my eyes want to cross. I much prefer having a mechanical problem to fix, a tool in my hand.

"I haven't seen anything like this before." Her fingers slow, occasionally tapping out small sequences as she attempts to go deeper into Jinx's operating system. I shift my weight from side to side. Suddenly, it feels like a violation—Jinx has seemed so real to me, it's as if we are performing brain surgery, not just looking at his code. My biggest fear is that we might damage some vital part of him.

"There are some lines of code here…" She lifts her hand up to the screen. "That keep jumping around. Look!" As we're watching, the code moves from one portion of the screen to another. "It definitely *shouldn't* be doing that. But whoever wrote this program is good. Very, very good. It has a kind of…elegance to it that I haven't seen in a long time. Ah!"

"What?"

"See this?" She points to a line of code. At first, I can't see what's caught her interest in it. But if I squint, I can tell that the letters and numbers look slightly different than the ones around it. "So obvious, right?" She looks over her shoulder at me.

I raise an eyebrow at her. "Obvious?"

She lets out an exaggerated sigh at my coding incompetence. I grin back and squeeze her shoulders. "I wondered why there were these big chunks of ugly, blocky code in the midst of all these otherwise *beautiful* lines. They're totally out of place—I can't believe you can't see them, I mean, it's like a bunch of weeds growing in a row of neat roses."

"I sort of see…" I say, while squinting.

"That's the black mark. It's written to infect the operating system while it's attached and stops any of the programs from functioning. There's no way to get this off?"

"I don't think so."

"Huh. Okay, well, I'll try to read around it." She stares intensely at the screen as she scrolls through the code, occasionally stopping to zoom in on particular sections. Every now and then she scoffs at one of the lines, or makes a sound that I *think* is a small sigh of awe. After about ten minutes of doing this, she lifts one of her braids into her mouth and begins chewing. That's how I know things are *really* serious.

Even though I'm afraid of what she might find, it swells my heart to see her acting like this. It means the old Zora I knew is still there.

I distract myself by tidying up some of the boxes around the locker, and start to scrub down some of the paint from the *TRAITOR* sign. Don't need to be looking at *that* every time I come down here to work. Plus, people might start asking questions. Zora already tried, but I can't break the Profectus NDA to tell her about baku battles and my teammates.

I pull down a few boxes and something else tumbles off a high shelf. The box from the Moncha store. The poor scarab beetle baku is still encased in his packaging, returned there after Zora worked on him. He has no one to love him. He thought he was going to be leashed, but he never was.

For some reason, guilt gnaws at my stomach.

Zora sits up straighter on the stool, and that attracts my

attention. I put the beetle box back up on the shelf. "What is it? Did you find something?"

"I'm not sure…"

"What exactly are you looking for?" I ask.

"Coders often leave a signature—it's pretty hard not to write something as extensive as this and not leave bits of yourself behind. And although there would have been a team of people at Moncha writing this, I think I see enough hallmarks of a single person here… This doesn't feel like an 'on the books' kind of project. Hang on…"

She types furiously, but all I can see now is that code is dropping off the screens, falling like rain droplets in a storm. In its place is blankness. "What's happening?" I ask.

"There's…something…another…layer…"

Briefly something flashes up on the screen, another layer of code, but instead of written in neon green, it's a flash of bright gold, like the sparks of a firework. Then, as fast as it appeared, it vanishes.

"No!" Zora slams her hand down on the keyboard, but the screens in front of us are dark. Zora is breathing hard, as if she's just finished sprinting around a track as opposed to sitting in a chair, typing. Her brow is covered in a sheen of sweat. She hasn't finished typing, though. She keeps trying to draw back the regular code, but nothing happens. The screens remain blank.

She whirls around on me. "What is this thing? Where did you get it?" She jabs her finger at Jinx's inert form.

"I don't… I told you…" The tidal force of her anger almost knocks me over.

"All that code we were looking at? Those elegant phrases interspersed with the uglier sections…"

"His code and the black mark."

"No. All of it was an illusion. Like an overlay. A false front. I've never seen anything like it. I broke through, but…" She throws her hands up at the screen. "He shut me out." She stares down at the small robotic creature curled up on the desk as if it is something alien.

"But he's got a black mark on him—he can't *do* anything." I unleash him from the computer and gather him up in my arms. I'm afraid of the look in Zora's eyes, I realize. I don't know what she's going to do. She might take him. I can't let that happen.

"You have to hand him in."

"Zora, you can't ask me to do that."

We face off, staring at each other, Jinx in my arms, and Linus at Zora's ear. Finally, Zora's shoulders slump. "I won't tell anyone. Promise you'll be careful. Your baku isn't normal. You don't have control. He's not the companion you thought he was."

I open my mouth to protest. It doesn't matter to me what Jinx is. I still love him.

But she continues. "Look around." She gestures at the *TRAITOR* sign on the wall, and I wince, at the remnants of coffee mugs and ramen cups, and I wince again, at the bags under my eyes and greasy hair I haven't had time to wash. "I know you want to believe that you are in control of this situation. But, Lacey…" In that moment, both Linus and Zora fix me with the same wide-eyed stare. "I'm not sure just who here is controlling who."

33

FOR THE FIRST WEEK BACK AFTER MR. BAIRD'S
shocking reveal, I'm as skittish as a mouse, imagining someone
coming to take Jinx around every corner.

But nothing has changed. Even Carter seems to have dropped
his vendetta. My former teammates still ignore me, but as I walk
past Kai in the hallway. he flips a bottle of spray paint over in his
hand. At least I know who is responsible for the *TRAITOR* graffiti.

I go to each class as normal, keeping my head down, and use
the isolation to regain some focus. For once, history and French get
my full attention—much to the surprise of my professors.

There had only been one odd moment to remind me of the
wild happenings of the week before.

The morning after the baku battle, when it was established
that no other team had managed to repair their bakus enough to

take any points from me, I had to meet with Mr. Baird to remove Jinx's black mark.

I'd tried to make as little eye contact with him as possible, but he acted as if nothing unusual had happened the night before. I guess he's had a lot of acting practice in his years as a corporate spy.

"Well done, Lacey," he said, once the mark was off. "Good luck with the next battle."

"Th-thank you, sir," I stammered out.

But it was once I'd gotten to my desk that the strange thing happened.

>>You looked at my code.

*Yes, with Zora*, I replied.

>>Did you find anything?

*No... I'm sorry, Jinx.*

He beeped, which I interpreted as a sigh.

>>Don't worry, I'm doing enough to figure
this out for the both of us.

*What are you doing?*

He didn't reply.

*Jinx? What do you mean?*

The questions spilled out of me, then.

*Do you know how you came to be at the bottom of the ravine? Do you remember anything of the time before I brought you back to life?*

All the things I'd wanted to ask but hadn't.

Then the biggest question of all. *Do you remember who made you?*

>>No.

For the first time his robotic tone had lost any of its warmth.

But I'm getting close.

Even now, he refuses to explain more. I don't care. I'm glad to have Jinx with me and everything back to normal.

At the end of the week, I stay behind to talk to Mr. Baird.

"It doesn't seem like anyone is after Jinx," I tell him. "I know you think I might be in danger, and I appreciate the warning. But Jinx isn't what you are looking for. He's not some rogue baku—he's normal. And I also want to let you know that working for Moncha Corp is still my dream. I want that internship more than anything. That hasn't changed."

It takes him a moment that seems to stretch into a lifetime. Then, he nods. "It doesn't look like I could change your mind even if I wanted to."

"But…I also wanted to let you know that your secret is safe with me."

Mr. Baird's eyes search my face. "I appreciate that."

I turn to go, but Mr. Baird speaks again. "You know, Lacey, if that rogue baku did fall into the wrong hands…then there could be more at stake here than a school competition."

I swallow. "I understand," I say, even though I'm not sure I do.

When I leave Mr. Baird's classroom, I'm surprised to see Jake waiting for me. He has a friendly smile on his face, which almost breaks my heart. I haven't seen a friendly face at Profectus Academy this whole week. "Just checking you haven't found some other new rule that means you're not participating tomorrow? Or if you're going to be fighting with ten bakus instead of one?"

I shake my head. "No tactics, no strategies. I just need to find a way to get through this."

He raises an eyebrow. "Get through? Not to win? Even with a summer internship at Moncha HQ and one-on-one with Monica Chan up for grabs?"

I swallow. He's read me like an e-book in oversize font.

He laughs at my expression. "All my money is on you, by the way."

"That seems like a bad bet."

His eyes twinkle. "Well see, that's exactly where you're wrong. Of course I'll be putting money on you. Money, Monchacoin—heck, I'd even take homework passes. You're on fire. Or, if you maybe need help dodging questions you don't want to answer, I'll take a couple of *your* homework passes to act as a bodyguard. Speaking of bodyguards… Are you sure you can't sneak me on the behind-the-scenes Moncha HQ tour?"

I shrug. "No dice. Captains only."

"Shucks. Thought being your only friend left at school might have *some* perks."

That hurt, and he notices. He squeezes my upper arm. "Forget 'em. You have a great baku, you're a better fighter in your first year than people who have been here for years. You're on track to go right to the top of Moncha. Just don't forget the people who were nice to you on your way up." He winks at me.

"Never," I say.

"Good luck, then!"

"I hope I can deliver." Preparing for the battle hasn't exactly been at the top of my agenda—not with all my attempts to stay under the radar, worrying about people coming for Jinx.

"If it were only you, I might be worried. But with that baku by your side? Lacey, you're unstoppable."

PART FIVE

# MONCHA HQ

## 34

I STARE UP THROUGH THE GATES AND AT THE entrance to Moncha HQ, Jinx pacing at my feet.

With everything that's happened, I've barely stopped to register where I am. I exhale sharply, my breath streaming out in front of me, a white cloud into the cold air. I'm outside the building I've dreamed of working in my entire life. The building where Monica Chan works.

Where bakus are created.

Where the magic happens.

*And where once upon a time, Dad came to work every day.*

I shift from foot to foot, wriggling my toes to keep them warm. The headquarters are just east of downtown. Around the corner is the BakuBeats warehouse, where I celebrated with my former teammates. I remember reading that this area was once Monica Chan's favorite part of the city—a blend of old red brick and modern glass towers, a collision of history and modernity that made her happy. Plus, it was the location of her favorite coffee shop.

When she made her money, she bought out the historic buildings and built her headquarters.

It was a controversial move. So many people protested this young tech CEO coming in and commandeering a place that had been not only a great tourist attraction, but a movie set and a place of historic importance for the city. But Monica won everyone over, keeping the historic feel and spirit of openness to the public, while shrouding the actual headquarters themselves in mystery. The headquarters took almost a decade to complete—a lifetime in an era where entire sixty-plus-story condo towers shot up like weeds in the space of a few months. Plenty of rival firms sent drones overhead to find out exactly what was going on with the building, bribed employees and workmen to act as spies. But there's never been a public leak. It's like the Willy Wonka's Chocolate Factory of tech—totally out in the open, and yet fully concealed.

And I'm about to be allowed in. I hope it doesn't disappoint. I crane my neck as employees walk past me and into the building. From what I've glimpsed so far, the lobby interior looks like any other corporate office.

Jinx sits at my feet, grooming himself. I didn't know what to wear, so I'm in the most sensible corporate-type clothing I own—a plain black dress that I borrowed from my mom, a dark red cardigan underneath my puffy jacket to ward off the cold November air, and a pair of thick black tights and boring patent leather Mary

Janes that make me feel like I'm both five and forty years old at the same time. How does that work? With my asymmetrical bob falling over my eyes and thick glasses, I don't think I'm fooling anyone into thinking I'm cool enough to work here, and—seeing the streams of Moncha employees entering in sweats and oversize parkas, I wish I had gone with my normal *out of school* uniform of boots, jeans, and a band T-shirt.

Jinx buzzes.

>>Teacher and hostiles approaching.

I look up and see Mr. Baird, with the other team captains. I swallow down my feelings of insecurity, and my mixed emotions at seeing Tobias again. His face is buried in the hood of his jacket, his posture hunched over, his back turned to me.

I can't tell what is worse—him ignoring me, or the open hostility on the faces of Gemma and Elektra. They've both got new versions of their bakus to replace the ones that were destroyed by Jinx in the baku battle.

Tears threaten to prick at my eyes, but I hold them back. I'm here at Moncha headquarters now. I'm going to make the most of it.

"Before we go in," says Mr. Baird, his voice tense, "I'm afraid I have to black mark all of your bakus. Security reasons."

>>No, I don't want...

Jinx wriggles in my arms, trying to escape, but Mr. Baird latches the mark on in time. I feel sick, as if I've violated Jinx's trust. But maybe it's better for us both—at least he won't attract any unwanted attention while he's in that state. I take a deep breath and remind myself that I'm about to embark on a tour of a building I've wanted to see all my life.

We head in through the automatic doors, and I gasp.

What I'd seen before—the lobby that looked like every other boring corporate office block—was an illusion. A hologram laid behind the doors, to fool anyone who was looking in from the outside.

The real lobby?

It's a cathedral of light and space and green and *curves*. The building is not the vision of the future I saw in old sci-fi flicks, all shiny chrome and glass (only the bakus wandering around are evidence of that). This is warm, red brick and tiled mosaic floors, renovated to take advantage of the natural light, streaming in through iron-clad squares of window. There are trails of hanging vines and ivy, and bright pops of color from the occasional bloom. A fountain bubbles up from the center, adding to the serene atmosphere. There are perches everywhere for flying bakus, obstacle courses around the walls for land-based ones, and snugs for leashing up.

We're greeted at the fountain by a young woman with a stunning lynx baku. She steps forward to shake Mr. Baird's hand. "Are these the team captains?" she asks, giving us a beaming smile.

"All present and accounted for," says the teacher.

"Well then, if you guys would like to follow me, I can give

you the grand tour! My name is Nina Fiore, and this is my baku, Flare. I'm a high-level baku designer here at Moncha Corp. We have about an hour before the baku battles, so lots to cram in." She leans in toward us conspiratorially. "So many of us have requested the afternoon off to watch—lots of former baku battle alumni in this building! Looking forward to a great show! I especially can't wait to see that eagle baku in action. I remember when he was just a few sketches of a pencil on paper in the Moncha brainstorming lab." To my shock, she actually wipes a tear away from her eye. But then my heart swells with pride. I knew the people who worked at Moncha really cared about what they were creating, and here was direct proof.

"Speaking of," Nina continues, after gathering herself. "Let's head to the brainstorming lab now. It's as good a place to start as any…"

If I could have bottled my own feelings in the hour that followed, I would have. My emotions swung between elation and wonder, delight and curiosity and awe. Any unease or discomfort I had is wiped away. Being here is better than Disney World, better than Christmas—the inner workings of Moncha are exactly what I had envisioned and more.

More, because people seem to actually *enjoy* working here. The brainstorming lab was filled with people collaborating, using their bakus to project ideas onto large white tables. We get a glimpse at the manufacturing plant, which is like my basement locker on steroids: I glimpse every different kind of material and machinery I could ever imagine working with, all state-of-the-art, and the companioneers inside all smile and wave at us as we pass by.

Nina informs us that Moncha HQ is totally self-sufficient, the machines and computers running on green energy provided by solar panels on the roof, and even the water is recycled daily so nothing is taken from the city's main lines. It's nothing like the depictions of working life on TV, the daily grind, bracketed by boring commutes. There's a genuine buzz in the air, electric in its intensity. These are people keyed up on a different plane. I wish I could have brought Mom and Zora with me. They would have understood, then, what I meant about not being satisfied with simply being content. I wanted to strive for more. I wanted to strive for *this*. For *joy*.

Me being me, all this is accompanied by an undercurrent of panic that maybe I won't get there. Not even the angry team captains can make me feel as bad as I manage to do to myself. The other captains seem so at ease with their abilities, their innate confidence shining through. They don't doubt their place here. But even though I've known my whole life that I wanted to be a companioneer, even as the ring around my finger tells me that engineering is in my blood, even as Jinx and Aero and Jupiter are working proof that I have some skills, I still worry that I don't belong.

*No, it's not that*, I remind myself. *The reason you don't feel comfortable is because you didn't earn yourself a place at Profectus. You were rejected. You didn't make Tobias's team; there was a mistake. You were never a wild card. It was a fluke. Your true baku is sitting in a box on a shelf in your storage locker and you should be at St. Agnes.*

But then there's another voice. A voice that says: *Fluke or not, you're here now. You have to embrace it. You have to live it. And you have to run with it, as fast and as hard as you can, to make it that much harder for anyone to take it away from you.*

Maybe it will all come crashing down. But I won't be the one who presses on the detonator for the explosion.

We travel down several flights of stairs, the tension rising in the air between the other captains as battle time draws near.

Even though we're underground, the hallways are wide and spacious, the ceiling height generous—so it feels as if there is a lot of light. There are even "windows" at specific intervals, programed to show off different outdoor scenes—like a stunning waterfall or leafy forest.

Nina stops outside a black door, marked with a stylized *BB*. My fingers fidget against Jinx's body as I realize that the final baku battle is about to begin.

"I hope you enjoyed your tour of Moncha HQ! I look forward to welcoming one of you back here for the summer internship," Nina says with a wink. "Good luck—and may the best baku win."

The door opens and Mr. Baird beckons us through. We're led into a room where the other teammates are waiting. I hang back as the captains join their teams, then head toward a paper sign that has my name on it. All the other teams have their names designed up—Gemma's are in neon lights, while Tobias's are in a series of neat gold sans serif. Dorian's are in black-and-white 1920s Hollywood-style font, and Elektra's team are in an elaborate cursive, while Pearce's are the most outrageous, in a font that looks as if it's styled out of lightning bolts.

"Competing bakus in the center."

The other captains know the drill, but I know nothing—I wait and watch. There's a stand in the center of the room and one by one, the fighters—Tobias, Pearce, Dorian, Terence (from Team Elektra), and Kayla (from Team Gemma)—strap their bakus down on the table.

When I step forward, I place Jinx down gently and tie up the straps. Mr. Baird stares at Jinx with laser-like intensity as he removes the black mark from his paw.

Jinx springs to life, and he tenses immediately. He's not able to move because of the straps—although I can see he desperately wants to.

>>What happened? Where am I?

*We're inside Moncha HQ, and you're in the baku circle, ready to enter the arena for the final baku battle. Don't you remember? They made us put black marks on you when we entered the building.*

>>No. Let's get out of here.

*Jinx, it's okay. We have to do this one final baku battle and then we never have to do this again. If you don't want to fight, I won't make you.*

"Miss Chu?" says Mr. Baird, one eyebrow raised. "Back to your station, please."

I take a step back to my paper sign.

>>Don't leave me here.

*Just this battle.*

>>And then we can go?

*I promise.*

It's the first time I've seen him panicked. Maybe even afraid. I don't understand, and it's making me even more nervous than I was before.

"Fighters, this way," says Mr. Baird.

There are choruses of *good lucks* directed at the fighters by the other teams, but no one to cheer me on. I grit my teeth, determined to make quick work of this—so that I can get back to Jinx and find out what's wrong. We're led into another room filled with glass cylinders: the elevators that will lift us up into the arena. My cylinder is sandwiched in between Dorian and Tobias—an uncomfortable place to be.

"All right, battlers. There are five hundred points up for grabs here—meaning a win here for any of you would put you in with a chance at the grand prize: the summer internship right here at Moncha HQ in a department of your choosing. The last baku standing—or any bakus on the field after thirty minutes—will be declared the winner, with other teams given the opportunity to repair their bakus before tomorrow morning. But if you pull your baku before thirty minutes are up, then you will not be eligible for points. Does everyone understand?"

We nod.

"As Ms. Fiore said: May the best baku win." For a moment, Mr.

Baird sounds sad, losing his normal cool, and he presses his fingers against his eyebrows. I take a step forward out of the cylinder, but the glass slams shut around me and Mr. Baird leaves the room.

Now, the chat starts.

Dorian snaps his fingers at me. Reluctantly, I turn my head in his direction. His thick black hair is gelled into place so it creates a perfect crest of a wave on his forehead. "Good luck, newbie. You're going to need it."

My throat is so dry, I don't respond. Instead, I turn to the other side, where a few feet away is Tobias. His fingers are balled into tight fists at his side. He must sense me looking, as he turns his head my way, his eyes dark. He says nothing.

But I don't have time to think about it. The elevator shakes, and I'm lifted up into the arena. I can barely hear myself think over the roar of the crowd—all of the students from Profectus, and lots of Moncha employees too. I blink several times, trying to take in the sheer size of this arena, which must be double that of the one at Profectus. Huge spotlights shine down on us, so bright they're almost blinding. I lift my hand to shield my eyes until they can adjust.

To my left is Dorian and his wolf.

To my right is Tobias and his eagle.

But in front of me, there's nothing. Jinx isn't there.

He's gone.

**35**

THE OTHER BAKUS LEAP INTO ACTION AROUND ME.
But it barely lasts a moment before a whistle blows, and everything
comes to a grinding halt.

The teacher who blows the whistle isn't Mr. Baird, but Dr.
Grant. "Battlers, halt!" she cries out to us. The other participants
look at one another in confusion, their bakus frozen in place, while
the crowd's mood shifts from frenzied to annoyed.

Tobias is first to realize the problem. "Where's Jinx, Lacey?" he
calls out to me from his spot.

The place where Jinx is supposed to be is empty. My heartbeat
pounds in my ears. "I...I don't know?"

Dr. Grant's voice rises above the crowd. "Miss Chu, your
baku needs to be in play, or else we will have to suspend the entire
tournament. All bakus must be present and accounted for, and all
teams must have at least one baku in the arena."

I don't know where Jinx is. I don't know what could have happened to him. *And where's Mr. Baird?* This was a mistake. I should never have left Jinx alone. Panic rises in my chest, but I also see an opportunity. "Disqualify me, then," I say quickly. My eyes scan the crowd, and I see Jake's face fall at my words, then cloud over with annoyance. I'm going to lose yet another friend, but in this moment, I don't care. "I forfeit my points and my place in the competition. The other teams can battle for the internship." I hate how squeaky and desperate my voice sounds, but I've seen a way to end this agony and I'm going to take it.

"Yeah, let her quit!" says Gemma from her team box, gleeful at witnessing what she thinks might end up being my downfall. I wince at the word *quit*, but it's true—I want out. I want out and to go back to being a seventh grader, a teammate, not a captain—the mechanic behind the scenes.

And I want to find Jinx.

Then I want to go home and explain everything to Mom and Zora. They will help me figure out a solution.

Dr. Grant shakes her head. "There won't be any quitting. The rules are clear. Captains must participate once they've signed up. The battle will resume again tomorrow. If your baku does not appear again, then the punishment will be a weeklong suspension from school—and we will be forced to review your place at Profectus."

Tears prick my eyes. Suspension, and possible expulsion.

But it's not the dread of being kicked out of school that's worrying me. *Where are you, Jinx?*

I scan the remaining players, all glaring at me—except Tobias, who refuses to make eye contact—but I can barely see straight. The floor beneath my feet vibrates, and one by one we're taken back down into the holding pit. The groans and boos from the crowd—who were expecting an exciting battle—follow me down. I think I even get hit with someone's balled-up popcorn wrapper.

My mind is racing too fast to care. *What has happened to Jinx?* I hope he's run off and hidden somewhere. But my gut is telling me that something else has happened.

As soon as my feet touch the ground, Tobias shoulders past me. "Great, now we have to do this whole charade over again. Come on, Aero," he mutters to his baku. "Let's go train. Might as well do something productive out of this wasted evening."

"Thanks, Lacey," says Gemma, who bursts into the team room to meet Kayla, sarcasm dripping off her every word. "Why are you trying to drag out the inevitable? You're going to lose, that little machine you love so much is going to get destroyed, and that's it. Game over."

"There's more to life than baku battles, Gemma," I snap back.

She stares at me, then shakes her head. "You had so much potential. I thought you were one of the good ones. Looks like you're the same as everyone else."

She and Kayla leave the room, and I'm alone.

*Jinx?*

There's no response. Nothing from him whatsoever. I touch the spot on the stand where I last placed Jinx. There are no clues as to where he might have gone.

The panic that I had been suppressing rises now. I'd been relying on the fact that this is something Jinx sometimes does. He runs away. He disappears on me. But he always comes back.

*What if this time he doesn't?*

*What if now I am alone?*

That can't be the case.

There's only one thing that could have happened. *He's been taken.*

I run from the room, straight into the back of Dr. Grant. "Where is Mr. Baird?" I ask.

She frowns and clucks her tongue against the roof of her mouth. "He's been fired.'"

The color drains from my face. "What?"

"A few moments before the battles began. I sent him away to pack his things and leave. Now, Miss Chu—I'm very disappointed in…"

"Sorry, Dr. Grant, I have to go. Need to find my baku before tomorrow, you understand."

Normally I would be cringing inside at being so rude to the Profectus principal, but I don't have a moment to waste. I bolt from the competitors' room.

"Miss Chu? Miss Chu!" her voice calls out to my back, but I don't stop.

I run up the stairs two at a time, using the momentum of my sprint to swing around the banisters and launch myself forward even faster. I reach the beautiful atrium again, but I can't even in take in what I'm seeing. My thoughts are focused on a single goal. I need to catch up to Mr. Baird.

I dash around the outside of the building to the parking lot. I spot Mr. Baird getting in to his car and manage to reach him just in time.

"Where is he?" I slam my hand on the roof of his car, then peer in the back windows, trying to see if Jinx is hidden there. All Mr. Baird would need is a black mark and he could smuggle Jinx out of Moncha HQ no problem.

He certainly looks shifty as he rolls down the window. "Where is who? What are you even doing here?"

"What are you talking about? Where is Jinx? You took him before the battle, I know you did."

"Took Jinx? What? He's missing?"

"Of course he's missing, otherwise I'd be battling at Moncha HQ—you know that full well. No one else would steal Jinx. You as good as told me you wanted him. Give him back now, or else …"

"Or else you'll do something even worse than get me fired from my job? I was trying to protect you. But you're too blinded by loyalty to Moncha Corp to understand."

I take a step back, panic and anger over Jinx's disappearance warring with the shock of what Mr. Baird is saying. "Get you fired? I didn't do anything! I haven't told anyone about you. And you repaid me by stealing Jinx. I told you he's a normal baku."

He stares at me, his eyes scanning my face. Slowly, the outrage that had been etched on his face drops. "You didn't tell anyone?"

"No!" I repeat.

After a moment, he says, "I believe you. And I didn't take Jinx."

"Oh." I slump down against the car door, tears spilling out onto my cheeks. Anger had been keeping me upright, but now I feel as though I'm going to collapse under the worry. "Then...who did?"

He shakes his head. "You said he was taken before the battle?"

I nod. "The last time I saw him, I was placing him on the stand. But he never showed up in the arena."

"So Moncha Corp has taken him," says Mr. Baird, his voice tight.

He's voiced my worst fear out loud, but I still shake my head. "You don't know that. It could have been..."

Mr. Baird looks at me with pity in his eyes. "It's a shame. I think he was a marvel. Maybe I should have been stronger with my actions—prevented you from bringing him straight to Moncha HQ. But you convinced me he was normal. Now you have to accept that he is gone. If Moncha have their hands on him, they will have destroyed him. Here." He hands me over an old-fashioned business card since I don't have a baku for him to send his contact details directly to. "If Moncha isn't for you...maybe you'll consider BRIGHTSPRK."

I take the card with trembling fingers and step back as he rolls up the window and the car drives away. My head hangs low.

*You have to accept that he is gone.* Mr. Baird's words ring in my ears.

But I won't accept it. Not yet. Not until I have proof that Jinx is really gone. I won't give up on him.

36

I WANT TO MESSAGE ZORA, BUT WITHOUT A BAKU, I'm cut off from communication. I also have no money on me—no way to pay for public transport up to St. Agnes. I'm so reliant on Jinx for practical things as well as for companionship.

I've never felt so alone. I have no choice but to walk, conscious that every minute that goes by without Jinx is an opportunity for someone to destroy him.

It takes me almost an hour, and when I arrive at St. Agnes, I'm red-faced and breathless. I walk straight through the front doors as if I belong, thankful now that I didn't have to wear my Profectus Academy uniform to Moncha HQ. I have no idea where in the school she is, so for a moment, I'm at a loss. But there's one place inside the school where I know I can at least send her a message.

I make a beeline up to the library, where I know there is a bank of old desktop computers gathering dust. I duck past the librarian—trying to be inconspicuous—and take a seat at the nearest computer. I clear a thick layer of grime just to be able to see the keys. The machine boots up incredibly slowly, but eventually it sputters to life. I stare at the screen for a few seconds. I've almost forgotten how to use an old operating system, but I find my way to an old messaging program.

I type in Zora's "number" (it's really Linus's unique identity code) and start typing.

**LACEY:** Are you there? It's me, Lacey.
**LACEY:** SOS.

Within a few seconds, I get a reply—and I breathe a sigh of relief for the fact that Zora constantly monitors her inbox.

**ZORA:** Everything OK? SOS?
**LACEY:** Jinx is gone. I think someone stole him.
**ZORA:** ???!!!???
**ZORA:** How are we messaging right now??
**LACEY:** I'm on an old computer in the St. Agnes library.
**ZORA:** WHAT?! I'll be there. Wait for me.

True to her word, within a minute, I hear the clomp of Zora's boots on the linoleum floor.

"Jinx is missing," I say again, once she catches up to me.

Zora is all business right away, pulling over one of the wheeled office chairs to sit in front of the screen with me. "Let's check his last GPS location. You can do it through the old Moncha database."

I smack my palm to my forehead. *Why didn't I think of that?* I type in the address for Moncha Corp database, then I stare at the log-in screen. I haven't had to use my old log-in and password in over a year. I set it up when I got my first cell phone at ten years old. Finally, from somewhere deep in my memory bank, I dredge up the password.

Then I scream in frustration. There's a second layer of security. How did people used to do it back in the day? Remember the random combination of letters and numbers, of mother's maiden names and first streets and pet names, whether something is in upper or lower case, whether it contains numbers or symbols or letters or some combination of everything. Eventually, however, I remember what ten-year-old me's answer to *What's your favorite movie?* is, and I crack my way in to my old Moncha homepage.

The layout of the page is so clunky, it makes me cringe to think this was once the norm. I type Jinx's unique identity code into the section which would show his last recorded GPS location.

Of course. Of course, it says Moncha HQ. Why did I expect anything different? According to the computer, Jinx should have been exactly where I left him—in the arena.

"Have you reported it to police?" Zora asks.

"Not yet…"

I log out of my Moncha account and turn off the computer. Linus races down Zora's arm. "Here, use Linus to make the call."

I nod. "Linus, call Moncha's stolen baku line."

There's a brief pause as Linus connects.

"Moncha guard. How can we help?"

"My name is Lacey Chu and I need to report my baku as stolen."

"Baku unique identity code please."

"J1NX89."

There's a silence that feels a moment too long. "I'm afraid we have no baku registered to you under that number."

"J1NX89," I repeat. "I'm a student at Profectus school…"

Zora raises one of her eyebrows at me.

"There's no baku registered to you at all, Miss Chu."

"What? That's not possible. You can look at my records—"

"I have to warn you that we take prank calls very seriously. This is going down as a warning on the record of Miss Zora Layeni and her baku Linus354. Goodbye."

Linus switches off the call and crawls back up Zora's arm, as we stare at each other in disbelief. "Not registered?" Zora's eyes open wide.

"They've wiped Jinx from the database," I say, frozen with shock.

"That means Moncha Corp knows he's the rogue baku," says Zora, biting her lower lip.

I nod, tears welling up in my eyes. "Zora… They're going to destroy him."

She leans forward and grabs my hand. "What are we going to do?" asks Zora.

I blink, squeezing her fingers back tightly. Never have I been so grateful to hear the word *we* in my life. "I need help. I need someone with at least a level three baku."

Zora breathes out heavily, clutching level two Linus to her chest. "What are you thinking?"

"I think... I think I need my teammates back."

37

ZORA PROMISES TO MEET ME AFTER SCHOOL, AND in the meantime calls me a car to take me to where I *think* my old teammates will be. We hug each other tightly before leaving.

"Don't worry," she tells me. "We'll get him back."

The drive over to Companioneers Crescent disappears in a flash, and the car pulls up at the edge of the recreation ground.

I can see Team Tobias wrapped up in their brightly colored coats, huddling up for a strategy session with red cups of hot chocolate steaming at their sides. I snuggle down into the collar of my down jacket, but then force myself to lift my head up high as I approach.

It's Tobias who sees me first. He scrambles to his feet, and the others follow, taking a defensive stance behind him.

"What are you doing here?" he demands. "Come to cheat some more?"

The accusation stings, but I don't let it get to me.

"Please, guys... I need your help. Jinx is gone. They're saying he never existed. But I think he might still be at Moncha HQ somewhere."

"Wait a second. You want us to help you?" says Tobias, his hands on his hips. "You have some nerve, Lacey. You led us all on, letting us think you were a part of our team when really you were a wild card all along." He shakes his head. "You know what? If I were someone else—like maybe Gemma—I could be impressed by your ruthlessness. It's impressive. But I didn't think you had it in you. So no, don't come crawling back here for help now."

I can't take Tobias's intense angry gaze anymore, so I look at the other team members. But there's no sympathy on their faces either. No one wavers. Not Kai, not River, who's always sort of liked me, not even Ashley, who remains stony-faced. They're all behind their captain. They're a real team—tightly bonded, woven together, strong. I was the loose strand. Something that could be snipped off at any convenient moment.

I just didn't expect to be the one holding the scissors and making the cut.

"It was a mistake to come here," I say.

"Yeah, it was," grumbles Kai.

"Come on, guys, we have a battle to prepare for," says Tobias.

Without another look, they spin around and walk out of the rink, shutting off the lights as they leave, leaving me alone in the cold and the darkness.

I head home. There's nothing left for me to do. There's no way I can track Jinx. I can't go back to Moncha HQ. Even worse, I don't have anything to remember him by. He's gone forever.

I lock myself in my room and cry into my pillow, the fabric turning damp beneath my cheek. Mom asks me what's wrong, but I can't bring myself to explain. Not yet.

I've done everything I can think of, and I'm exhausted.

Well, *almost* everything.

Jinx is smart. More than that, he makes his own decisions.

What if Jinx tried to get a message out to me? There's no way he could. I'm totally out of reach—I have no phone and no baku. I wish I hadn't recycled my old phone, smashed-up screen and all.

Then I remember. I *do* have a baku. On a shelf in my locker.

"Mom—I'm going downstairs. I'll be back later."

"Honey, are you sure? I don't think you should be alone right now…"

"Mom, I'm okay." I give her a quick kiss on the cheek. "I promise you I will tell you everything. There's just one thing I have to do for school first."

Her face searches mine, and then she nods.

I race downstairs, and when I leave the elevator, I see Paul walking toward his locker.

"Paul!" I cry out.

"Oh, hi, Lacey!" He must catch sight of the look on my face because his brows furrow. "Are you okay? What's wrong?"

I can't help it—I burst into tears again. I turn into a sniveling, sniffling mess in front of him, my chest heaving with sobs. "It's Jinx... He's gone."

"Gone? What do you mean?"

"Taken. He... He was special. Different. Someone wanted to destroy him, and I delivered him straight into the wrong hands." It's the first time I've said it out loud to anyone except Zora. I can't hide it any longer.

He doesn't ask me any of the questions I expect—like whether I've contacted Moncha security. He doesn't even seem surprised by my statement. Instead, he stares at me with his intense gaze. His lemur does the same. "He wasn't a normal baku, was he?"

"No," I say, but the words come out as a whisper.

The feeling of Jinx gone is a sucker punch to my gut.

"What are they up to in that fancy building of theirs?" His words trail off as he stares into the distance.

"Paul?"

He blinks a couple of times and comes back down to earth. Then he puts one hand on my shoulder. "I know losing Jinx might feel like the end of the world. But your future isn't decided by your baku, Lacey. It's up to you."

I smile weakly and squeeze his hand in thanks. But he doesn't understand. "I'd better continue..."

He nods and lets me pass. But before I go, he says one final thing: "Listen, little tinker. You fixed that baku from nothing. I've never seen anyone work harder than you did this summer. Whatever Jinx is, he is because of you. Don't let anyone take *that* away from you."

"I won't," I whisper back. I hadn't realized how closely he'd been watching my progress. My heart swells to know that he does know how much this means to me after all. "Thanks, Paul."

"And if I could give you once piece of advice?" I nod, waiting for him to continue. "Contact Monica Chan. This sounds like something she should know about."

"But how do I do that?"

He shrugs. "If I knew that, I would tell you. Good luck, little tinker."

*Contact Monica Chan.* Paul is right. Destroying a baku—even a rogue one—doesn't sound like something Monica would want her company to do.

But I need to get myself a working baku first. I let myself into my locker, not even bothering to turn on the light. I open the box containing the scarab beetle. "Well, hello old friend," I whisper to it.

I wipe down the front of the box with my hand, removing some of the film of dust. He really is a beautiful little creature, even if he isn't very powerful. He has an emerald-green carapace that glitters purple in low light. His legs and pincers are a glossy obsidian, little slices of companioneering perfection. I slide him out of the package, gently using the pads of my fingertips to pry him from his plastic enclosure. He sits on my palm, almost covering it completely, and I can feel the little rubbery pads of his fingers that will give him incredible flexibility and strength. He'll be able to cling onto my skin, no matter how much I shake him around. He's a brilliant little companion—for someone.

"I'm sorry," I whisper again. I should have been happy to have him. I almost feel unworthy now, because I looked down on him so much. He's not only what I deserve; he's what I could afford.

I should be okay with that.

I take a deep breath, then I lift him to the leash at my ear. I feel the sync—a tiny spark—and the beetle comes to life, his legs wriggling against my neck. This is the experience I was supposed to have a few months ago.

A strip hologram projector lifts a series of texts into the air above his back.

>>Hello, Lacey! My name is...

There's a pause as he waits for me to fill in his name. I hadn't thought that far ahead. What am I supposed to call him? It doesn't seem right to give him a boring name, but I can't think for too long about it... I have a job I need him to do.

I think about what his coloring made me think of. An oil slick.

"Slick," I say out loud.

>>Hello, Lacey, my name is Slick! Nice to meet you.

"And you," I reply.

>>I'm downloading your preferences now, so we can be lifetime companions. Oh! I see that you're a big fan of ramen noodles. Me too. I'll help you locate the best ramen restaurants in the city.

I can't help the small smile that creeps onto my face. "Oh, well, thank you."

>>You're a very popular person, Lacey. I'm receiving a lot of messages for you. Would you like to read them now, or do you want me to save them for another time? Whatever is convenient for you.

He's so polite! I can see how it could be addictive, having something so nice and sweet in your ear. But I miss Jinx's cheeky little asides and backtalk—not to mention the fact that reading the text is a lot more cumbersome than having his voice in my head.

"Let's go ahead and read the messages."

>>Here you go.

I'm flooded with connections—missed messages from Zora, a few Flashes, notifications from my social media, and an email from Profectus saying that since the battle was called off, lessons have resumed as normal. My absence hasn't gone unnoticed. I don't read any of them, just flick through notification after notification, hoping for something from Jinx.

But there's nothing. Nothing that seems even remotely out of the ordinary.

>>Excuse me, Lacey?

"Yes?" I rub my eyes, racking my brain to try and think of another way to find Jinx.

>>There's a video here that's been sent to your spam. Do you want me to auto-delete anything that is flagged as spam, or would you like to view?

My instinct is to insta-delete—that's definitely what you should do if you get sent strange videos over the internet. But this might be a way for Jinx to get through while staying under the radar.

"Let me see this one," I say.

>>You got it.

My heart leaps into my throat as the video projects onto the wall in front of me. It's video feed from Jinx. He flicks his tail and shows me a tiny portion of his body. I would recognize it anywhere. It's him.

"Slick, please make sure you are recording backup footage of this," I say quickly, in case the stream stops running or gets deleted. "And make it as large as you can."

Slick enlarges the view so it's as if I'm immersed in the video. I use it to look around, trying to take in every detail. He's being carried in a cage by someone. I catch a glimpse of a moving picture on the wall, the dreamlike image of a waterfall, and the Moncha logo with a cluster of stars in the background.

Mr. Baird was right. Moncha Corp has taken him back.

My heart sinks. Maybe Monica has known about this all along.

*No, not Moncha.*

The view shifts so I catch sight of a snout, the curve of a tusk. A boar baku.

*Carter has him.*

My heart beats so fast inside my chest, it threatens to burst out. I was so caught up, I didn't even think to check whether Carter was in his team box at the baku battles. He must have nabbed Jinx while I was in the cylinder. But what is he doing with my baku?

There's a crackle, and suddenly there's audio alongside the video. Carter is on the phone with someone. I can only hear one side of the conversation. "Dad? I've got the baku. No, I really think you need to see this… Well, come back then! If you get on the jet now, you can make it back this evening… Yes, I'm alone!… No, she's not going to know where he is. I put one of those black marks on, so he's totally out of it."

The audio crackles and dies.

Carter. I should have known. I'd seen the predatory look in his eyes as he looked at Jinx.

Now he wants to bring him like some sort of prize to his father. He probably thinks that's a way of getting in his good books.

I ball my fingers into my fist and collapse down onto the floor. The sight of him locked up in a cage has cut me down to the core—but at least he's in one piece still. And I'm not going to leave Jinx. He might be a robot, but he has no one to protect him. I'm not going to give up.

*But how, Lacey? How are you going to get through Monica's security alone?*

There's a tiny tapping sound at my locker door. I open my eyes from my position on the floor. At first I see a pair of sparkly, silver Converse, and next to them—the paws of a spaniel baku. Jupiter.

## 38

I SLOWLY SIT UP, PUSHING MYSELF INTO AN upright position.

"Ashley?" I say, blinking slowly—as if I expect in the span of one blink for her to disappear. But she's still standing there.

"Hi, Lacey," she says. "Can I come in?"

I scan her hands for cans of spray paint, rolls of toilet paper, or something worse, but there's nothing. She even holds her hands out in the open to show she's unarmed. "I just want to talk."

I nod. "Okay." I undo the bolt on the cage door to my locker and let her in.

Jupiter runs up to me, and I pet her on the head, before gesturing for Ashley to take a seat. She doesn't. Instead, we stand there, looking at each other. I roll back and forth on my left sneaker, not sure what to say.

"I…" Ashley's mouth opens and then closes again. She looks down at Jupiter, and tears well up in her eyes. "I'm not doing this for you," she says, her voice fierce.

"Okay…" I say, not sure about where this is going.

"This is for Jupiter. If it wasn't for what you and Jinx did… Carter would have destroyed her beyond repair. I know that. So if there's anything I can do to help find him…then I want to."

I worry at my bottom lip for a moment. "Really?"

To my surprise, she steps forward and engulfs me in a hug. "Are you kidding? Of course. I don't know what I'd do if I lost Jupiter—or if he was taken from me. It would be horrible."

I lean into her hug, feeling how genuine her concern is, and appreciating it. When we finally separate, I nod. "It is horrible. The worst."

"So, let's find him. What do you know?"

I take a deep breath, before launching in.

And yet, before I can, there's even more commotion. "So that's where our missing teammate has got to."

Ashley and I both turn at the same time, to see Tobias, Kai, and River outside the locker.

"You can't skip out on a team meeting like that," says Tobias, his arms crossed.

For a second, I think Ashley is going to take back her offer—but she doesn't. "The team meeting ended, and I have a right to do what I would like with my spare time."

Kai and Tobias exchange a glance.

"Well, come on, guys," says River. "Let's not stand here. If we're going to help get this baku back, then we need a plan."

Tobias turns to me. "We're all going to help you," he says.

"Oh, thank you—" I stammer. I can't believe my luck.

"No," Tobias interrupts me. "Don't thank us yet. We're not helping you because we like you. Well, at least, that's not why I am doing it. The way you played us was harsh. We're doing it because it's not right that someone stole your baku. And whether we like it or not, you were once part of our team. And even though you're now our opponent, we need you if we're going to win fair and square. If that means helping you get that stinking cat back, then so be it."

He might be telling me not to thank him, not to be grateful, not to grin widely, but I can't help it.

"I do know something about where he is," I say finally. I hesitate for an instant more—especially as this means giving away my biggest secret. But if I can't trust my teammates now, I might never save Jinx.

And that's not a risk that I am willing to take.

"I was sent this video." I play the stream back for them. "Do you recognize it, Tobias?"

His face is stern, his normally full lips pressed together into a thin line. "Yeah, I do. Why on earth is your baku in the Team Happiness wing of Moncha HQ?"

**39**

"CARTER IS THE ONE CARRYING HIM IN THE VIDEO,"
I say.

Kai lets out a low whistle. "And it looks as if he's upgraded his
boar already. Look at the point on that tusk."

"But wait—what is that?" asks River. I look up and see he's not
watching the video—he's staring at me, pointing at Slick on my
shoulder. My new baku.

I cringe. "I had to leash a baku in order to send and receive
messages…and this was the one I originally bought."

"But that's a level one scarab beetle."

"I know," I say, my voice small.

"You're not even allowed onto the *grounds* of Profectus with
something like that," says Kai.

"Don't you think I know that?" I say. Then I sigh. "Look, I was
rejected by Profectus at first. But then they changed their minds…"

Kai turns to Tobias. "Okay, man, are we really going to waste our evening? I mean, she has a scarab baku. She doesn't stand a chance in the final tomorrow. We don't need this."

"We don't need this?" Tobias laughs. "Kai, Oka was mincemeat because of this girl's baku. I want to compete against the best—that's the only way you know if you're the best."

"Whatever," he says, crossing his arms. But I can tell he's in by the way his brand-new version of Oka steps forward into the circle.

"Right, so let me get this straight—if you bought a beetle baku, how did you end up with Jinx?" says Tobias.

I shrug. "I kind of…found him by some railway tracks. Then I brought him back here and fixed him up like new."

"And no one came to claim him? He didn't have any record of previous owners when you leashed him?"

I shake my head.

"And now Carter has taken him."

"Yes. And he wants to give Jinx to his dad."

Tobias frowns. "But why? What's so special about Jinx anyway?"

"Apparently, at the beginning of the summer someone at Moncha developed a one-of-a-kind prototype baku with…unique characteristics. It wasn't quite ready for release yet, and then it went missing," I say. "Moncha have been searching nonstop to try and get it back. And Carter thinks that Jinx might be it."

"What do you think?" Tobias asks, one of his eyebrow arching into his forehead.

I open and close my mouth. "I…I don't know," I say finally.

"Does it matter?" asks Ashley. "The point is, he was Lacey's baku. Carter stole him, and we can't stand by and let that happen."

"We don't have long," I say. "Carter told his dad to get on a jet."

"He's in Singapore, according to latest news reports," says River, scanning some information on the back of his new frog baku. "If he literally got on a jet an hour ago, he could be back in six hours."

"So that's how long we have to figure out how to break and enter into Eric Smith's private wing at Moncha HQ, find Jinx, steal him back from Carter, and get out of there without getting caught?" says Tobias.

"That about sums it up," I say.

He sighs heavily. "Well, you don't make things easy for us. And then what happens when you get Jinx? Carter's not going to go down without a fight, and if Eric Smith wants it back…"

"Yeah," says Kai. "You know technically, even though we all 'buy' a baku, they still belong to Moncha Corp? It's buried deep in the terms and conditions. No one ever reads those things, but I do. And if you found yours, you'll have even less claim to him than normal."

"That can't be true!" scoffs Ashley, hugging Jupiter tight to her chest.

"It is. So if Eric wants Jinx back, he can take him from you. You'll need an additional plan."

I nod. "I've thought of that. I'll get in touch with Mr. Baird."

"But he's just been fired!" says Tobias. "I heard it's because he's a corporate traitor. That he works for BRIGHTSPRK or something."

"Well… That's true," I say. I figure now that he's been fired, I don't need to worry about keeping his secret anymore.

There are gasps all around the locker.

"But he's going to help me. He's said he'll protect me and Jinx. He can arrange for us to get picked up once we get Jinx back. And then I'm going to find Monica Chan and tell her what her partner is up to. She'll put a stop to his plans once and for all, I know it."

"Dude, you have to tell us what is going on with Jinx," says River.

"Does he have some sort of new technology?" asks Tobias.

*He's real*, is what I want to say. But the words balance on the tip of my tongue without slipping out. It's too unbelievable, I can't say it out loud. I know I need to give them something, though. "It's buried in his code. Something that Moncha doesn't want to get out."

"Ooh, ooh, is it mind control?" asks River. "That's what all the conspiracy posters on Reddit say is the next step for exploiting baku owners."

"What? No!" I say, although I suppose telepathic communication isn't *that* far off.

"Huh, like some sort of proprietary software or something?" muses Tobias.

I nod. "Yeah, more like that."

"Well, I guess it doesn't matter. Let's prepare a strategy," he says, rubbing his hands together.

"This is Carter we're talking about. Not some sort of mastermind villain. We'll be able to take him down easily," says Kai.

"But we're running out of time," Tobias says, looking down at his watch.

"I'll call Mr. Baird," I say. I pull out the business card from my pocket, then I dig out the ancient rotary phone. "I don't think I should use a Moncha Corp baku to call someone at BRIGHTSPRK."

"This is like a Bond movie!" exclaims River.

I dial the number, waiting for it to ring out. "Hello?" says the voice on the other end.

"Mr. Baird? This is Lacey. Jinx and I need your help."

## 40

"WE'RE PART OF CARTER'S BAKU BATTLE TEAM,"
Tobias says to the security guard at the front desk, Aero spreading his
wings—simultaneously looking impressive and partially obscuring us
from view. We know that Carter trains here with Gemma's team, so
we're hoping the guard hasn't paid too much attention to which particular students have been coming and going.

"He's signed in, you're right, but he didn't mention anything
about a team…"

"We have a standing order to practice whenever possible. Eric
Smith said we could," says Tobias, putting on his most authoritative-
sounding voice. Aero squawks loudly. This is stage one of the plan.
All we need to do is get in, find Carter, get Jinx back, and then Mr.
Baird will be waiting outside to take Jinx and me to safety. What
I'll do from there… I'll figure out later.

The security guard frowns. I'm hoping the fear of ticking

off Eric Smith is greater than the desire to check if we're really supposed to be there.

Then Tobias pulls out his trump card. It's a pass he stole from his dad's home office, emblazoned with the same logo we saw on the video—the logo for Team Happiness. The guard's eyes widen at the sight. "All right, go on through—but try not to create too much of a mess this time around, okay, guys?" His sleek black panther baku sniffs us each as we pass, but with my level one baku especially, I don't attract any special notice.

We walk casually toward the elevators. Tobias leans down to talk in my ear.

"Okay, the four of us will take on Carter—we shouldn't have any trouble. You focus on getting Jinx."

I nod. "I will."

Tobias and I head down in the elevator, while the others take the stairs, following Tobias's directions. Thankfully there aren't many staff around so late at night, so less chance of us running into anyone asking awkward questions.

There's no denying that we might have a better chance against Carter if we use the element of surprise, but we've decided our first course of action is for Tobias to try and reason with him.

Tension radiates off him. I want to make things better between us. I hesitate. But this might be the last time I will get to see him for a while.

As the elevator doors slide closed, I reach out and touch Tobias's arm, just above his elbow. He looks down at it, but doesn't shift his position. I swallow. "Thank you for doing this."

He sighs and turns to face me. "I want…" But he doesn't finish the sentence. The bell dings for our floor, and for once I wish that technology wouldn't work so well—that it would break down, leaving us stranded together, trapped in the elevator until we sort things out. Aero flaps out first, and Tobias follows, moving so quickly my hand drops.

*Jinx.* I remind myself. Jinx first, and then I can focus on rebuilding my relationships.

"This way," Tobias says, looking at the map that Aero projects in front of him. "Through here." He leads me through a sliding glass door emblazoned with the constellation on it, into a long hallway—the one I saw in the video, with the waterfall window. This wing, however, feels different to the other parts of Moncha HQ that I've seen. For one thing, the walls seem to shimmer as we walk quickly past, making my eyes go funny.

"All the walls here are screens," says Tobias. "Eric wants Team Happiness to be able to code whenever inspiration strikes."

"Wow," I say. If I weren't so focused on finding Jinx, I'd be way more impressed. "How are we going to find Carter in this labyrinth, though?"

Tobias gives me a small smile. "That, I think, will be the easy part. Aero, call Hunter."

Aero obeys the command, and a second later we hear the snuffling sound of the boar from farther down the hall. We race to catch up with the sound, then pause outside the door.

"Ready?" Tobias mouths to me. I nod.

We open the door.

Carter is standing at the far end of a huge open-plan space, similar to the brainstorming lab we'd been shown earlier. "No one is supposed to be in here!" says Carter with his back to us, sounding panicked. "Do I have to spell out every single instruction…"

He stops talking when he turns around and sees us.

"Give back Jinx, you animal!" I blurt out, *so* not the approach Tobias and I had discussed. Tobias throws his arm out in front of me to stop me from doing something stupid—like launch myself toward him.

"What Lacey means to say is, she knows you have her baku and we would like to ask for it back—nicely," says Tobias. Aero is down by his side, and I see him furiously typing a message on his back to communicate our position to the others.

Carter looks as if he is going to lie to us, but then he moves his body to reveal the cage that holds Jinx's inert body. "There's no way you're getting this machine back. It wasn't yours to begin with. You don't even know what that thing is. But my dad knows. He's been looking for this baku everywhere. And I'm the one who's going to return it to him."

"Carter—listen. There's two of us and one of you. Let's make this easy and give us the baku back," Tobias says.

Carter laughs. "Hunter can easily take Aero, and Lacey doesn't even have a baku." As if to prove his point, the upgraded Hunter steps forward. His bodywork has changed—there's no attempt to make him look like a realistic boar—he's a brute of titanium and chrome, with two layers of supercharged, razor-sharp curved tusks that look especially vicious. "But did you really think I would come down here with no backup whatsoever?"

Three other security bakus, the thick-legged, sinewy black metal panthers, jump up onto the tables behind the boar. I swallow. Aero's not going to be able to handle this on his own.

Luckily, we're not alone either.

Oka bursts through a door at the far end of the room, Lizard and Jupiter not far behind. We've come at Carter from both sides. Now it's a fair fight.

Carter grunts, but still doesn't look afraid. "Hunter, get that eagle."

Aero flaps his wings, raising up off the ground. But the boar is good—so good—and Aero is restricted by the ceiling height. Hunter has had upgrades to his back haunches, and with a powerful run, he launches high into the air. He sideswipes at Aero with his tusks, almost taking a slice out of the eagle's wing.

Tobias is forced to send Aero into defense.

The panthers divide up the remaining bakus between them. Oka and Lizard rally around Jupiter to attempt to protect her. Ashley barks at them to leave her alone—she can do it. I feel a surge of pride for my friend, especially as she launches Jupiter over the top of Oka and into the oncoming path of a panther.

Carter has underestimated me again. That's always his mistake—to see me as the weak link, the one who shouldn't have made it, the underdog. I place Slick down on the floor and send him scurrying around to Jinx, while I distract Carter by facing up to him directly. My hands ball into tight fists. He's used to having baku fight baku. Well, he's about to deal with me.

Carter grins as he sees me approach. "What you going to do, Lacey, hit me?"

"If you don't give me back Jinx, then yes."

"Well, I have another surprise for you. In school we might only be able to fight baku against baku. But here? The security bakus can fight *you*."

My heart stops, and I spin around, screaming, "Watch out!" to Kai, River, and Ashley as the panthers leap *past* their bakus and aim their attacks at the people themselves. It goes against everything I believe Moncha Corp stood for. And it's the opportunity that Carter needs. While Tobias is distracted by my screams, he sends Hunter up to bring Aero down. There's a sickening crunch of metal against metal, as Hunter's tusk pierces Aero's belly.

But despite the noise and action, I manage to slip Slick past. He gets to Jinx just as one of the panthers jumps at me. He misses—but only because Tobias shoves me out of the way. I roll on the ground, directing my fall toward Carter, then lunge at him to take him out at the ankles. Caught by surprise, he tumbles to the ground, and I pin him there. "Got you, you thief!" I shout. "Call off your bakus! Call them off!"

"No way!" he says, defiant even with his cheek pressed on the ground. But I see exactly what I need spilling out the top of his backpack. Black marks.

Risking taking a hand off Carter for an instant, I chuck the bag of black marks at Tobias. "Use these!" I shout. Tobias snatches the bag out of the air and uses the marks to subdue Hunter and the security panthers.

Carter wriggles underneath me, and I use both hands to subdue him again.

He writhes. "What's the point of you 'saving' that thing? Moncha owns the baku, not you. My dad is going to hunt you down. Hunt you down and find that baku—no matter where you go."

"No," I say, my voice firm. "You're going to tell your dad that you made a big mistake. You *thought* you had a special baku, but it turned out to be normal. Otherwise, you're going to have to explain to him how you had Jinx in your hands and let him slip away. Another failure in your father's eyes. Is that what you want? Because you can come looking for Jinx. But you won't be able to find him."

For a moment, Carter looks scared. "You don't understand. He won't stop there. You don't understand what this baku means to him. It could have implications for the whole company. If BRIGHTSPRK gets him…"

"No one is going to get him. No one is going to use him."

Carter shakes his head. "You're so naive. Dad has resources you can only dream of. One baku isn't worth it. It'll be your whole career. Your future."

I don't doubt it. But I have to be brave. "Friends are always worth it."

"I've got Carter," says Tobias, touching my shoulder gently. "You go get Jinx."

I scramble to my feet gratefully, then walk over to the cage, where I see Slick working hard to remove the black mark from Jinx's paw. Just as I reach them, the mark pops off. I stretch my arms toward Jinx, my heart soaring as he saunters out of the cage, looking (as far as I can tell) unharmed. He leaps up into my arms.

My relief is heightened when I hear his voice in my head.

>>You came for me.

*Of course I did.*

>>Thank you, Lace.

*Any time.*

Carter looks small, defeated, as Tobias lifts him up to standing. I almost pity him. He thought this was the best way to impress his dad, but it's backfired. "Go home, Carter," Tobias says, giving him a shove. Carter picks up his inert boar, struggling under the weight of it.

"I'll make sure he doesn't cause any trouble," says Kai, who is the first of my teammates to recover. He has a scrape on his arm from his altercation with a panther, but a big goofy grin on his face—as if he *enjoyed* it. That's Kai for you. He grabs Carter under the arm and frog-marches him from the room.

Now I have to trust Mr. Baird can find a safe place for Jinx and me. Somewhere far from Eric Smith's reaches. Until we can get ahold of Monica and get her to sort this all out for good.

"Come on, let's get out of here," says Tobias. He's got one arm around Ashley, who is bleeding from a scratch along her hairline, the other arm supporting River, who is getting shakily to his feet. I nod.

"I couldn't have done it without you guys," I say, with a smile to the rest of the team. I squeeze Jinx in my arms, ready to walk out of there—and to safety.

But, to my horror, Jinx bolts.

41

I CAN ALMOST SENSE IT BEFORE HE DOES IT. The tensing of his small electronic body in my arms, the way his ears twitch—left and right—his whiskers taking in the surroundings. I instinctively adjust my grip, trying to hold onto him tighter. He can't do this. We're so close to being safe. Mr. Baird is waiting for us outside. Every moment we stay at Moncha Corp is another moment we are in danger.

But Jinx leaps from my arms, able to wriggle out of the tightest grip I could muster.

"Jinx, no!" I shout.

Tobias and the others gape after me in confusion. I sprint after Jinx, who darts through an opening I didn't even realize was a sliding door. It slams shut as I cross the threshold. I'm separated from the team now, but I can't look back—not when Jinx is running away from me. A strangled cry escapes from my throat, and I drop to my knees with the momentum of trying to keep up on the slick hardwood floor. Jinx nips through another door. If I don't hurry, I'm going to be the one locked out next.

I scramble on the floor, hurling myself down the hallway. But the door slides across before I make it there. I slam my hand up against the glass, and I see Jinx stop and stare back at me.

"Don't leave me again," I cry out. "I just got you back."

>>I'm sorry, Lacey.

His voice is soft inside my ear.

>>I need to find out who I really am.

"But you belong with me," I say, my eyes welling with tears. I want it to be true so badly.

>>It's all been leading to this.

*What do you mean?*

>>Ever since I was hit with that blaster,
I've been looking for a way back here.

My mind flashes back to the hole in his side when I found him. Caused by a blaster. That's one mystery solved, but it brings me no satisfaction.

>>When you passed by me in the ravine, I
knew you could be my ticket back here.

You'd just had your leash installed. I used a proximity signal to find out more about you. I learned you had the skill to fix me. I ran through all the possibilities, factored in all the variables, examined every permutation… In the end, it was simple. I could see the path that would lead me back to the heart of Moncha HQ. No one would suspect the baku of a young student. The hacking was easy: Getting you into Profectus, getting you onto the right team, getting a wild card place so you'd be in the final battle. The things I didn't factor in were the Black Marks. But you rescued me. And now I am so close to finding out the answers my vast databases couldn't solve.

*You…used me?*

He flicks his tail.

>>I need to know who I am.

I nod, even though it hurts every fiber of my being.

Then he spins around and, in a couple of bounding leaps, is off beyond my sights.

I think I hear a siren from behind me. Maybe Carter managed to alert Moncha security. Jinx might not think he needs me, but I'm not going to leave him until I know he is safe. How can I find a way to follow?

>>I can open the door for you.

I hear a polite voice. Slick. I'd almost totally forgotten about him.

Slick crawls out of my pocket and onto the door's lock. One of the beetle's front legs disappears into the keyhole, and in a few moments he breaks through the security.

"How did you do that?" My jaw drops. I'm sure that's not standard for a beetle baku.

```
>>My code has been adjusted by a Miss
Zora Layeni to add some specific features
and update some of my applications. As a
result, I am excellent at picking locks.
She wrote in a message for me to pass on
to you when you discovered this feature:
"so you never get locked out of your cave
ever again."
```

My throat feels tight. Zora did this for me as thanks for fixing Linus. I'm so shocked, I could kiss him. He vibrates with happiness. The door clicks open, and I'm through.

Then, I stop. It's like I've traveled through a portal and out into…suburbia? It's like a set on a movie studio lot. I appear to be on a street lined with trees on either side that can't possibly be real—the ceiling above us looks like open sky, but I know it has to be an illusion. I turn back toward the door—the only thing that looks out of place. Otherwise, I could be outside and back in time.

"Jinx?" I call out tentatively.

There's a light on in one of the houses a few feet away. There's a red mailbox out front with the letters CHAN written in gold along the side. A shiver runs down my spine. The house is the type almost no one can afford anymore, unless you're on Companioneers Crescent: wide-fronted, with two huge windows downstairs, and four on the upper level. It's painted a warm, creamy white, with deep, olive-green shutters.

Is this where Monica Chan lives?

On a fake street buried beneath Moncha HQ? Why would she choose to do that?

No. Something is not right. I need to go in and find out what's going on, once and for all. A blinking red light catches my eye. I look up and I see cameras in the trees—and thick iron bars concealed among the greenery.

That's when I realize: it's not a home at all. It's a prison.

I slowly walk down the path, treading on each flagstone carefully as if each one might be booby-trapped. Who knows in a place like this? But I peer through the front window and spy a flash of Jinx's tail, giving me the push I need to enter the house. The door is unlocked. I knock on it once, unable to shake the politeness from my system, but go in without waiting for a response.

"Hello?" I say tentatively.

The door swings open into a wide hallway, intricately patterned rugs covering dark hardwood floors and vibrant paintings of the countryside in oversize gilt frames on pale green walls. I feel like I've walked into a dream. None of it seems real. I wrap my arms around my waist, a deep sense of *wrong* pervading all my senses.

A giggle from the front room catches my attention. I walk in without hesitating any longer. Sitting cross-legged on the floor, stroking Jinx, is my idol and tech icon—Monica Chan—her signature jagged bangs grown out of shape. Jinx rolls onto his back, allowing her to stroke him in his most vulnerable state, and a pang of jealousy spikes through my belly. Monica is talking to him, laughing—and, I realize as I get closer, crying too. Tears are rolling down her cheeks, dripping onto Jinx's fur. "I thought I'd never see you again!"

She looks up as I walk in and doesn't even blink. It's as if my presence is not a surprise to her. "Are you the one who did this? Are you the one who brought him back to life?"

"His name is Jinx," I say, through my teeth.

"Jinx. Oh, a perfect name. A perfect name for a perfect creature. My little trickster. He looks very different now, but I would recognize him anywhere."

"There wasn't much to work with," I say, bristling at the implied insult at my handiwork. Then I soften. "You created him?"

"Created him?" She continues to brush Jinx's fur with her fingers as she talks, as if she wants to touch every part of him. "I suppose you could say that. It would be more accurate to say that he created me. He showed me the light." At that, her eyes seem to glaze over. "I…can't think like that. It's too difficult. I am happy now." Her fingers lift from Jinx's fur, hovering just above him. She wants to touch him, but something is stopping her.

Jinx rolls over onto his paws now. He nuzzles up to her, then hops into her arms, climbing to her shoulder. Absentmindedly—more habit than purposeful movement—she runs her fingers around Jinx's tail, holding it up to the leash around her ear. "Do you mind?" she asks, her eyes suddenly bright as if she's woken from a trance. It's as if the artificial light from the basement prison she lives in is replaced with inner light that shines from her face like moonlight. This is the woman I recognize from all the videos I've watched. The woman I've idolized for so long.

I hold my breath as she connects Jinx's tail to her leash. And yet... Nothing seems to happen. I breathe a sigh of relief, despite myself.

Monica closes her eyes. When she opens them again, she deflates. "I suppose things have moved on for both of us. Come on, let's drink some tea. We won't have much time—and I don't know how much longer I'm going to be this lucid—but I do know that a cup of green tea can fix anything. Something my mom said once."

"My dad used to say something similar," I say, my voice sounding small.

"He must have been a smart man, your father."

I don't elaborate—because I don't want memories of my dad to ruin this moment. But Monica continues. "Is that who gave you that ring?"

My eyebrows raise in surprise, but then I realize I've been playing with it again—it must have caught her eye.

"I had one of those once," she says.

"I know," I say sheepishly. "It's another one of the reasons why

I wear it. You're like—my hero," I splutter out, before I can stop myself.

Monica blushes and it covers both her cheeks, traveling down her neck—reminding me of how I react when I blush. The fact that someone so powerful and confident can still be reduced to redness like me endears her to me even more. Does she have to be perfect in every way?

"If you put him back together after what he endured, you must be a pretty incredible companioneer. Has Eric tried to offer you an internship yet?"

"I don't think that's likely. I think Mr. Smith hates me. At least, his son does."

"And why is that?"

I shrug. "Because I beat him at everything?"

Monica chuckles, then beckons at something behind my head. I turn around to see a sloth baku walking into the room, two teacups balanced on its back.

"Take one," she says to me.

I do as she says, but I can't hold my questions in any longer. "What's going on? Where are we? Why are you here?"

Monica sips at her tea. Then, she frowns. "I did something… bad. Bad for the company."

I drop out of my chair, so I'm almost sitting at her feet. "Do you know what Eric is doing to your company in your absence? He wants to destroy Jinx, you know. His son tried to steal him away from me."

Her eyes darken. "Yes, the Smith family seems to have made a habit of trying to take things that don't belong to them. I should have acted sooner." She levels her gaze at me. "If you're a companioneer, then you know something about the magic of building. Of creating. I wanted to keep challenging myself. Keep pushing the envelope.

"But I was so focused on my race to invent, that I forgot about my responsibility to the company that bears my own name. I'm not a natural CEO. I'm a creator. An inventor."

"A companioneer," I say quietly.

"Exactly. You understand that drive to work. That's when I was happiest. Jinx was my project. You must know that feeling, as an inventor... There's the work you're supposed to be doing, and then there's that secret thing that sets your heart on fire, the one you don't share with anyone, the one that consumes you. That was this idea, for me—this question I wanted to answer. I'd created a perfect companion. But could I go a step further?

"Could I create something that *chose* to be my friend? Not a slave—but a true friend? I spent every waking hour working on him, refining every component and aspect of his design, tinkering with his code, inching closer to perfection with every step.

"The closer I got, the more protective I became. I didn't want to share what I was working on with Eric. He begged and cajoled me, but nothing worked. I could tell he was getting frustrated, but also I knew he would wait. His frustration stemmed from the fact that he knew whatever I came up with would be a game changer for the company. So many of the updates I'd made—had they come to light—would have triggered a jump in Moncha's shares. But I wasn't ready to share him yet. *I wasn't ready for him to belong to anyone but me."*

"And did it work?" I ask.

Monica laughs, scratching between Jinx's ears. "What do you think? No. I ended up with scratches up and down my arms, having to use the black marks to keep him powered down—every time I leashed him up, he would rebel and act like an out-of-control wildcat. Nothing I tried made him *want* to be leashed up to me, apart from to use me as a power source. And with advances in piezoelectricity and solar energy, he didn't even need me for that. You've noticed that, haven't you? That he doesn't need to be leashed to you to keep his charge?"

I nod, biting down on my lip.

"That was *one* of the breakthroughs I'd made creating Jinx. He is the culmination of all my hard work… I thought maybe my code was the only thing not up to scratch. That was always my biggest weakness, when it came to building the bakus. So I decided it was time to share with Eric what I had created."

She pauses then, her eyes staring off into the middle distance.

"What happened then?" I prompt.

She sighs, her shoulders collapsing down. "He panicked. He couldn't understand what I was playing at—trying to create something that didn't obey. It didn't make any sense. He tried to alter the code I'd already written, but it backfired. The baku rejected the update—he wouldn't accept Eric's code! Even more than that, he started *rewriting* Eric's code, infecting and dismantling it. We had to wipe the entire project to stop the baku from destroying *everything* on the Moncha cloud. It would have been chaos.

"I couldn't tell if Eric was angry or amazed. He called my baku a monster. A virus. He wanted to destroy the baku then and there—he tried to! But I grabbed him and ran. This was my baby that Eric was trying to mess with. I triggered an old alarm that I'd set up a long time ago, in case something like this would ever happen. A mutual promise with an old university friend of mine who worked at BRIGHTSPRK to offer each other sanctuary, no questions asked. But Eric sent security after me. They took me down, and that's when I lost the baku into the ravine…

"Next thing I knew, I woke up here. Leashed up to Pardem here. And curiously…happy." She gestures over to her sloth baku, who gives her a sleepy smile.

"But, Monica—how can you be happy knowing what Eric is still trying to do? That he's taken over the running of your company. He's told everyone you're away on business! When you've been stuck down here all along."

She doesn't immediately reply, but she cocks her head to one side. "You have to get out of here," she says softly. There's no sense of urgency in her voice, even though her words quicken the beating of my heart. "If they find you, then he will arrest you."

"I can't leave you here!"

"You must."

>>And what about me?

322 | AMY McCULLOCH

*Well, Jinx, it's up to you. You can come with me, and I will promise to do anything I can to stop Eric from getting to you.*

Monica looks up at me. "You two... You're communicating, aren't you?"

I nod.

She smiles, her face lighting up with the wideness of her grin. "Don't you see, Lacey? You've done what I couldn't. You don't need a leash to be attached to Jinx. To know what he's thinking, to communicate with him. You're not leashed to him right now. You're leashed to that beetle."

I stare down at my shoulder, where Slick is sitting. I can't believe I didn't realize it before. Jinx and I *are* communicating without officially being leashed.

"Because you two chose each other. That's what true friendship is. That's what life is. Being presented with options and choosing your own path. Maybe not every choice makes you happier. Maybe not every decision will be the right one. But if you think carefully, I know you will know what to do."

My eyes fill up with tears. "But Monica, I can't leave you..."

The sloth nudges Jinx out of the way, and Jinx steps back from her.

>>Lacey, she's right. We have to leave.

"I'm so sorry, Jinx," I whisper to him. Slick crawls up onto my shoulder and raises one of his small beetle legs in solidarity.

Pardem approaches Monica, climbing up onto her lap with

his painstakingly deliberate movements, his arms wrapping around her neck in a slow, loving embrace. As he leashes to her, her demeanor changes again. The tension in her shoulders slips away and she sinks into the cushioned back of the armchair, her muscles relaxing. A small smile creeps onto her lips, and I can't deny it—she looks peaceful. Serene. But the light is gone.

Jinx leaps up into my arms.

>>So, that is my creator?

I squeeze his body tightly. *She might have built your body, but, Jinx... I think the point of all this is that you created you. Through your choices, your decisions.*

Jinx rolls his spine and arches his back in my arms. I carry him out of the perfect house, down the perfect pathway, toward the Hollywood suburban dream that his creator is trapped in. He purrs softly, but I know it's not me who needs comforting, but him. I hold him close, stroking him.

*I can't leave her here... It's terrible. Moncha needs Monica Chan.*

>>We won't let Eric Smith take over. We'll
figure it out.

*But how? I don't know if I'm capable. I'm a kid. I'm not a superhero. I'm not special. I'm just me.*

>>Lucky for you, I *am* special. We will do
it together.

Suddenly, Slick beeps and flashes wildly. I look down at his carapace and see he's flagged Moncha security guards approaching.

*We'd better move, Jinx.*

He doesn't reply, but he doesn't wriggle out of my arms either— which I take to be a good sign. I run out of the creepy fake suburb, the movie set ideal of perfect happiness.

Jinx directs me the quickest route outside, using an unmarked exit that means we don't have to go through the main atrium. But instead of following his directions to Mr. Baird's car, where I know Tobias and my teammates are waiting, I turn and head in another direction, down a narrow alleyway running behind the building. Relying on my memory, I try and orient myself in the streets. Slick beeps in my ear, but for this—I ignore him.

>>Where are we going?

*Don't you remember this place?*

I turn the corner, and we arrive at the park where Jinx and I saw the wild cats. I place him down gently on the ground. Then he hears the first meow, and his ears prick up to attention.

"This is what you want, isn't it, Jinx? To find your place in the world. You can live here and you don't have to belong to anyone."

It's more than that. It wouldn't be right to take Jinx to BRIGHTSPRK, to force him to help me save Monica, or even to bring him home with me. He's my entire world, but that doesn't give me the right to decide what's best for him. He needs to make that decision all on his own.

I don't want a friend I have to force to be with me. Friendship is about choice, not obligation.

I know that now.

My heart feels as if it is ripping in two, but I summon some courage. "Go," I say. "Be free."

I don't know if it's the right decision. But it's what feels right to me.

I'm not starting out a campaign for Monica's freedom by keeping my baku on a leash against his will.

More than my baku. My friend.

>>I love you, Lacey.

Without a second pause, Jinx runs away from me and my heart lurches. Then he stops at the gate to the park, his head cocked to one side, ears perked up into triangles. My heart swells at the sight of him, his tail gently swaying from side to side in the breeze.

"I love you too," I whisper.

He lifts up onto his haunches then, pivoting around in the strange sinewy way that cats move. But before he disappears from view, he turns his head and looks back at me. I wonder what he is thinking. What funny quip he might say at that moment. But I don't need to wonder whether he is happy.

I just know.

He'll come back and find me. If he wants to.

But I'm not done with Moncha Corp. Not with my idol locked up in the basement of her own headquarters and Eric Smith taking over. I'm going to find a way to save her, and then save the company that I've admired for so long. I've got my teammates, and I've got Mr. Baird and the resources of BRIGHTSPRK. We can expose Eric and bring Monica back to the head of her own company.

"Slick, take me to Mr. Baird," I say, leashing the beetle to my ear. Slick beeps, a series of tones I haven't heard before.

>> I'm sorry, I can't do that.

His robotic voice is hard in my ear.

"What?" I frown. "What do you mean?"

>>I'm sorry, Lacey.

He says it again, this time more softly.

A jolt of electricity shocks me through the leash, and I collapse to the ground.

# ACKNOWLEDGMENTS

As a science fair nerd (and proud of it!) throughout middle school and high school, my first thanks go out to the amazing young people innovating and creating in STEM fields: you guys are my inspiration, and I can't wait to see what the future will look like in your capable hands.

Huge thanks to the team at Sourcebooks Young Readers and especially to my editor, Annie Berger—I've been truly blown away by your passion and enthusiasm for this book. A special shout-out to Lauren Dombrowski in production and Stephanie Graham and Mallory Hyde in marketing for all your hard work. Also thanks to my editor in the UK, Lucy Rogers, and the whole team at Simon & Schuster UK, for their unwavering support.

To my agent, Juliet Mushens of the Caskie Mushens Agency— you are my rock, always willing to jump into the arena for me at a moment's notice! What a journey this has been, and I'm so grateful to have you in my corner. Thanks also to Molly Ker Hawn of the Bent Agency, for bringing Jinx and Lacey to North American audiences.

To Kim Curran—thank you for being with me on every step of this journey, and for your patience and guidance through multiple drafts! I have so many writing friends to thank who have supported me above and beyond over the past year: Amie, Laura, James, Juno, Will, Laure, Tom, Neil, Keith and Zoe. You are all superstars.

To Jessie (and Jinx-inspiration Margot), and Adam, Tania and Scarlett—you guys gave me the space and time to write when I had nowhere to go, and I can't thank you enough.

And finally, to all my family and friends who have boosted me up over this past year, you have no idea what your support means to me. I'm lucky to have you all.

# ABOUT THE AUTHOR

Amy McCulloch is a writer, editor and part-time adventurer. She was born in the UK, raised in Canada, and currently lives in London, UK. She is the author of six books for young adults, including The Oathbreaker's Shadow duology and The Potion Diaries series. She loves nothing more than to travel the world and climb mountains, all while researching extraordinary settings and intriguing stories for future books.

Find her online at amymcculloch.net, or say hi on Instagram @amymccullochbooks.